PRAYING MANTIS

DOMINI TAYLOR

JOVE BOOKS, NEW YORK

This Jove Book contains the complete
text of the original hardcover edition.
It has been completely reset in a typeface
designed for easy reading, and was printed
from new film.

PRAYING MANTIS

A Jove Book / published by arrangement with
Atheneum Publishers

PRINTING HISTORY
Atheneum edition published 1988
Jove edition / April 1992

ISBN: 0-515-10827-8

Jove Books are published by The Berkley Publishing Group,
200 Madison Avenue, New York, New York 10016.
The name "JOVE" and the "J" logo
are trademarks belonging to Jove Publications, Inc.

PRINTED IN THE UNITED STATES OF AMERICA

10 9 8 7 6 5 4 3 2 1

PRAYING MANTIS (*Mantis religiosa*) An insect of the order Orthoptera, akin to the cockroach, widespread in tropical areas. This interesting creature is named, in various vernaculars as by the scientists, from the curious way in which it positions its forelegs when eating or reposing, remind observers of the folded hands of a nun at her devotions. We have seen the name rendered 'preying mantis'; this apparently careless usage may in fact be better than a slip of the pen or a solecism (may even be a deliberate pun), because it is believed that the female insect regards the male only for the purposes of procreation and social display, and when he has performed these functions to her satisfaction, she kills and eats him, in the manner of the venomous American 'black widow spider'. The writer has not personally witnessed this ruthless ritual, but it is always folly to dismiss as pure fancy anything which has been firmly believed for a long time.

Edwardes, Major K.L.E., late Royal Engineers:
My Six-Legged Friends, being Entomological Notes from Many Lands. Privately printed, Calcutta 1882.

C·H·A·P·T·E·R

1

Victoria Lambert thought it was the oddest thing she had ever done. It was outrageous and shameless. There was no harm in it. She had never done anything like it before. All her life she had erred, if at all, on the side of modesty, priggishness. She was not at all certain why it had happened. It had simply seemed a reasonable thing to do. Now that she was in such a bizarre situation, there was no reason not to enjoy it. She did enjoy it.

It was three o'clock in the morning on the Thursday of the last week of June. It was a fine night, windless, warm: there was no moon, but a brilliant scattering of stars. The weather was like an oasis in that dreadful summer—an oasis in reverse, a blessed patch of dryness in the boggy desert of unremitting wet. There was a glow, sensed rather than seen, of a million street-lamps. There was an intermittent murmur of distant traffic, streets away.

Victoria Lambert stood naked on the lawn outside the back door of her house in Battersea.

Nobody could see her. Practically nobody could have seen her, except from her own house, even at midday. The garden had high brick walls on both sides, and trees on both sides of both walls. At the bottom, hidden by more little trees and by climbing shrubs, was the blank back of a warehouse.

Victoria stepped out, away from the house, into the middle of the lawn. The grass, new mown, felt dry and springy under her bare feet. The air was the most lovely temperature; she felt its touch as she moved; she felt conscious of every square millimetre of her skin. Glancing down at herself, she found that to herself she was visible, small high breasts, flat stomach, long slender legs, a milky glow in the starlight.

Perhaps to someone in a top-floor window of a neighbouring house she was visible, to someone with naval night-glasses peering out of a bedroom window, at three o'clock in the morning, to spot naked females on lawns. The notion was ridiculous and unworrying. And she was beautiful. She had grown used to being told so, and she knew it was true. It was not a thing anybody intelligent could be unaware of. She had been told about her beauty the previous week, not once but again and again, in the Royal Enclosure at Ascot, in the Paddock and in White's Tent and in the boxes of friends. It was funny to compare that careful and daily-changed elegance of silk, underclothes, nylon, hat, binoculars, with this glorious feeling of freedom, this sense of being a living thing among living things, as perfectly natural as they.

All that previous week she had proclaimed her identity, like everybody else in the Royal Enclosure, with the little card pinned to her coat: 'The Hon. Mrs G. Lambert'. Some of their more elderly acquaintances had to put on spectacles, embarrassed, in order to read the card and remember who she was. Now she seemed to have no name, no identity; she had shed more than clothes and card; she was simply a living thing among many in the garden.

How goggle-eyed their friends would be, to see her now, just a week later, just as she was. Many of them were a good deal older than herself, inevitably—Gerald's old friends, his generation. There had always been a risk that she would lose touch with people of her own age, less rich, less eminent, much less leisured—that she would be swallowed up altogether by these older and more sophisticated people: but Gerald, typically, had not allowed it to happen and now some of her best-loved friends were even younger than herself.

Slowly, luxuriously, Victoria walked to the end of the lawn, to where the Iceberg roses overhung the grass. She saw better and better as her eyes grew used to the darkness. Scores of white blossoms, as palely visible as her own body, opened their abundant petals to the starlight. Victoria felt one with the roses, one of the roses. She giggled at the thought of herself infested with greenfly, and being sprayed with an aerosol insecticide. There were real similarities, though, recognisable without feyness. She and the roses needed food, attention, medication sometimes, loving care always. She and the roses received all these things, and in consequence were healthy and beautiful.

Victoria knelt in front of the roses, to sniff the sweet and delicate perfume which was enhanced by the darkness. She found herself in an attitude of prayer; she found herself praying. She prayed thanks, on behalf of the roses and herself, for health and beauty and loving care. She prayed for her husband, that he would keep for as long as possible, for a little while at least, his strength, virility, activity, energy, that he would be able to enjoy, for a little while at least, his full life and his friends. Appalled but realistic, Victoria knew—and she knew that God knew she knew—that it would not be so very long. Her friends, his, had always been worried by the difference in their ages. The problem was no less real for having been faced and dismissed. His hair was thinning. That was unimportant. The thread of his life, invisibly to the world but with horrible obviousness to Victoria, was thinning too, weakening, fraying, not so very far from shredding into nothing. Victoria did not think God would intervene with a miracle to save him; but she did not think He would mind being asked to.

She did not think He would find it impertinent or blasphemous, that she should address Him naked, under the stars, among roses.

Some of the roses were in tight bud. She prayed for their health and beauty and vigour as they expanded. She prayed for the tiny bud inside herself, the baby conceived on May Day, to be born about the beginning of February. She wanted the baby's spirit to be full of starlight and the scent of roses. It was their first. She knew with certainty that the child was a son. She could not explain this certainty to herself or to anyone else.

She thought of her husband that May Day midnight, there in the bedroom whose windows were catching the radiance of the stars. There had been no words between them. It was one of the times when they understood one another perfectly: desire and delight were equal, awe and amazement, absolute joy. Victoria remembered the feeling, ridiculous but familiar—how can anything so exciting be *allowed*? He had slept afterwards, as quietly as he was sleeping when she slipped out of bed ten minutes before. Why? Why not? She had been lying most unusually wakeful, looking at the big pale oblongs of the windows, listening to the almost inaudible whisper of her husband's breathing, fancying that she could smell the roses in the garden. Sleep seemed unattainable and unnecessary. She slid out of bed, naked as always in such weather, and softly opened and closed the bedroom door. For some reason she had not bothered with her cotton summer dressing-gown. To grope for it, and struggle into it, seemed a needless bore, a complication, a concession to irrelevant convention. For some reason she had crept downstairs, across the hall, through the dining room and kitchen, and then through the French windows onto the paved terrace. Yes, into the open air. Very extraordinary behaviour.

She felt not at all cold, not at all sleepy, and only slightly peculiar.

She sighed, and rose to her feet. She brushed from her knees some grass-mowings which had escaped the box of the mower. She felt so great a surge of love for the physical universe that she wondered, for a groggy moment, whether she was having a genuine religious experience. She thought she was the very last person she knew likely to have such a thing—to see a visiting angel, or hear St Joan's voices, or receive miraculous wounds. In the ordinary way she was, she thought, almost depressingly down-to-earth, competent, common-sensical. Not altogether unimaginative, perhaps, not at all immune from most forms of art, but very, very realistic. This made it all the odder that she should be doing what she was doing, all the odder that she should feel this flood of love for all created things. But it was in character that she should be careful not to bring a lot of grass-mowings into the house.

She wiped her feet on the mat just inside the kitchen French windows. The doormat was prickly to the soles of her narrow feet. In the morning it would be taken up, carried across the flagstones, and shaken out onto the lawn.

Victoria crossed the polished wood of the kitchen floor and the Wilton carpet of the dining room. Even in these familiar surroundings she felt her way carefully: the fact that she loved the Regency chairs in the dining room would not make a stubbed toe less painful. Some wayward and transient gleam came through the fanlight over the front door, across the hall, through the open door of the dining room; it kindled for a second the cut glass and ormolu of the Empire *tazze* on the sideboard, the George II silver candlesticks, the big silver-gilt tray engraved with Gerald's family's coat of arms.

Victoria went out into the hall. A car passed, slow, quiet, most unusual in that cul-de-sac at that time of night, probably looking for a place to park. Victoria saw with astonishment that a young woman, a beautiful young girl, was standing naked ten feet away from her, pallidly lit for a long moment by the headlights of the car. The naked girl stood tall, proud, unabashed, infinitely graceful. She was slim, with beautiful long slim legs. Her hair was dark, long and straight, untidy from the pillow she had left. Her skin was altogether pearly white except for the accents of pink nipples and black hair. She had a look of happy wonderment. She looked as though she loved and was loved. It was Victoria's reflection, in the glass-fronted cabinet at the bottom of the stairs.

Behind the glass was Gerald's inherited collection of Chinese porcelain. The hall was not the best place for it, but there was no room for the cabinet in the drawing room. Gerald had been offered a great deal of money for the collection, which had been looted by an ancestor from the Imperial Palace after the capture of the Forbidden City. They might one day decide to sell. It would be like losing a tooth, or a lifelong friend, or a favourite tree.

They were perfectly all right for money now, but the things that would have to be considered were medical expenses and the child's education. Victoria was to an unusual extent aware of their financial situation—it was one of the things Gerald had taught her. The accountants and solicitors, after their initial surprise, had agreed. They had spread out papers in front of her, and explained everything. Nobody came out and said so, but it was probable that she would outlive him by many years. She had to be able to manage her own affairs. In the event, and reluctantly, she found herself managing most of Gerald's affairs.

The porcelain would pay for a single-premium, tax-effective insurance policy to cover the boy's years at Eton and Oxford. With his genes, he would hardly fail to get into either. His father had extraordinary abilities, not a tenth of which were obvious to people who knew him only slightly—painting, music, lyric poetry in various languages; in practical tasks, his hands were virtuoso in their deftness—he could rewire a house, fix any machinery, mend an antique clock, renovate the plasterwork on a Chinese Chippendale mirror—it was astonishing that he had mastered such a variety of skills when he had really had so little time.

Now that he had the time, he no longer had, perhaps, quite all the skills.

As an outcross to those genes there were her own. (Genetics, as related to the thoroughbred horse, was one of the subjects that Gerald had made his own.) Her father an actor and musician, her maternal grandfather a professor, she herself well able to manage a portfolio of investments and to help a dramatist with the structure of a play.

If the boy combined the best of his parents, his would be a life it would be fascinating to watch.

'His *will* be a life it *will* be fascinating to watch,' said Victoria wordlessly to her vanished reflection.

Her husband was still deeply asleep. It was only recently that the doctor had put him onto sleeping-pills (just as it was only recently that she had persuaded him to have regular scalp massage). They did not make him snore. He only snored when he had had too much to drink. That was more often than people realised, because he carried it extremely well. He was a gentleman, by this definition as by all others. He drank selectively, with knowledge and love especially of the red wines of France. He drank too much of them simply because he was such a good host, endlessly generous, anxious to share with anybody worthy any discovery he made, any lucky buy at auction, any little-known and underpriced château. Victoria's own wine education, sketchy before their marriage, had benefited enormously. Almost too much—she could now hardly endure bad wine; and some of their friends were young and pretty broke. You could not have an after-theatre supper in the studio of a struggling painter, and turn up your nose at Italian plonk. It was a problem which, as a girl, she had never expected to meet. It was a problem that followed entirely on too much good luck.

Victoria knew she was the luckiest person she knew, even to having a husband who did not usually snore.

She climbed delicately into the huge bed. She pulled the sheet and the single blanket up to her chin. She was careful not to waken the beloved man beside her.

She was sure now that she could smell the special and magical fragrance of the white midsummer roses. Perhaps she had brought it with her, into the house, into the bed. She had brought the starlight, and the love of all things. Part of her wished she was still in that lovely and extra-ordinary situation, kneeling naked under the stars among the roses. Part of her was there.

Fourteen minutes away by moped—considerably more by car—Victoria's daughter, Charlotte Bramall, was at that moment celebrating her twenty-second birthday. The party was in her flat, on the third floor of a Council block off Peckham High Street.

Lottie was a bouncy girl, an evident enthusiast, a little overweight, with strong features and very short blonde hair. She looked exactly twenty-two, except for an occa-sional wariness which made her look either much older or much younger. It was the look in the eyes of a dog with an unpredictable owner; it was the look in the face of somebody twice or thrice shy after being badly bitten. She was wearing baggy black trousers, home-made, mid-calf in length, red ankle-socks, no shoes, a shirt outside her trousers in red and white checks like the tablecloth in a French café. The red of the checks near enough matched her socks, but clashed with the puce plastic golf balls of which her necklace was made. She was sitting on the floor at the feet of her boyfriend, smoking a Gauloise without inhaling and drinking the last of a litre of anonymous red from a supermarket.

The walls of the room where they sat were a lurid royal blue. The two boys had painted them the previous week, as a birthday present for Lottie, with the racing from Ascot unheeded on the TV in the corner. Lottie's boyfriend James Drummond, who was a painter and a waiter in a wine bar, had done wild drawings of centaurs, in imitation of Picasso, with the blue paint and a half-inch brush on the dingy mustard of the walls. Lottie had wanted to keep them—to leave the walls as they were, with the randy centaurs prancing all the way from skirting-board to ceiling: but the boys were more conservative—because of, or in spite of, being older and better educated—and they insisted on extending the paint all over the surfaces. The floor was of an unidentifiable substance, blotched with areas of red, as though the room had been used as a slaughterhouse. Over the place where the fireplace would have been, if the building had not been designed by planners, there was a large unframed painting by James, on loan, acrylic on hardboard—an urban landscape by night, in his neo-realistic manner. Lottie required anybody who came to the flat to admire it. She tried to sell it, on James's behalf, but her notions of price were unrealistic. On the other walls were posters, showing a concern with high fashion, rock, and political commitment.

The furniture was mostly cushions. They had eaten dinner off a table nine inches high. Lottie's flatmate Mary-Emma Black—M.E., Emmee or Emmeeeeee—had made covers for all the cushions, as she had made Lottie's trousers.

James would be borrowing the picture back for the exhibition, shared with two others, which would be held later in the year or early the next year, in a barn in Sussex which had been half turned into a gallery. It was time James had a break. He was twenty-six, and after the Royal College he had been painting professionally for four years. He was not totally unbought, but he was not making a living. Lottie had known him since the New Year. They had been on holiday together in May, backpacking in Italy. He was six foot three, thin, clumsy in movement as though he had suddenly shot to this height in the previous week and

was still unable to control so many cubits. His hair was
the same colour as Lottie's; it was the same length and cut
in the same style, because Emmee had cut the hair of both
of them the previous day. Emmee said that she would not
squat down to a birthday dinner with people who needed
haircuts.

Emmee was a tiny girl, five foot nothing and skinny,
who looked like a racing car whose chassis, brakes and
transmission were not rugged enough to cope with the
full power of the engine. Her hair was mouse-coloured,
copious and curly; she had a long face, enormous grey
eyes, a small mouth and a tiny pointed chin, so that she
resembled an over-filled ice-cream cone. She and a partner, a beefy cousin, ran a market-stall in Covent Garden, Portobello, Camden Passage and other places, selling whatever clothes, new and second-hand, they judged
would be tomorrow's fad. They had guessed right about
old woolly long johns, dyed and sold for a fiver to girls
like themselves and Lottie to wear at parties. They had
guessed right often enough that they were suspected not
of anticipating trends but of starting them. It was a job
that led absolutely nowhere, but it was better than Lottie's
jobs—house-cleaner, stand-in waitress, artist's model—
which seemed to be going backwards.

Emmee, a year older, thought she had a duty to be
motherly about Lottie, who would otherwise starve or
become a white slave: but she was careful not to let
this show. Lottie, four inches taller, thought she had a
duty to be motherly about Emmee, who would otherwise
shake herself to pieces, the overpowered machine crum-
bling the little brittle body: but she hoped she did not let
this show.

Emmee's boyfriend of nearly a year knew that he had
a duty to be responsible for all of them, because he was
nearly thirty and a commercial designer. He did too many
other things to be an unqualified success as a designer,
such as being responsible for his friends, painting people's

walls, and playing rhythm guitar in a group called Robert Smith Surtees. He was always called Thurber, because of his resemblance to a large, sad-eyed dog. He was thankful for this nickname because his real name was Sebastian Mallinson; his parents were great admirers of Evelyn Waugh. He had a sufficient but irregular income; he had bought the three litres of wine which were all the four of them drank.

The lasagne had been cooked by Emmee and Thurber. The can of lychees had been opened by James, who had cut his finger on the jagged edge of the lid. Lottie had not been allowed to do anything, except stick the Elastoplast on James's finger.

Lottie had not wanted a larger party, because there were not enough cushions. The cushions they had came from Emmee's mother's house in Buckinghamshire, where there were far too many cushions.

'Anything from your Ma, Lot?' asked Thurber suddenly. His own parents were in Guernsey. They were frightened for him. They never forgot his birthday.

'No,' said Lottie, the wary expression re-entering her eyes, as it had when she saw James pick up the can-opener. 'I haven't seen her for a year.'

'I find it extraordinary. She only lives a long spit away.'

'A spit into a different world,' said Emmee, who had seen Lottie's mother's house. 'Up a bloody mountain from the bottom.'

'This isn't the bottom,' said Thurber. 'Beautiful walls, beautiful picture, beautiful dinner.'

'Beautiful girls, beautiful wine,' said James.

And so to Lottie's relief the subject of her mother passed.

It was indeed a year, exactly a year. It had been her twenty-first birthday. Her mother gave a party for her, the first and last, because it would have looked so odd to her friends if she had not done so. Lottie had taken Giles to the party. That was a calamitously stupid thing to have done.

Giles was an asset to any party, though in some ways he was a liability.

Giles. Lottie's memory of her meeting with Giles still made her near to laughing and to weeping.

It was early April of the previous year, nearly fifteen months before. Her father's death, following hard on her brother's death, had severed what frail threads bound her to her family. Rienzo had been a thread, felt more by her than by him, until he borrowed his father's Jaguar once too often, and turned it over half-a-dozen times in the eastbound fast lane of the M4. Her father had been a rope, a narrow pipeline of contraband supply, too loyal, too punctilious to say anything to Lottie about her mother, but loving Lottie and very nearly saying that she had had a lousy deal. He was sorry that she had run away, but she thought he understood why she had done so. He understood that the charge of ingratitude was ridiculous.

After four years at one of the most expensive boarding schools in Britain, Lottie, at the age of sixteen and with one O Level in art, had joined the population under the railway arches. It was not comfortable, and she was not street-wise. After a week she managed to get her father on the telephone with her mother out of earshot. She had money after this, as much as her father could send her without her mother knowing. She found somewhere to sleep, and resumed the habit of eating. Much more than a week under the arches, and she might have been driven home by squalor and hunger and fear. Sustained by contraband tenners, left for her with the hall porter of White's, she managed all right.

That club had become the only place where her father was a completely free agent, writing what letters he wanted, and spending, cautiously, what cash he wanted. As a post office it was beyond price. Lottie used to wonder what the hall porter made of her, dressed the way her world dressed in second-hand shreds from street markets. But the porter was friendly, because he very obviously liked and respected her father.

Lottie learned quickly. She supplemented the tenners with scrubby little part-time jobs in the black economy. She shifted herself and her sleeping-bag from one condemned house to another, in Shepherd's Bush and Brixton and the East End. She bought an elderly bicycle from a black boy for a fiver; he did not pretend it was not stolen. She was not reduced to selling herself, body or soul.

Rienzo, two years younger than she, was in his third year at Eton. She went and saw him there once, but he was ashamed of her. She looked pretty good, but not to him. It was difficult for her and her father to meet. He was nearly seventy, retired, with less and less excuse to come to London. His wife kept an eye on him. She said it was because she was worried about him. She kept him at home in Berkshire; she answered the telephone for him and read and answered his letters. He and Lottie met in bizarre and furtive places, station waiting-rooms and pub car-parks.

Lottie was not so much unforgiven as a nuisance, an irrelevance. The Berkshire sun rose and set round Rienzo's shoulders. There was an aureole about his smooth dark head. All his life his mother had made sacrifices at the altar of Rienzo, and one of the lambs was Lottie.

Lottie's life went from bad to bad, and only sometimes to worse, for nearly three years. She finished growing. She grew in the kind of sophistication learned in squats and the kitchens of restaurants. She became friendly with Mary-Emma, whose mother was not an enemy but simply a citizen of a boring world, speaking a boring language. Lottie and Emmee became a team. Lottie was welcome at Emmee's mother's boring house, but not at her own mother's house.

It was just before Rienzo's seventeenth birthday that, at two in the morning, he celebrated failing his examinations at the wheel of his father's car.

Lottie wrote to her parents, addressing them jointly. It was a terrible letter to write. She did not suppose her father ever saw it. She did not expect a reply, and did not receive one.

It rained on the day of the funeral. Lottie, with faithful Emmee, huddled unseen at the back of the church. She tried telepathically to comfort her father, who looked broken, shattered, aged. He was still not seventy. Her mother's face was hidden. People supported her. As far as Lottie could remember, she was barely forty. Her figure was still slender, superb. Her black silk coat was close-fitting; she wore sheer black stockings; her veil covered only her face. Emmee, who had never seen her, was astonished that Lottie had such a mother. Her own mother spent her whole life in an apron. Emmee was astonished that Lottie was not with her parents at such a moment, in the church and at the graveside under the yews.

Lottie's flowers were hidden under mountains of flowers. She wept among the weeping yews. She was too far away to hear the parson's words at the graveside. Emmee was shocked.

Lottie had explained it all to Emmee, and did so again in the train both coming and going. Objectively Emmee understood, recognising that the situation was not unprecedented, that she had heard of other families which had simply fallen apart out of dislike or indifference. But emotionally it was all double-Dutch to her. Her experience of mothers did not equip her to understand Lottie's mother. She despised Lottie's father for being so completely under his wife's thumb, but as she had never in her life been under anybody's thumb, she had no experience to equip her to understand that, either.

The remittances continued, and the girls found the flat in Peckham. Emmee was more frequently in love than Lottie. Lottie had no chance of personal contact with her father, the summer after Rienzo's death; there was no point in writing or in trying to telephone.

Her father's death in October was a tragedy and a disaster rather than a surprise. Lottie thought he died of Rienzo's death. It was lucky, if any part of the whole thing could be called lucky, that somebody showed her the notice in *The Times*. There was a brief obituary, because although Gerald Bramall had not really been a public figure, he was popular and successful and he had had a very good war; he had been twice torpedoed as an officer in the R.N.V.R. It was terrible to think of that brave man and famous sportsman dwindling into the tottering wreck they had seen at Rienzo's funeral.

The paper said he died 'as the result of an accident at home'. None of Lottie's friends speculated, in her hearing, about the accident.

The funeral was in the same place and in the same weather. Lottie and Emmee sat in the same pew in the church, and stood under the same yew tree in the graveyard.

Emmee constituted herself a busybody. She sought out one of the undertaker's men, and got the name of the company. From the mortician's office, by telephone, she got the name of the executor of Lottie's father's estate, a lawyer in Abingdon. She told the lawyer's office where Lottie could be reached. Lottie did not resent this well-meant interfering, but she knew it was purposeless. She got a short letter from the lawyer, all kindness and condolence, in which there seemed to be astonishment and apology between the lines. Lottie was astonished at the astonishment—her mother had had full power over her father for all those years, and she had never expected to get a penny.

Lottie's mother immediately put the Berkshire house on the market. It sold very well very quickly, in spite of the unfavourable time of year, property values in the area having increased dramatically. The house and its out-buildings and the land fetched nearly half a million, on which no Capital Transfer or Capital Gains Tax were payable. Her husband had also left her a substantial fortune in equities and he was heavily insured.

She bought a house in London, had it redecorated from top to bottom, and furnished it with the very best of the very good pieces she now owned. The rest of the furniture, pictures and carpets went to auction. Nothing was put into store. The executor knew how Lottie could be reached, but her mother did not avail herself of the knowledge for six months.

That was the situation the following April, a bright blowy Tuesday, a day to fill you with optimism and benevolence. Even living in the middle of a desert of bricks and mortar, life was a lot easier in summer than in winter. Emmee and their friends were beginning to plan Lottie's twenty-first birthday, as Lottie and their friends had planned Emmee's the previous year.

Lottie found herself in Oxford Street at three o'clock in the afternoon, a bouncy, energetic, independent girl, handsome rather than pretty, untroubled for the moment by romance, with a new job in a deli. She was pretty smart by her standards, because of the job interview with the Cypriot manager of the deli, a man of old-fashioned ideas. She had dressed with Emmee's assistance and some of Emmee's clothes. For this reason among others she had left her bicycle at home; she joined a queue for a bus to Waterloo, by way of which she would ultimately reach Peckham.

In front of her in the queue stood an Asian woman with a gentle face, the shape of a vegetable marrow, swathed in shawls many of which would have been saleable by Emmee. Lottie forbore to make an offer for them.

In front of her stood a tall man in his late twenties. He was strikingly handsome, almost impossibly so. His hair was a bright chestnut, wavy without being curly, brushed back as smoothly as its natural spring and the April gusts would allow, cut not as short as a soldier's. His face was visible in profile when he turned his head to look across Oxford Street. His brow was high; he had strong cheekbones; his nose was hawky; he looked like an aristocratic Red Indian with an Irish grandmother. His nose was slightly irregular, as though it had long ago been broken. You could assume it had been broken in some gallant and glamorous way—on the polo field, in battle, or protecting an old lady from a gang of drunken muggers. This irregularity made him not less beautiful but more attractive, being not a flaw but a point of interest and humanity, something with a history, something over which hung an irresistible question mark.

His eyes seemed to be greeny-grey, an anonymous Anglo-Saxon colour, as far as could be judged in profile.

His clothes began conventionally with collar and tie, but became increasingly eccentric as the eye moved downwards.

His shirt was in bold checks, very much the sort Lottie's father had worn in Berkshire, the sort he would never have dreamed of wearing in London. Lottie thought it was frayed but had been trimmed with nail-scissors.

His tie was black, possibly silk, oddly teamed with the hearty country shirt, tied with a large knot. Lottie knew such knots. Some of the boys she knew had occasional cause to wear ties; the ties cost a few pence from sources socially lower than Emmee's market-stall; they had to be tied either with very large knots or with very small ones, in order to hide fraying, cigarette burns, or immovable stains.

Lottie wondered for a moment if you got a cigarette burn in your tie from your own cigarette or somebody else's.

The stranger's coat was of decent elderly tweed. It had been made for a man of less height but greater breadth of shoulder. This man looked fit and he held himself well, but he was very slender, and the shoulders of the coat extended beyond the angles of his own shoulders. The coat would have fitted Lottie's father pretty well.

Below the tweed coat, visible when Lottie peered with growing and amused curiosity round the shawls of the Asian woman, were unmistakable evening dress trousers—black, perhaps midnight blue, piped with a broad silk double band at the seam. They might have belonged to the same man as the coat: they had not been made for the wearer.

The man was burdened. Under his left arm he was carrying two bulging brown-paper parcels. In his right hand he held a suitcase, dented and torn in such a way as to show that it was made of cardboard; the handle had come adrift at one end, so that it was vertical in the bearer's hand, and the suitcase hung at an angle.

He looked like a Squadron Leader in a crack regiment of cavalry; he was dressed like an eccentric teacher in a progressive school. Lottie wondered how he would manage, if he got on a crowded bus. He wouldn't be able to hold on to anything, and he wouldn't be able to get to his pocket for money. Lottie hoped he was going somewhere where somebody would look after him.

An explanation came to her. He had been shell-shocked in battle. Possibly he had been kicked after a fall in the hunting-field or in a military steeplechase, so that his nose was broken and his mind permanently damaged. There was something innocently benevolent about the way he looked at the people in Oxford Street. Lottie had seen that look in the eyes of bullocks who had never heard of beefsteak.

Her bus came. The route was in general demand. The queue surged forward, under moderate discipline. The laden man seemed totally undecided whether to get on the bus or not. He looked at it with amiable doubt, as though it were an old friend whose invitation to lunch was probably convenient but possibly not. Some school-children, a black girl, the Asian woman, a fat young man all climbed on the bus knowing exactly what they were doing and where they were going. The bus was nearly full. There were people standing. There were still people on the stairs.

Lottie wanted to get on the bus, but she thought somebody should take responsibility for the brain-damaged man with the bundles.

He solved her immediate problem by suddenly deciding that the bus was an answer to prayer. He stepped onto it with a grace and assurance which fitted his face but were at odds with his clothes and belongings. Lottie followed him, at the last moment, less gracefully although she was carrying nothing.

The inside was full. The conductor sent them upstairs. The man understood that he was to climb the stairs of the bus, which was now swooping past Selfridges. Lottie was immediately behind him, holding tight to the handrail. Without a free hand the man lurched, staggered, seemed in danger of falling downstairs onto Lottie. He dropped one of his parcels. The remaining staple securing the handle of his suitcase came off, so that the suitcase tumbled. Suitcase and bundle both burst on Lottie's knees and shins, piling many books and a few garments round her legs as though she was the pier of a bridge in a river full of debris.

'That was inevitable,' said the man.

He now held the remaining parcel under his left arm, and he was at last, somehow, holding to the handrail with his left hand. His right hand gripped the handle of the suitcase, a five-inch curve of imitation leather of no further use.

To the handle he said: 'It was lunacy to trust you.' To Lottie he said: 'I beg your pardon, Madam. Please feel at liberty to tread on my possessions.' To the bus at large he said: 'Salvage will now commence.' His voice was light, pleasant, educated and apparently sane.

The bus braked sharply to avoid a daredevil courier on a Yamaha, causing the man to swing on the handrail, to drop his remaining parcel, and to embrace Lottie round the shoulders.

Lottie began to laugh. The people on top of the bus, to whom the episode had been invisible, saw nothing to laugh at. The man laughed with Lottie, continuing to embrace

her in order to save himself from falling downstairs. They
swayed together, as though in an old-fashioned nightclub.

'What are you going to put it all in?' said Lottie.

'I'm not,' said the man. 'I'm going to abandon the lot
of it. I'm going to jump off the bus when the conductor
isn't looking.'

'You *can't*.'

'Is it litter? Would it be antisocial just to leave it? I
suppose it is blocking the stairs. I would like to keep the
books.'

Lottie began picking up the books, while continuing to
hold on to the handrail. She tried to pile them into the
man's free arm, but they tended to fall off his arm and
down the stairs. The bus slowed for a stop. People wanted
to come down the stairs. It was their clear right to do so.
Lottie and her new friend had to come down the stairs
to get out of the way. The people made what seemed a
genuine effort not to tread on the books and clothes, but
some things got trodden on and some pushed further down
the stairs. A shoe landed at the conductor's feet as the bus
stopped.

The bus turned down Regent Street. By the time it
reached Piccadilly Circus, Lottie and her friend had gathered most of the things that had not fallen off the bus into
the street. The conductor helped them, when his duties
allowed. Other people helped them. There was an atmosphere of goodwill and amusement. A club formed, speedily
dissolved, devoted to reassembling the man's goods. People glanced at the titles of his books, and saw that they
were in foreign languages. A new population inhabited the
bus, who were not members of the club.

The conductor got around to asking Lottie and the man
for their fares. Lottie bought her ticket. The man asked
for an address on the Bayswater Road. He was told he
was going in the wrong direction, that he had caught an
eastbound bus instead of a westbound, that he should have
been waiting on the other side of Oxford Street, that he

was being rushed further and further away from where he wanted to go.

His good humour was unimpaired.

'I don't really want to go there anyway,' he said. 'It's just an address I was given.'

'Where do you want to go, cock?' said the conductor, who was already editing the story for his mates in the canteen.

The man looked at Lottie, smiling, as though asking her opinion. Where did he want to go?

'I think,' said Lottie, half in love, 'you'd better come to Peckham.'

C·H·A·P·T·E·R

2

Emmee was at first nonplussed by Lottie's new companion. She thought Lottie was being conned. She herself was inclined to collect lame ducks, but she tried to protect Lottie from doing so. This man was beautiful, and he had the most charming old-fashioned manners (something about which Emmee herself was old-fashioned) but at his age and with his education he ought not to need the help of someone like Lottie.

Emmee saw that she was being expected to mother Lottie's new friend as well as Lottie herself. Before she consented to any such thing, she wanted a lot of straight answers to straight questions.

'Don't be such a bully,' said Lottie, softly, in the kitchen.

'I just want to know what we're letting ourselves in for,' said Emmee.

'It needn't be anything to do with you.'

'You're so bloody trusting.'

The stranger was given a mug of instant coffee, and invited to sit down on a cushion. He lowered himself gracefully and sat on the cushion elegantly, which Lottie had seen very few people do. He was perfectly agreeable to answering questions.

'My life is an open book,' he said, in his pleasant, educated, light baritone. 'No secrets, or if there are I shan't tell you about them. No criminal record, except for the time I was arrested in Barcelona for eating flowers. No vices, not even sloth. I think I may once have coveted my neighbour's maidservant, but that was when I was six. I have often been in love since, but never with such absorbing passion.'

'Can you read this?' said Emmee, holding up a paperback of Dante's *Inferno*, in Italian, rescued from the bus.

'Well, yes, I spent a year in Italy.'

'*Ha fatto che cosa?*' said Lottie, who had tried to get an Italian O Level and who, when being a waitress, had practised on many Italian waiters in London.

'*Quasi niente.*'

'*Che peccato.*'

'*Si.*'

'Stop showing off,' said Emmee.

Emmee's examination of their guest was prolonged, discontinuous owing to other calls on her time, and not conducted according to the chronology of the subject: but they got it all in the end.

His name was Giles Lambert. He was the younger son of an Anglo-Irish peer called Lord Enniscorthy, now elderly and confused and living in a nursing-home in County Wexford. Giles's mother was dead. He had been an unexpected and unwelcome son of their old age. The early Georgian mansion of Lambertstown, in the West, had been gutted by fire in the Troubles. Giles's older brother, heir to the title, was fifty years old and farming in New Zealand; he had paid for Giles's education. The family, though obscurely noble, was not related to the differently spelled Lambarts, the Earls of Cavan.

Education? Winchester and a scholarship to New College.

'Then you've actually got a degree?'

'Well, actually not. There always seemed to be so much else to do. And then, you know, it was a bit like a pious Christian suddenly losing his faith. We were studying the history of mediaeval France, and I was invited to write an essay on the Cathars—'

'The what?'

'Albigensians. Manicheans.'

They looked at him blankly.

'Heretical sect in Languedoc, destroyed in large part by Simon de Montfort. They built a lot of little castles on hilltops. They probably invented *cassoulet*, which is really only pork and beans.'

'No it's not,' said Emmee. 'There's a lot more to *cassoulet* than that, and there are lots of ways of making it.'

Emmee had few books, but among them there were big ones on French and Italian regional cookery.

Giles grinned.

Lottie saw that he was one of the people whose faces were lit up by a smile, as though by a brilliant internal lamp. His face was handsome in repose; smiling, he was beautiful. She could not take her eyes off him.

'Well, what about your essay?' said Emmee, returning to the examination, like prosecuting counsel after a recess.

'What essay? Oh, the Cathars. I suddenly decided I didn't care about them. I wasn't interested in them or the Pope or St Dominic or any of it. I didn't care what they believed or what happened to them. I do now, partly because I've been there and it's wonderful, but at that moment I didn't. I told my tutor so. That was the beginning of the end of my academic career.'

'Didn't you care about *anything*?'

'Oh yes, all sorts of things, too many things, that was the trouble. That, I suppose, is why I've had so many different jobs. I've always been able to get jobs, but I've never wanted to keep them. Really what I want to do is sit and write a book.'

'What sort of book?'

'That's what I can never quite decide. Sometimes I think a volume of critical essays, destroying established reputations and elevating certain unknowns to the eminence they deserve. Of course I should be a subjective critic. Sometimes I think an autobiography, and sometimes a novel. But the novel would really be an autobiography, and the autobiography would be dreadfully like a novel.'

He had material for an autobiography, undoubtedly. A wild Irish childhood, running far out of the ken of elderly parents, near-fatal scrapes and brilliant success at school, a prolonged party at Oxford (pretty girls, punts, champagne cocktails), his year studying Italian and art history in Rome, Florence, Venice, his periods—some of more than a year, some apparently of days or even hours—as art dealer, journalist, wine merchant, assistant racehorse trainer, travel-agent's courier, film extra, advertising copywriter, and minicab driver.

'That was my briefest career,' said Giles. 'They told me to go to an address, and I couldn't find it. I got completely lost, going round and round Belsize Park. I was running out of petrol. So I drove into what I thought was a filling-station, but it was a flight of steps going down to a tunnel under the road.'

'How could you have thought that was a filling-station?'

'Very silly of me. They look quite different. It wasn't a job I was cut out for. I realised that, when we got to the bottom of the steps.'

'Were you hurt?'

'Only spiritually. My pride was hurt. The car was hurt worse. It scraped all its insides out of itself. I tried to drive it up the stairs on the other side, but it thought it had done enough. I thought I'd done enough, too. I can't imagine how they got it out of that tunnel. I cleverly joined a crowd of people which collected to stare at the car. We all got very friendly, wondering aloud to one another who could have been such a monumental fool as to drive a car down a flight of steps. I remember expressing myself pretty satirically about it. We had a good laugh.'

'You just walked away and left it?'

'After a decent interval. Without unseemly haste. But time was speeding by and I wanted another job. I became a cabinet-maker. I never understood why so called, because one of the rarest things one is called upon to make is a cabinet.'

Lottie thought the minicab part of his autobiography was, indeed, very like a novel; in fact she had the idea that she had read the novel, long ago, perhaps at school.

'Where have you been living and where are you going to live?' asked Emmee.

'I've been away from London for a long time,' said Giles. 'The property market seems to have gone mad.'

'Marcus Hills has a spare bed . . .'

Lottie nodded. The thought had occurred to her. Marcus lived directly below them, his flat served by the same awful staircase. His flat-mate Elmer was doing three months for stealing from cars. Marcus was deeply in love with Elmer. 'I shall wait for him,' he said. Their relationship seemed to be stable, so it was unlikely that Marcus would fall in love with Giles.

Lottie seemed to herself to be falling in love with Giles. She supposed Emmee was doing so too; they had never fallen in love with the same man before, and it might put a strain on their friendship.

Lottie was energetic and independent, and since her father's death she had paid her own way. That made her, she thought, the sort of person who would be useful to the sort of person Giles was: charming, educated, talented and beautiful, but without sense of direction. Lottie had no sense of direction, either, but she expected to have one by the time she was Giles's age. Meanwhile she thought she could help Giles find one.

Even dressed as he was, Giles could go anywhere. He was clean and well-shaven. He had had a bath in the last twenty-four hours, and a shave in the last twelve. Emmee could see that as well as Lottie could.

One other thing was to be got straight. Emmee thought

it needed to be clearly stated, out in the open, although to
Lottie it was clear already. Emmee was not abashed at asking the question—it was difficult to imagine her abashed at
asking anybody any question. This particular question need
not immediately have arisen, except for Marcus Hills.

Giles was surprised by the question, more so than by any
of Emmee's other questions; this was apparently because it
had not occurred to him that the answer was not obvious.

Emmee was reassured. Giles was entirely heterosexual.
There was not the slightest danger of an entanglement with
Marcus, the consequences of which would have been miserable. Girls had been a part of Giles's undoing at Oxford
and ever since.

Why never married, at his age?

'I'm not so very antique,' he said, still sweet-tempered
in the face of what might have been thought Emmee's
impertinence. 'Actually there have been a number of narrow escapes. Not me escaping—I was all for it. The girls
escaped. They saw it wouldn't do. Sometimes the family
got it through to the girl, sometimes she realised it all on
her own.'

'What wouldn't do?'

'They thought I wouldn't do. When I was younger,
they were right. I was too young, and I'd been terribly
spoiled. They don't always realise it, but most girls want
a solid rock, a sturdy oak tree. I could never pretend to
be one of them. You know what people expect one to
be? Predictable. I do see the point. Life for most people is only livable by the exercise of empiricism. If we
didn't know, from experience, that tonight would follow
today and tomorrow tonight, then where would we be?
Floundering. Disoriented. Unequipped to make any plan
or decision. If circumstances oblige or tempt me to cross
this room, I do so in the reasonable confidence that there
will not be a trapdoor in my path, depositing me in an
oubliette a hundred feet below. That is the lesson of experience, of a lifetime of crossing rooms. One chapter of my

autobiography will be entitled "Rooms I have crossed, with notes on the absence of trapdoors in modern domestic architecture".'

'None of those girls would marry you,' said Lottie indulgently, 'because you talk too much.'

By nightfall Giles was re-equipped, in a sufficiency of particulars, with clothes to replace those that had fallen under the traffic of Oxford Street. This was an area in which Emmee was an expert, and had expert contacts. Oxfam and street-markets. She had a tape-measure and she knew where to go.

Giles now had a dark greeny-brown, medium-weight tweed coat with a faint red overcheck, not new but perfectly presentable, its lining needing a little attention. It fitted him well: perhaps the sleeves were a fraction short. His previous coat went in part exchange. He had dark grey worsted trousers, pretty new, newly cleaned, with creases down the front and pockets entire. They were a lucky buy at six pounds because his legs were unusually long. He had two Viyella shirts, in small checks, scarcely frayed at all. Unfrayed shirt-cuffs were important, as Emmee pointed out, since the sleeves of the jacket were a bit short. His tie was in a discreet Paisley pattern, and when tied any part of it could be displayed. His shoes were heavyweight loafers, made in the state of Maine, which could be made to take polish although they had not done so for some time. Socks, underpants, handkerchiefs and nightclothes had survived the disasters of the bus. He would not be needing an overcoat or a heavy sweater for some months.

Giles wore his new clothes as though they were his clothes. Lottie never saw him look in a mirror. While Emmee was conducting the various negotiations, he waited quietly. His wavy chestnut hair became tousled when he was trying on clothes; he pushed it back with his hands; it looked fine. He still did not look in a mirror.

Emmee's attitude to Giles seemed to change, during the

afternoon, during their conversations. When they got back
to the flat, she did not ask Giles to sit on a cushion on the
floor, but fetched a stool from the kitchen. He half perched
on it as though in a fashionable bar, as though posing
for a photograph by Lord Lichfield for an Aquascutum
advertisement in the *New Yorker*. He was their senior, of a
different generation, a kind of uncle. He was sophisticated,
widely travelled, deeply informed about all kinds of things
of which Emmee and Lottie, their education interrupted,
had hardly heard. It would have been unthinkable now to
subject him to the kind of questioning to which Emmee
had earlier subjected him.

There might be things about Giles which were whimsical, even freakish, but there was much that was impressive
and nothing that was boring.

His grin still lit his face like a brilliant internal lamp.

They pushed a note through Marcus Hills's letterbox,
asking him to dinner if he was back on time, and mentioned
a desirable potential tenant. They had bought enough dinner
for Marcus as well as for Giles.

Marcus appeared shortly after eight o'clock, fat, well-
scrubbed, bespectacled, a year or two younger than Giles.
He had a high voice and a West Country accent. In face
and manner he was like an old-fashioned servant, or like
the man who had cut Lottie's father's hair at Trumper's.
From the neck down he was in a prison uniform of blue
denim. He was tired after a day of trying to rig lights
in a place where it was impossible. He took one look
at Giles, and said that his slum was totally unfitted for
housing such a person. He took Giles one floor down to
look at it, however, and came back beaming.

Something was bothering Marcus later in the evening.
Lottie realised that it was that he needed a bit of rent but
did not like to ask for it. She reassured him, while he
helped her get the coffee. He said the arrangement could
only be until Elmer came home.

Giles kissed Lottie goodnight, when he went downstairs

with Marcus—an avuncular peck, somewhere in the region of the left eye. He kissed Emmee too. Marcus kissed them both, with far more of a flourish, as he had long been in the habit of doing.

Lottie concluded that she was really in love for the first time in her life.

Marcus Hills was apologetic about everything, but there was really very little to apologise about. The flat was like all the others in the gigantic Council block. It was cleaner than many, and hung with minimalist paintings by a friend. Elmer's bed, to be used by Giles, was in the sitting room. It was intended to resemble a sofa by day. Marcus made up the bed with a clean sheet and a clean duvet cover. He showed Giles where he could hang his clothes, and gave him half a dozen wire coathangers. He apologised for the wardrobe and the coathangers.

'I don't believe anything about that man,' said Emmee to Lottie when they were both in bed. 'I don't believe anything about today, that bus of yours, that life-story of his, the minicab in the tunnel. We'll wake up and find that it's yesterday morning, that today hasn't actually happened, that we dreamed the whole thing. I thought I might fall in love with him, but I could see you were doing that, so I thought I'd better not.'

Lottie did not answer. She was already asleep, emotionally and physically exhausted.

Marcus Hills called Giles at eight o'clock with a cup of Earl Grey tea. He prepared coffee and wholemeal toast, while Giles was drinking his tea in bed.

Giles, half-dressed and full of breakfast, said that he would do the washing-up. Marcus forbade this, on account of fears for the Luneville breakfast cups and for Giles's trousers. Marcus himself had been wearing his apron, which

was a cheerful design of scarlet poppies on a yellow
ground, and had been a birthday present from Emmee.
Giles said that he would wear it when he washed up.
Marcus had to go out, to travel all the way to the outer
suburbs to be both an electrician and a creative artist; his
last words were to forbid Giles to do the washing-up.

Marcus got home very tired at seven-thirty, with a poly-
thene bag full of groceries. He found the flat empty. He
remembered that he had not given Giles a key. He half
hoped that Giles had disobeyed him about the washing-
up. Giles had; everything was washed and dried and put
away.

Emmee called in. Lottie was out working in one of
the places where she worked, and she had taken Giles
with her.

'I'm not sure about Giles as a waiter,' said Marcus. 'I'm
not very sure about that at all.'

'Lottie wouldn't dream of letting Giles be a waiter,'
said Emmee. 'She's setting her sights much higher. So
is he. He's going back to being a wine merchant or an
art dealer or something. What she's doing this evening is
getting him a free meal.'

'I've got dinner. I went shopping at lunchtime.'

'Then let's have it.'

Emmee in the event produced some of the food. They
talked about giving a party for Lottie's twenty-first birthday, not three months off.

Giles and Lottie came back soon after midnight, Lottie
now dressed as the waitresses were dressed in the restaurants where she imagined her mother had dinner, if her
mother had dinner in restaurants. Giles, in his smart and
slightly countrified clothes, looked a member of a different
species. He looked as though he frequented the restaurants
where Lottie's mother could be imagined going.

'Tomorrow is another day,' said Giles. 'My batteries are
recharged by hospitality, generosity, *escalope de veau*, and

a wine over which it would be kindest to draw a veil.'

'Ungrateful pig,' said Lottie, with such love in her voice that Emmee and Marcus glanced at one another, touched but troubled.

'Tomorrow will see Lambert Enterprises switching smoothly into top gear, into overdrive. Nervous persons are advised to stand clear. What contacts have we got, to provide openings for a young fellow who simply needs a chance to prove himself? You must remember that I've been away from London for a long time.'

Marcus, thus challenged, revealed predictable contacts in various fringe worlds of theatre, music, the arts.

'I see myself as an actor,' said Giles. 'Not Hamlet. A different sort of actor.'

'No, you don't,' said Lottie.

'There might be a problem with an Equity card,' said Marcus, trying in as kindly a way as possible to divert Giles's mind into more fruitful avenues.

'Cards,' said Giles. 'One of the things I have never been is a card-sharper. I should like to have worn a white fedora hat and a tie made of a black bootlace, and plied up and down the Mississippi on an old-time steamboat. The drawback is that I don't like Bourbon whisky.'

Emmee's contacts were extensive, running like the wiring of a jet's instrument panel through all the trades of all the markets where she sold things. It was not a world which Giles would understand or which would understand him. She had many friends also in the block where they lived: some of them were friends because they lived there, and some lived there because they were friends. A few were fugitives from Giles's native world, which, come to think of it, was Lottie's native world. Most were younger than Giles. They were on their way to some place at which they had by no means arrived. None had an entrée to Agnews or Justerini and Brooks.

Lottie's father would have been a help. It did not occur to any of them to think of approaching her mother.

They went to bed with Giles's latest assault on the world unplanned.

Two evenings later, Giles returned to Peckham in triumph. He arrived on the pillion of a motorcycle, shrouded in a plastic overall and camouflaged by a spherical white crash-helmet. The driver was a girl in black leather with metal studs. Giles stood talking to her for a time, before she roared away. She did not take off her helmet, so they never saw her face.

He had a job in a shop selling prints, near Charing Cross station.

'Prince who?' said Lottie blankly.

'Etchings, engravings, woodcuts, lithographs and the like,' said Giles. 'Any two-dimensional specimen of the visual arts which has been mechanically reproduced.'

'That's a field where you have to know what you're doing,' said Emmee. To her, the serious sellers of etchings were a kind of aristocracy of her world.

Giles intimated, unboastfully, that he knew very well what he was doing.

He mentioned, with easy familiarity, a number of Italian, French and Flemish names. Some, he said, were currently underpriced, and should be bought and held for a year or two. Others were overpriced, and should be unloaded on the first punter who had the money.

Lottie hugged him, crowing. She looked at Emmee with a triumph as great as Giles's.

'Who was your friend on the motorbike?' said Emmee.

Giles did not know. He had met her in the Strand. He did not know what she was called, what she did, or where she had really been going. It was just lucky that she had spare overalls and skidlid.

Lottie thought it the most natural thing in the world. Giles needed transport from Charing Cross to Peckham, so a girl popped up with a motorbike and a spare skidlid— of course she did.

Emmee was not yet used to the idea, so obvious to Lottie, that the whole world was designed to be at Giles's disposal. The motorcycle, its rider, the spare crash-helmet, all in the right place at the right moment, were in effect invented at that moment. They were called into being because Giles required them. The girl had not roared off to anywhere—she had gone back to limbo. Lottie had been on that particular bus, at the beginning of the week, because Giles wanted her there. She had not gone back to limbo because he still wanted her. Emmee had been on hand because Giles wanted her. Elmer had gone off to prison because Giles needed a place to stay. When Giles moved on, if he ever did, what would become of them all, suddenly no further use to Giles?

That was Friday. Giles was starting in the print-shop on Monday.

Lottie was busy all weekend, because overtime was crucial to her budgeting.

Emmee worked all Saturday, but she was free on Sunday. She thought Giles should meet his new neighbours, many of whom had nothing to do and nowhere to go on Sunday.

Giles had already met a surprising number; he had been into a surprising proportion of the flats, been given coffee or wine, been the recipient of many hopes, fears and other confidences. He had not knocked on people's doors, nor they on his. It had all happened almost overnight.

Giles on Monday was a new Giles. He was purposeful, executive, early rising. He left before Marcus did, and when Lottie was sleepily rubbing her eyes, in her dressing gown, by her bedroom window, Giles was off to the station. He was a cog in the commercial life of the capital, a wage-earner, a burden on nobody, independent and self-respecting. A part of Lottie's mind regretted this foreseeable development: a part of her would have liked him to be helpless.

• • •

Marcus and his director ran a lighting rehearsal. The company was very professional for people who were not being paid. He came back, late and very tired, to find that Giles had cooked dinner. Giles was wearing the apron with the design of red poppies, with less apparent self-consciousness than Marcus felt when he wore it. Giles had produced a dinner on the elaborate side, for working men dining *à deux*. He had broken nothing; if he had spilled anything he had wiped it up.

The communal, student-like spirit of the block accepted Giles with initial surprise, because he looked like a country gentleman, but with rapid and increasing affection. Although he remained inevitably an exotic, he was one of them. He was friendly and funny. He was evidently Lottie's property, but that did not stop some of the girls—hopeful actresses and artists—from trying to challenge her ownership. Giles treated them all politely.

Giles was a man who got to his feet when a female—any female—entered a room. He opened doors for women, and lit their cigarettes. Some of the people in the block had never seen such behaviour before: some only in the performances of William Powell in pre-war black-and-white comedies on late-night television. It was so popular with the girls that it began to be imitated by the men.

All this happened inside ten days.

Giles's second weekend in Peckham, the end of his first fortnight there. Emmee was away Saturday afternoon and night and most of Sunday because her mother needed help with the spring cleaning. Marcus was away seeing Elmer, and checking up on Elmer's family, and trying to ensure that Elmer was not bankrupt when he came out.

Giles and Lottie were surrounded by friends, but they were cocooned in the special, peaceful isolation of a Sunday in London.

• • •

Lottie had a rule that she only made love when she was in love. It was a rule that she had never broken, and it meant that her experience was limited and recent. Nobody who knew her thought she was a tart. Men who started by thinking so, customers in the wine bars where she worked as a waitress, were disabused before they spent much money.

Lottie sent messages of apology to Emmee's mother, who was probably expecting her for the weekend to help with the spring-cleaning. Probably Emmee's mother thought both girls needed feeding up. Emmee understood the whole situation; she felt envious, sentimental and troubled.

'You're too young,' said Giles. 'The temptation is enormous, but I don't think this is something that I ought to do. I've always suspected myself of a streak of old-fashioned morality, probably instilled when I was beaten so often at my prep school. A man of my age and experience is not supposed to take cynical advantage of the generosity and affection of a girl who is not even twenty-one. I am honoured and flattered and excited and tempted, but my conscience tells me that this would be wrong. The main and most obvious potential of this situation is that you will get hurt. Your personality is generous, trusting, affectionate and essentially simple. These qualities make it easy for you to get hurt. Your capacity for loving is a capacity for suffering. I can't do it, Lottie.'

Lottie was not going to have any of that nonsense.

On Sunday they did not dress until after lunch. Lottie spent part of the morning wearing the apron with the red poppies, and nothing else. Giles sat watching her, with what he said himself was a silly grin on his face. He offered to help in any way at all. She forbade him to help in any way at all. He compared her unfavourably to Marcus.

Before lunch he counted out, from the pocket of the

jacket he was not wearing, money which covered all that Emmee, Marcus and Lottie had spent on him. This included the smallest details, which he had painstakingly listed—bus-fares, wine, his share of the half-pound of New Zealand butter which Marcus and he had been eating for breakfast.

After lunch they put on some clothes, and went for a blustery, sunshiny walk on Peckham Rye Common. There were blacks and lovers and dogs and families with young children. It was a short walk, because they were preoccupied with one another, and with the thought of getting back to the flat with plenty of time before the others returned.

With an expression of absorbed solemnity, Giles unbuttoned, unhooked and unzipped all Lottie's clothes, and took them off garment by garment, while she stood in a trance in the middle of her bedroom floor. He let all the clothes lie where they fell. He took off his own clothes in about three seconds, letting them lie where they fell.

Giles was slim and athletic. There was no hair on his body except where it was to be expected. There were visible ribs, and visible, usable muscles in his diaphragm and thighs. Lottie prodded his muscles in wonder. His muscles felt like bands of leather, like the trousers of the girl who had given him a lift on her motor-cycle. He snorted, because she was tickling him.

Afterwards, her close-cropped head on his chest, he began to talk in a roundabout way about marriage. They were still talking about it, not having moved, when Emmee came home just as it was getting dark.

Emmee made a noise like an apologetic steam-engine, and went into the kitchen to put the kettle on for tea.

'It will appear to you,' said Giles later in the evening to Emmee, 'that I have done exactly what I swore to myself that I would not do. That as an experienced worldling I have taken advantage of the generosity and vulnerability of a very young girl. In the event it was not quite like that. I was picked up by a tornado, like the girl in *The Wizard of Oz*. I was whisked away and deposited in another country, inhabited by angels, where rules were different. You know her better than anybody else. Can you wonder that I'm in love with Lottie?'

'Now,' said Emmee to Lottie, 'you'll really have to get in touch with your mother.'

'If I write to her, she'll just throw the letter away.'

'It's not possible. Her only daughter, her only child?'

'It's not just possible, it's what would happen.'

'Ring her up.'

'How can I?'

'I suppose she's in the book.'

'She'd just hang up on me.'

'I don't believe it.'

'Then you try.'

Emmee tried—not just then, late at night, but in the middle of the following morning.

The voice to which she was connected, by way of a servant, was one she had never heard before—immediately friendly, cultured, rather high and light like a young girl's voice, hesitant, possibly shy, with no trace of arrogance or bitchiness, with an attractive hint of breathiness, of childish excitement.

'I have tried to blank Charlotte out of my life,' said this nice voice, the voice of this apparently nice person, 'because it is so unpleasant having one's heart broken. But if she sees this as a—a reason, an excuse, a platform for us being together again, for her being my daughter again . . .'

'Then?' said Emmee, feeling as though a new sun were rising in a new sky.

'Then I shall be very joyful to be a mother again.'

Lottie's mother said that she was absolutely committed to going abroad almost at once, to stay with friends near Biarritz and then other friends in other places. She expected to be back in about six weeks.

Emmee thought this a little odd. She would have expected Lottie's mother to have dropped everything and rushed round to Peckham, or to have required Lottie to drop everything and rush round, with or without Giles, to Battersea. But she knew that the old had an obsession about adhering to arrangements. Her own mother was hardly sane on the subject: no visitor, having been asked, could be put off—no invitation, having been accepted, could be ignored. Emmee accepted that Lottie's mother was not available for motherhood for some weeks.

Emmee cautiously mentioned Lottie's approaching twenty-first birthday. There was a sort of shy whoop at the other end of the line. Lottie's mother would give her a twenty-first birthday party. That would be a reunion in which all the misunderstandings would melt.

Catching Lottie's eye during the conversation, Emmee saw in it the look of wariness which had been frequent but had become rare.

Hanging up, Emmee was a little jealous that Lottie's mother, rather than she herself and their friends, had taken charge of Lottie's birthday. But it was obviously a good thing all round, for Giles and for their future together as well as for Lottie and her mother.

The wary look remained in Lottie's eyes, until Giles came home from work in the evening.

C · H · A · P · T · E · R

3

The engagement was announced in dribbles. It did not occur to Lottie that her private affairs were matter that should be published in a newspaper. If it occurred to Giles he said nothing about it. Few of Lottie's friends ever saw *The Times*, or would have dreamed of buying space in it.

One of the first to hear was the boss at Lottie's new part-time job, the Greek Cypriot who managed the deli off Oxford Street. He heard because Lottie asked for time off, to go shopping with Giles. It came out better if you said 'my fiancé' than if you said 'my boyfriend'. The manager was a strong family man, like all his people, and he thought Lottie was not too young to be engaged, but if anything too old. His complete approval was heartening, and ensured that she got the time off.

Gradually, gradually, during the rest of April and the whole of May, the engagement between Giles and Lottie became established by virtue of its being known. It became certain that they would eventually marry, because so many people knew they would. It was history in reverse—not general knowledge based on evidence, but evidence derived from general knowledge.

Lottie sailed about London on her bicycle in a cloud of such happiness as she had never known. Strangers smiled back at her smile. Armoured by love, she took insane risks, unscathed, in heavy traffic.

In the second week of May, Giles moved from the Charing Cross print-shop to another, in the Tottenham Court Road, more specialist and more expensive.

'I feel a nostalgic affection for the old place,' he said. 'A poor thing, but our own. The trouble was the commission. I would have negotiated a profitable sale, in my most winning and boyish manner, and Mr Harris would appear, from nowhere, his head in the region of my solar plexus, and suddenly complete the transaction. The purchaser flattered by the personal interest of the proprietor. The latter charmed by not having to pay commission to his employee. Lambert out on a limb.'

'Limbert out on a lamb,' said Lottie. 'Limbert the lamb. Limbert the lambkin.'

'I am either much too young for all this,' said Emmee austerely, 'or much too old.'

For his new job, Giles needed new clothes. The quality of the prints he was selling required a dark suit. The one he got, with the help of friends of Emmee's, was dark grey barathea, by Huntsman of Savile Row, made for a tall, slender man who had hardly worn it.

Dressed in his dark business suit, Giles looked utterly incongruous among the people of the Peckham block.

The suit needed new shirts, ties, shoes. Giles could now afford them.

Giles did not do anything so pompous as to teach Lottie. He did not give her lectures, sit her down in front of art books, prescribe a course of reading, or oblige her to listen to tapes of classical music. He rammed nothing down anybody's throat. He did not even seem to talk much about art in any of its forms, history, his travels, fine wine, or other unattainable things that he knew about.

But Lottie had the sense of being educated by Giles.

Through his pores when they lay in bed, from the atmosphere which surrounded him when they sat talking, she absorbed a sensitivity to the beautiful and the excellent which was completely outside her previous perceptions. Other people remarked on it. She was accused of becoming highbrow. Probably, because it was all new to her, she talked about it too much—far more than Giles ever did, even to her.

They did go to exhibitions and concerts together. Giles knew where they were and whether they were worth going to. Almost imperceptibly, Giles helped Lottie to appreciate what she saw and heard.

Marcus understood, because he had been trying to do the same for Elmer, before Elmer's unfortunate misunderstanding. Marcus thought Giles's taste was hopelessly traditionalist, because he preferred Beethoven to Berg, Rembrandt to Rouault. But Marcus admitted that, in the discredited academic sense, Giles knew far more than he did.

Lottie felt like one of the Japanese paper flowers that visitors to Court Farm had given Rienzo and herself as children—flowers which were pallid dry nothings until you put them in water, in your toothglass, but which, after a little, expanded and blushed and opened and came to lovely life. It was as though Giles had plugged her into a source of power she had not known existed: as though he had opened doors onto gardens previously invisible, forbidden, unguessed.

She realised for the first time what a pity it was that she had run away from school when she did, half educated, ignorant of anything important. Avidly she made up for lost time, lost ground, lost chances.

'You ought to disagree with me more,' said Giles.

Lottie knew what he meant. She was to develop personal standards on which to base personal judgements. But, try as she might, she never found it possible to disagree with him.

• • •

Physically, their relationship was stunning. Lottie had never dreamed of such sweetness and excitement.

The moment that moved her most was when, lying quiet after passion, she felt tears on her cheek which were not her tears. If Giles had old friends, he never seemed to see them. And he must have—his Irish childhood, Winchester, Oxford, his travels, his many jobs. Where were they? He never greeted people at exhibitions, in the intervals of concerts, in theatre foyers.

Lottie began to have the sense that he was avoiding people, his own previous and proper world—that he was refusing to recognise people that he perfectly well recognised. She accused him of being ashamed of her, of not wishing to be seen with a common-looking ratbag like herself.

He silenced that one pretty quick, leaving her breathless with adoration.

He explained it obliquely, by reference to an experience in a fairground in the South of France: one foot on the carousel, one on its static rim.

'A sense of otherness,' he said. 'It was foolish to get in such a predicament. I should have chosen to revolve amongst the horses and camels, or remain unmoving amongst the anxious adults. By embarking on one environment while remaining in another, I risked probable injury and certain ridicule.'

'Which am I,' said Lottie, 'a camel or an anxious mother?'

'An anxious mother camel,' said Giles; and she felt his smile, under her face, in the darkness.

At the beginning of June, Lottie's mother began to make amends, in Emmee's eyes, for the unaccountable indifference of the previous weeks, to say nothing of the previous years.

The telephone rang several times. When Lottie or Giles

or anybody else answered it, the line went dead. When Emmee answered it, a voice she knew said, 'Mary-Emma Black? This is Charlotte's mother. Are you alone? I want to talk to you absolutely privately.'

Emmee was not alone, and did not foresee being alone in the flat for the rest of the day or night. She agreed to ring up Lottie's mother from Covent Garden, from a box. She wrote down the number. She was thoroughly puzzled and fairly suspicious.

The reason for the furtiveness was made clear, later in the morning, when they talked again. Lottie's mother was bent on giving the party, but she wanted it to be a surprise. The hesitant, very young-sounding voice seemed to appeal to Emmee for her understanding, her indulgence, her cooperation. What kind of party would Charlotte like? What time of day? Formal or informal? Who should be asked? Probably the numbers should be limited to about thirty, because although the garden would more than double the amount of room it would be foolish to rely on the weather.

Lottie's mother talked for a long time, ringing Emmee back at the call-box when Emmee had exhausted her silver. What she was suggesting—simply suggesting—sounded glamorous and fun, a buffet supper with champagne for about thirty people, twenty to be nominated by Emmee as being the ones Lottie would most like to be there, ten asked by her mother as a leaven, to mix the ages, and as being those of her mother's closest friends whom the child would have most fun meeting, and vice versa. They would have candles in the garden, if they could. Music, of course, as long as they kept it low after midnight. Emmee went along with all this, planning, even as she talked, the extraordinary clothes she would herself wear.

Lottie's mother's voice was really attractive. She sounded attractive, longing to give the party that Lottie would most enjoy, longing to be rejoined to her daughter.

Emmee was half beguiled.

Emmee promised faithfully that the secret would be kept, that the surprise would be absolute.

Emmee was abstracted for the rest of the day. She wrote lists of names on bits of paper, and crossed them out again. Twenty people, including herself and Lottie and Giles. It was not very many for a twenty-first birthday party, but Emmee saw Lottie's mother's point. It was a lot of plates and glasses, and it was awful trying to eat in too much of a squash. They had to be people who would not look utterly bizarre in Lottie's mother's house, supposing that to be remotely as Emmee imagined it. They had to be people who would not get drunk, or break precious glasses, or think it funny to be rude to a retired ambassador. These and similar requirements immediately reduced the list, among their friends, to a point that made Emmee wonder if she could raise as many as twenty.

She discussed it with Giles, having sworn him to secrecy.

Giles was dubious, as soon as he understood what was proposed.

'In all my experience,' he said, 'I have never attended a surprise party that could be called a success. Nobody has. In all recorded cases, either the news leaked, or the party was a flop, or the guest of honour was sick in the hostess's lap. Always. One of those three. One or more of those three.'

'What a comfort you are, Mr Lambert.'

'I have got where I am by fearless realism. That is to say, I would have got to where I should have got to had I exercised fearless realism.'

'We won't ask anybody who'll be sick in Lottie's mother's lap.'

'Good thinking. Or anybody who'll blab. The party might still be a flop . . . No. I think this might turn out to be the exception. No party Lottie's at could possibly be a flop.'

Emmee was pleased with Giles.

They compiled a list together. There were one or two names unknown to Giles but urged by Emmee; he accepted her recommendation.

In Lottie's presence they both, jointly and severally, so studiously avoided the subject of her twenty-first birthday that she realised they were planning a surprise party. She hoped not to find out what form it would take.

Giles gave different accounts, all clearly fantastic, about the termination of his employment in the Tottenham Court Road. He moved on to selling antique furniture in Fulham. Fortunately he knew quite a lot about furniture, and could date and value most English and French pieces. Before he was hired, he was taken round the shop by the owner, and asked his opinion of the furniture there.

'He brought me face to face with an oval mirror, with a heavy gilt frame and blobs round the side and an eagle at the top. I said it was Empire. He said, but where was it made? I said I thought it was English but it might be French. He said he thought it was French but it might be English. So he's labelled it Anglo-French. On such things lifelong friendships are based.'

Lottie thought that if he walked into a shop that sold snakes, he would turn out to be a world-class expert on snakes.

There occurred a conjunction which none of them could have predicted: the meeting of Giles with a piano.

Chuck Deakin, some hundreds of yards away in the block, was typical of the population of the place in being on the way to somewhere, his present destination being different from that which had been pointed out to him when he started. He was enrolled as a student of architecture, but he had decided that his future lay in music. To this end he acquired, by commercially dubious channels, an elderly upright piano. To celebrate the fact, and to assemble an audience, he gave a party. He had a bit of money, from an optimistic stepfather.

Among the guests were Lottie, Giles, Emmee and Marcus.

None of them had had any idea that Giles played the piano. He went to concerts, yes. He put Bach and Schubert on Emmee's hi-fi, yes. These things were normal among people in the block, though most went to different concerts and played different tapes. But when he glimpsed the piano he was seen to sniff. He pawed the ground. He said Haha among the trumpets. Marcus said so afterwards.

He sat down and played for an hour and a half. If Chuck Deakin was chagrined, nobody else was. People drank while he played, and those who smoked smoked, but if anything was said it was said in a whisper. If anybody had spoken out loud, Lottie would have hit them on the head with a bottle.

He did not quite finish any piece he started. He had no music and he had not played for some months. He was a bit rusty and his memory uncertain. He started preludes, partitas and two-part inventions; he started Gershwin and Jerome Kern. People began singing and were silenced by Bach; people began dancing and were stilled by Scarlatti.

Chuck Deakin, putting a good face on it, kept Giles's glass filled. Nobody kept tabs on how much he drank. Some afterwards said it was three or four glasses, some— including Chuck—said three or four bottles. It was possible that latterly his accuracy was affected: possible also that his unpractised fingers were tired, or that he had started with pieces that he remembered best, and went on to ones he knew less well.

When he rose he did not stagger; when he spoke his speech was unimpaired.

Lottie caught Emmee's eye some hundreds of times during the recital. Lottie's eye said: *Look what I found! Look what I've got!*

Marcus helped Giles home to bed, very late, after the

party, with Lottie twittering behind. Both Giles and Lottie said that Giles needed no help, but Marcus helped him anyway.

In the morning Giles had no trace of hangover, and he ate his breakfast with his usual appetite.

Emmee had further conferences, on the telephone, with Lottie's mother. They became great friends on the telephone, although Emmee, knowing some of Lottie's history, kept an open mind. Lottie's mother refused all offers of help with the party. She was going to cheat, she said, and get in some caterers. The caterers would provide crockery, cutlery and glasses, as well as a dinner which Lottie's mother hoped Mary-Emma would approve of.

The party would begin at eight. They would start with champagne. They would switch to Traminer or a white from the Loire (Would that be right? What did Mary-Emma think?) with the smoked salmon . . . And so forth. It sounded like no dinner Emmee had ever had in her life, though she recognised it as being part of the original backgrounds of both Lottie and Giles.

Brought nearer the reality of the party, Emmee made some changes in her guest-list.

Giles flatly denied that he could draw. He had no talent for it whatever. The nearest he could come to a figure was a stick-man; the nearest he could come to a tree was a blob with a trunk.

Lottie, as flatly, refused to believe him. To her, he might as credibly deny that he could distinguish Burgundy from Bordeaux, Raeburn from Rubens, Mozart from Monteverdi. He could do everything.

Instead of painting a picture of her, Giles wrote her a poem in what he said was Silver-Age Latin:

> *Carlotta pulcherrima mea puella,*
> *Uxor promessa, marit' ultrabella . . .*

' "Ultrabella" sounds like a disease,' said Emmee.

'I think I've caught it,' said Lottie, and thereafter slept with the poem under her pillow.

It was extremely difficult for Emmee, keeping the numbers to the stipulated twenty, keeping the secret, soothing the feelings of the uninvited.

Clothes were one of the things that had to be discussed, first with Lottie's mother and then with the guests. The notion of a black tie party had only to be examined to be discarded. Lottie and Emmee could not summon ten men between them who had ever worn a dinner jacket in their lives. But 'informal' to the people they were asking meant informal indeed: the word would open floodgates to shirts unbuttoned to the waist, body-paint rediscovered from an earlier generation, khaki shorts over long johns, and jeans that could not be trusted on Lottie's mother's loose-covers.

'Oh—you know—dark suits, I suppose. Would that be all right?' Lottie's mother had said in that hesitant, almost bashful way of hers.

Emmee set herself to carry this instruction up and down the staircases of the block, where it caused ribaldry and consternation. There was extensive shopping in the street-markets not only for birthday presents for Lottie, but also for male garments that could be passed off as dark suits. Marcus Hills found a coat that fitted him, and trousers that fitted him; at a distance, and in a bad light, they looked near enough the same colour.

The girls could all dress up like parakeets at a few seconds' notice.

All this had to be kept from Lottie.

Many people showed Emmee the presents they were giving Lottie. Emmee was startled, as she had been at her own twenty-first the year before, at the generosity and ingenuity of their friends. Pictures, sculptures, ceramics, jasper, jade—Lottie would start crying early in the evening, and go on crying for a week.

There was only one solution to the problem of the people not invited to Lottie's mother's party—another party, in Peckham, earlier in the day or the day before or the following day. Since Lottie's birthday was on Friday, the following day was obviously right. Lottie could be allowed to hear about that one. Lottie wanted to know why the party couldn't be on her actual birthday—as many of their friends were free on Friday night as at any time on Saturday, and most of them could recover just as well on Saturday as on Sunday. Emmee and Giles and the others talked rapidly about other subjects. Lottie understood that there were still things that she was not being allowed to hear about.

Giles showed Emmee what he was giving Lottie. Emmee stared at it blankly. She had never seen such a thing before. She had no idea what it was called or what it was for.

It was a piece of furniture. It looked antique. That was all Emmee could be sure of.

It had a round top with a rim, three spindly and curving legs to the middle, in the middle a thing like a pineapple, with a small drawer below, and very widely and elegantly curved legs to the ground.

'I didn't think I'd take it to Battersea,' said Giles. 'I thought I'd give it to her here, the day after. Do you think she'll like it?'

'She'd like anything you gave her,' said Emmee. 'What is it?'

'An eighteenth-century wig-stand. I know Lottie doesn't usually wear a wig, but you can put other things on it. There was one at home, not as pretty as this. The idea was to put flowers on it, but there were never any flowers because the gardeners were drunk. If there had been flowers the housemaids would never have put them in vases.'

'Were they drunk too?'

'It was quite peaceful, because one liked port and the other one liked Jamieson's whisky. When gentlemen wore wigs—ladies too, come to think of it—they had blocks made the shape and size of your head. Not your head, their heads. You put the wig on the block on top of the wig-stand. The round thing is a pomander.'

'I thought that was something stuck with cloves.'

'That's the other sort. You kept scent in this sort. It made your wig smell nice. And then there's a drawer for your patches.'

'It's *beautiful*.'

'Those legs are pretty, aren't they? My boss let me have it for a song because it was broken.'

'It doesn't look broken.'

'No, I mended it.'

'I remember you saying you could do that. Lottie will value it all the more.'

'That I call a nice thing to say.'

'Of course you mustn't take it to Battersea. Give it to Lottie on Saturday. What's your idea of a song?'

Giles began to sing, in his pleasing baritone, *Voi che sapete* from *Figaro*. Emmee silenced him at last (he seemed to know the whole opera, and to be intent on sharing his knowledge) and explained that she wanted to know what it had cost and how long it had taken him to mend it.

'The work of a moment,' said Giles. 'Lunchtime moments. Done with one hand, with a sandwich in the other.'

He would not say what he had paid for it.

Familiarity made Giles no less incongruous in the Council block in Peckham. Going off in his dark suit in the morning, he clearly ought to have been emerging from a house in Chelsea or Hampstead. If he thought so he showed no sign of it.

Lottie was grateful to Marcus Hills for being such a

good friend to Giles. Emmee said Marcus was one of the people, of whom there were many women but fewer men, who needed to feel that they were needed. On this basis, Lottie could be grateful without jealousy.

On a more intimate level, there were certainly no grounds for jealousy. Giles proved his enthusiastic normalness as often as possible—it could not be too often for either of them—and Marcus remained loyal to Elmer.

Lottie surprised herself by not wanting to live with Giles until they were married. She certainly wanted to continue to go to bed with him, frequently, anywhere, but not actually to share the same postal address. This was eccentric in the mores of the block. Lottie could not explain it to herself or to Emmee.

But Emmee surprised herself by agreeing. Probably she would not have agreed if Giles had been properly one of the Peckham lot, any kind of student, younger, scruffier, street-wise, but Giles being what Giles was made it a different ball-game. It put the whole thing into a grown-up world from which, by and large, the Peckhamites had excluded themselves. Lunch parties where ties were worn, the crush bar at the Royal Opera, race meetings and pheasant shooting . . .

Lottie might re-enter the world from which she had run away nearly five years before: and the way in would be her mother's front door, and the date would be her twenty-first birthday. She would be coming of age in a larger sense than any of them had predicted. This was evidently Lottie's mother's plan. Emmee supposed it was a good plan.

Emmee had the feeling that she was going to lose Lottie—lose her to the people she saw going by in taxis when she went to the West End. Lottie would be all right because she had Giles to look after her, and he would be all right because he would have Lottie to look after him. Lottie was Giles's nanny and his pupil and his lover, and Emmee and her friends would become embarrassing outsiders.

It had not happened yet, but whenever Emmee saw Giles in his dark suit she knew it was going to happen.

Emmee had not had, for years, any sense of class, of snobbery, of social divisions. Any such sense would be ridiculous in Peckham, irrelevant to life as it was lived, rightly abhorred. She supposed that she came, herself, from the most boring middle of the middle-middle classes, which was one of the reasons why she was here and not elsewhere. Life did not permit the luxury of contempt, even disapproval. Emmee preferred people to be kind, honest, fairly clean, and even polite, but she made allowances in all these regards.

Now she became unhappily aware of social distinctions, because she had the sense of looking upwards from below.

The wig-stand prompted thoughts on these lines. Giles visualised real life—his real life, not the agreeable game he was playing for a spell in Peckham—as being furnished by objects such as Georgian mahogany wig-stands; the housemaids might be drunk, but there were housemaids; the gardeners might be drunk, but there were gardeners. Emmee doubted if anybody she knew, except Giles and Lottie, had ever so much as seen a housemaid in a private house.

Upwards from below. It had not happened yet, but Emmee knew it was going to.

Lottie was not allowed to do anything on Friday. The place where she was supposed to be working was told on the telephone that she was not coming in.

The whole day was a party, although the main parties were in the evening and on the following day. The objective was to make Lottie feel like a queen. From dawn, people began calling with presents and bottles. Emmee put away most of the bottles: it would be all right to get legless on Saturday, but not today. Nobody from Peckham was to be sick in Lottie's mother's lap, least of all Lottie.

Giles was out all day, working. His terms of employment were not as casual as Lottie's. He would be working on Saturday morning, too, which was one of their busiest times.

Giles was far too intelligent not to be self-aware.

He was aware of faults, even vices. He was aware of a degree of incompetence, irresponsibility, which could be said to amount to selfishness: he ascribed this without resentment to his impossibly indulgent upbringing. He was aware of moral cowardice, which in some moods he could describe to himself as kindness, as an unwillingness to hurt anybody's feelings. He was aware that he was accident prone, and suspected shortcomings in himself as the reason. There were limits to his energies for introversion, so he left it there.

The fault that he did not have was ingratitude.

He knew very well what he owed to Lottie, Emmee, Marcus and many others in that strange, classless, intermittently highbrow block of flats in the middle of depressing slums. (It was itself a depressing slum, but inhabited by people who transcended their surroundings.) He thought about it during Friday, the day of Lottie's birthday. It was his duty to think about it and he wanted to think about it. As he sold Victorian dining chairs to people who would have the seats unsuitably re-upholstered, he thought about it.

His luck had been fantastic. He did not deserve it, but it kept happening to him. Things turned up. The luck of the Anglo-Irish. His ludicrous predicament on the bus, all unsought, the result of absent-mindedness, of hangover, of having been away from London for so long . . . and then Lottie. Lottie the true, Lottie the brave, sent into the world Lambert to save, Lottie the loving, Lottie the sweet, Lottie he was damned lucky to meet, Lottie the sexy, Lottie the love, Lottie the angel sent from above . . .

The way to accommodate, mentally, the blocks of flats was to insulate the soul. The eyes must remain unfocussed, in order to see only in a blur the pictures they hung on their walls, the patterns they had on their plates. Was varnished furniture more horrible chipped or unchipped?

One walked up the concrete stairs with the object of arriving at the top. The walls, the stairs themselves, were to be ignored. It was like taking the subway in New York, the Airbus from London to Paris—the point was not the journey but the destination, Robert Louis Stevenson's lyrical apothegm exactly inverted. The thing was to travel hopefully but also myopically; to live so. There were meanwhile large mercies to be grateful for.

In planning his future with Lottie, Giles was aware that he had notions above his financial station.

There was no contradiction here, no failure of logic or morality. One was not less grateful because one's benefactor was without taste or money. One was *more* grateful because the benefactor was pretty broke.

The scent of old-fashioned beeswax furniture polish in the Fulham antique shop was to Giles, exiled, as might be the sudden arrival on the breeze, to an Englishman in the middle of the Sahara, of the scent of new-mown grass.

They told Lottie to dress up in her very finest, but not to be too bizarre. They said it was a grown-up party. In a sense, none of them except Giles had ever been to such a thing. Emmee and Marcus fiddled anxiously with the hem of Lottie's skirt. A girl who had been to drama school made her up to be a grown-up, but a very eager grown-up. Lottie hardly recognised herself. She still had no idea where they were going.

Something in Lottie's unfamiliar, sophisticated appearance reminded Emmee, by a trick of psychic association, that Giles's father was a lord, though Emmee had forgotten what he was called. Emmee was suddenly dubious about her own appearance, which was not at all usual for her. She had made her own clothes and Lottie's.

Giles got back at six-thirty. He had a bath, while Marcus ironed his dark suit and polished his shoes. Lottie thought she could hear him singing in his bath, but she decided that it was her own heart that was singing.

Lottie and Giles were reunited as though after years. The girl who knew about make-up hovered in a corner, ready to repair the damage caused by a lover's kisses. But Giles treated Lottie as though she were infinitely fragile, petals liable to fall and skin to be bruised. Her lipstick, the highlighting of her cheekbones, were unsmudged.

Giles said he would give her his present in the morning. He said that whatever anybody was giving Lottie, he was the one who was getting the best present. Lottie wanted to jump into bed with him immediately, but under the circumstances this was not considered possible.

Giles had telephoned for a minicab. He said that it was all right to take a minicab, as long as he was not the driver. It was still uncertain whether his minicab story was wholly fantastic or partly true.

They blindfolded Lottie on the way to Battersea, but not so as to smudge her lipstick.

'Darling, you take my breath away,' said Lottie's mother.

She took their breath away. She could not be less than forty—she must be more—but her legs and figure were wonderful and her skin flawless. She had dark hair, long, straight, glossy, so that side by side with Lottie's cropped blonde they made a stunning pair.

Lottie's mother made Emmee and Giles and Marcus graciously welcome. She really did seem to welcome them. She was not at all condescending.

She said to Emmee, 'Either you made that dress, or you've got a very rich sugar-daddy. Nobody of your age has enough money to go into a shop to buy a dress like that. Very few people even of my age could afford it. Quite triumphant. What a talented girl you are.'

This was definitely endearing.

Lottie's mother introduced them to some older guests, including one who was a general.

The general caught Giles's name, which Lottie's mother had perhaps not done.

'Lambert,' he said. 'Anything to do with Jamie Enniscorthy?'

'My father, sir.'

'Had a hunch he might be. I can see the likeness. I knew him in happier days.'

Lottie's mother took this in.

In his dark suit and understated tie, with his chestnut hair well cut and well brushed, with his startling, aquiline handsomeness, Giles looked exactly what he was—descendant of aristocrats, product of Winchester and Oxford, a man at ease in the company of an elderly general.

The wariness was back in Lottie's eyes.

Corks popped. The rooms filled. The party spilled out into the garden, lit by the French windows and by tall barbaric torches flaming among white roses. There was a conscientious attempt by the old to mingle with the young and the young with the old. Everybody was very polite. The champagne was non-vintage but genuine. There was no immediate threat of anybody being sick in anybody's lap.

Lottie was the guest of honour, and treated as such.

Lottie was confused. She understood the conspiracy of which she was the victim; she understood the generous motives of everybody involved; objectively, considering some other case than hers, she would have approved of the reunion of mother with daughter on the occasion of the latter's twenty-first birthday. But this was not some other case, and Lottie would not have come if she had known what she was in for.

She wanted Giles to be holding her hand all the time. She felt threatened, and he was the only one who could keep her safe. But she had been carried out into the garden by people and by goodwill, and Giles was indoors looking at the pictures and china.

Giles had come home. He had returned from exile to a home which had been burned down forty years before his own birth, to eighteenth-century furniture polished with beeswax and to pictures by Canaletto and Gainsborough. There was a lovely Chinese bowl on the Blüthner boudoir grand, full of pot-pourri which scented the room. The big rug was a Tabriz, and the card table was by Sheraton. Books lined one wall of the smaller sitting room. The sideboard in the dining room was superbly and shamelessly Empire; the chairs were of the same date but completely contrasting style; the combination was happy. Giles browsed among objects which seemed to welcome him home where he belonged; he felt like Odysseus returned to the household gods of Ithaca.

The air was warm and the wine cold. The younger guests sat on the grass. The caterers were deft and inconspicuous. Somebody brought out a many-branched candelabrum, and set it on a wrought-iron table on the lawn. The golden light touched the roses and the faces of the girls.

The music of the piano came out of the French windows onto the lawn. Giles was playing.

Still Lottie was fêted and flattered, by her own friends and her mother's friends. If the wariness was still in her eyes, it was not obvious in the candlelight.

'This is magic,' said Marcus to Emmee. 'This is a way of life I've never seen before. I could do with a lot of this.'

'I hope Lottie's enjoying herself,' said Emmee. 'But I'm not sure.'

• • •

It was one o'clock and time to go. Most people had already gone. Lottie was ready to go. Her conversations with her mother had been brief and stilted, but she was grateful for all the effort and expense. The garden had looked very pretty in the light of the candles and torches. She thought she remembered some of the things in the house, but when she had run away she had been incapable of appreciating them.

'Your mother sends her love and apologies,' said a thin woman of fifty. 'She was absolutely whacked, but she didn't want to break up the party. She took herself off to bed some time ago.'

Lottie nodded. She was tired too. Tomorrow would be a long and cheerful day, as today had been. She supposed she would ring up her mother in the morning, to thank her for the party. Indeed it had been marvellously organised, magically pretty, all that the others said.

'Giles, time to go home.'

Where is Giles?

Not in the garden. Not in any downstairs room. No sight reported, by the rump of the caterer's women still washing up, of a thirty-year-old six-foot man with chestnut hair. Overcome with sleep, even with wine, and gone to lie down? The bedrooms all empty, except the master bedroom the door of which was locked.

He must have gone home early, on his own, splitting headache perhaps, upset stomach perhaps, saying nothing to anybody so as not to spoil Lottie's evening. Probably he said goodbye to his hostess before he left. Yes, however rotten he felt he would surely have done that. But Lottie's mother not available to report. Shall we telephone? Not at this hour. If he went home it was because he needed to go to bed—unkind and counter-productive to wake him with the telephone now.

Lottie dubious, Emmee reassuring, Marcus twittering, everybody else gone.

• • •

Giles was not in Peckham.

At nine o'clock in the morning, while Marcus was having a lonely and puzzled breakfast, a man arrived at the flat. He looked like a chauffeur. He had a note for Marcus Hills Esq. The note was from Giles, written neatly on a piece of blank paper. The note thanked Marcus for all his kindness, said that Giles had intruded too long on that kindness, and empowered the bearer to take away all Giles's things. The chauffeur had brought with him a suitcase, for that purpose. The chauffeur was very polite, apologetic to be disturbing Mr Hills so early on a Saturday morning, and anxious to take nothing with him that was not Giles's undoubted property.

Still polite, the chauffeur would not say where Giles was, or where his possessions were going.

Among the things the chauffeur took was the Georgian wig-stand.

Emmee telephoned Lottie's mother at noon. Lottie, after a sleepless night, had fallen into a deep sleep.

Mrs Bramall had gone away, abroad. She had left for Heathrow an hour before. It was the housekeeper speaking. She had no forwarding address.

When Emmee asked if Mrs Bramall had been alone when she left, the housekeeper hung up.

Thereafter, the telephone was answered by a machine.

C · H · A · P · T · E · R

4

Victoria lay wakeful in the scented darkness, beside her sleeping husband. Yes, she had brought the scent indoors with her, gift of the roses, return for the love she had lavished on them. She had brought with her the baby, her yet-invisible son, whose soul was to be touched by starlight and the scent of roses.

It would be stupid to predict the details of his childhood, because he would from birth be his own person, with talents, tastes and temperament belonging entirely to himself. The parents were there to provide love and security—a push, perhaps, if it was needed, a hand on the reins of the impetuous, a beam of light on the signposts but no preconceptions of the road he would take . . .

There were starlight and roses in Victoria's own life, because she had gone out and found them. She had overcome a deprivation more savage than that of any third-world orphan, because the green grass was always visible, through an iron grille, from the desert where she lived. She made one vow to herself about her son's childhood: it would be unlike her own.

She did not often think about her childhood. She did not often want to. It was arid and exhausting and humiliating. But memories invaded, and she was at once too wakeful and too weary to repulse them.

There was, properly considered, much satisfaction to be gained by comparing her circumstances with her state as a child. Since that was the one good thing that her childhood could offer her, she allowed herself to remember it: she let herself be invaded: she submitted to rape by the mean and bestial details. She could not sleep, nor silence the voices, nor shut off the pictures. She let them all come. There was a kind of satisfaction in it.

It began with report rather than experience, the needful background to the seen: report that printed everything a disgusting shade of beige.

Her father was called Charles Courtenay. (A recent ancestor, called Boggis, had fixed on this incongruous patrician name.) He was born in 1910. His father was an assistant master at a dim, long-defunct, private boarding school near Northampton, an institution which existed for the sons of parents who were ambitious but gullible. He had married, no doubt in the school chapel, a girl who was assistant matron at the school. Victoria could imagine a spotty senior prefect leading the cheering outside the chapel. Of this obscene union there had been two children, Charles and Marigold, Marigold the younger by five years (a war baby) and the better educated. Charles had gone to the school where his father taught, not because it was a school any sane parent would have chosen but because there were substantial fee-concessions for the children of staff. The Headmaster could say to prospective parents: 'Look! My own staff send their sons here!'

Charles had from an early age the dangerous notion of being an actor, a performer. He learned the banjo, clog-dancing, the application of blackface. From the age of twenty he lived in the seediest boarding houses of South Coast resorts, a member of troupes of disappointed Thespians who appeared in shows on the piers of the towns. In the winter he did odd jobs.

By the workings of a providence less than usually scrutable, Charles fell in love in 1939 with a girl called Viola

Heath. Her father had nearly been a professor in a distant colony, early retired because of his health, dead in 1936. Viola was well though cheaply educated, and became an assistant librarian. She was still one at the age of twenty-three when she met Charles Courtenay at Brighton, or Margate, or Littlehampton, and was tempestuously wooed by him.

Probably he serenaded her with his banjo, in blackface; what assistant librarian could resist that?

The outbreak of war accelerated the courtship, and they were married somewhere in October.

Charles tried to enlist but the services turned him down because of his eyesight or bowels or something. He was sent to Sheffield to work on the clerical side in a munitions factory. Viola continued in her important war work as an assistant librarian. (Everybody in the saga was an assistant—assistant professor, assistant master, assistant matron, assistant banjo-player, assistant librarian; Victoria had a family tree of beige assistants.) Charles had occasional brief weekends of leave; he came south sitting on his gas-mask in the corridors of trains. At Christmas 1941 Victoria was conceived, a consummation which, knowing the two of them, was barely credible. After the baby was born, Viola went to live with her mother, impecunious widow of the near-professor, in a rented cottage on the edge of Farnham. Charles and Viola were reunited before the end of the war: either the army did not need those munitions, or the factory did not need Charles. Nobody did. He came and increased the overcrowding in his mother-in-law's cottage. Victoria was too young to remember that phase of her life, but she remembered the next phase all right.

Her father went back to the only life he knew, the only job for which he was even faintly qualified, as soon as the little theatres reopened on the piers of South Coast resorts. He played the banjo and performed clog-dances. He was employed by holiday camps, and wore a red blazer, while his wife worked part-time as a receptionist or telephone-operator in second-class hotels. They lived in the sort of boarding houses which catered to people like them. They never had a home of their own or a stick of furniture. They lived not out of suitcases but out of cardboard boxes. It was a rum life for an assistant librarian. It was a rum life for their child, who, when she was old enough to go to school, changed her school as often as other people changed their pants.

Victoria, from outside its fringes, saw the world she wanted to be in. Her nose was pressed against windows. The glass was transparent but unbreakable.

They found themselves in Eastbourne, jewel of the South Coast, where *Midsummer Madness* (or whatever it was called) played to a better class of audience, and where Charles's banjo was drowned by other and better banjos. And there they met—by a coincidence which was the less astonishing the more you considered it—Charles's younger sister Marigold. Brother and sister had not met since 1931, when he was twenty-one and she sixteen, when she ran away from home not to seek a fortune but because a fortune had lifted up a stone and found her underneath it.

Marigold's life to the point of the reunion was known to Victoria also only by report, but it was Marigold's report, and it was not beige at all. It was sky-blue and scarlet and silver and gold, old-rose and rich browns and greens, colours of Raphael and Rubens.

Marigold had loathed her childhood as much as Victoria was loathing hers. Like Victoria, she had seen from the dreadful school where her father taught the Gardens of the Hesperides through chinks in the walls that imprisoned her. A man with a big car (it was for sale: what he did was sell big cars) took her away just after her sixteenth birthday; he dressed her up in the very best the department stores of Midland towns could provide; he introduced her to terribly friendly roadhouses full of commercial gentlemen like himself, where she passed for a good bit older than she was; he introduced her to cocktails and badinage and sex, for all of which she showed a precocious natural talent.

She reacted against her background as her brother had done, but she was better at it.

That gentleman was the first of a series of gentlemen, each, successively, on a higher rung of the ladder which Marigold found herself climbing.

Under the auspices of one of the gentlemen, who had important friends in the world of the theatre, she joined the chorus of a touring company. The company may have played a town where her brother was performing on the pier: if so, neither was aware of it. At a party after a show she met a superior theatrical gentleman who inserted her into a company that played the ocean liners. The liners were full of gentlemen whose wives were prostrated by seasickness.

Marigold's life at that stage was undoubtedly a bit vulgar.

She was twenty-four when war was declared. Like many patriotic and generous-hearted girls, she married an aristocratic Free French fighter pilot in 1940. She hardly saw him after the honeymoon, which was a bit of a disappointment; he was shot down in 1942. She married an American Colonel, who divorced her in 1946. She met Sir Gordon Mackay between the decrees nisi and absolute.

He changed Marigold's life, and by doing so he changed Victoria's.

He was a baronet, divorced, childless, forty-one years old. Fortune and title came from brewing, but his father had sold the family company. His marriage had ended in divorce in 1945, owing to his wife's wartime infidelities with representatives, it was said at the hearing, of nine different nationalities. He had himself served with gallantry and distinction in the Guards Armoured Division, ending the war as a Major with the D.S.O.

He had the manner and manners of a playboy, but he seemed to make a lot of money.

He swept Marigold off her feet. All her life she had been looking for somebody like him. It was difficult to have a really good party in 1946, but Gordon managed it. He managed to get foreign currency, owing to associates in Switzerland and Italy. He managed to get gin and butter and petrol. Marigold liked everything about being Lady Mackay. She was still only thirty-one. She held her liquor and she played a good game of poker. She learned bridge and golf. Those accomplishments were all she needed—nothing else at all.

She grew into the role. If she worked at it, the work was nothing but a pleasure. In 1952, married six years, she went with Gordon to the Grand Hotel in Eastbourne, always one of their favourite spots, for a weekend in July. She ran into her brother in the street. He recognised her with ease, she him with more difficulty.

This was the aunt Victoria met when she was nine.

She and her parents had tea with the Mackays in the lounge of the Grand Hotel. Victoria had never set foot in it before: neither had either of her parents. They looked out of place there. She felt in place there. Sitting listening to the 'Well I nevers' of the grown-ups, embarrassed by her clothes and her ignorance and by the unfamiliar foreign biscuits, intensely embarrassed by the dinginess of her parents, Victoria soaked it all in. There were things she could identify, put a name to, because she had stared at them when her nose was pressed against the glass: furs, jewels, silk, a wave at a waiter. There were things that were yet without names, about Uncle Gordon and Aunt Marigold, and the Grand Hotel and everybody in it.

Marigold was childless, rich, good-natured, and serious-ly underemployed. Victoria became one of the hobbies of which she had too few. Victoria dated her birth from that stiff little tea party in the lounge of the Grand Hotel. What had gone before was merely the necessary provision by nature of bones and liver and the like; she had not been brought to life. She had been waiting for the touch of the sorceress, the kiss of the prince, the voice of a magic bird and the waving of a magic cheque-book.

Victoria thereafter divided her life between life and death.

Gordon and Marigold—generous, casual, rolling in money undiminished by Labour governments—began discreetly giving a dole to Charles. It amused Gordon to have a brother-in-law who played the banjo on the piers of seaside resorts. He was completely unsnobbish, to a degree which—a few years later, when she knew what was what—appalled Victoria. He actually claimed connection with a clog-dancer in blackface, who was a builder's labourer in the off-season. He made a good story out of it to his cronies at the poker-table, over the syphons and the spilling ashtrays. His kindness led him into tolerance of the intolerable. He brought up, for merriment, even for a sort of Bohemian glamour, what ought to have been buried deep out of sight.

Becoming Marigold's hobby, Victoria spent at first about a third of each year with the Mackays, then two thirds, in their house near Ascot. The house was not old but it was big. It was not beautiful but it was comfortable. Gordon had bought it just before the war; it was luxurious to the extreme pitch of 1939. Victoria encountered central heating, deep pile carpets, mattresses you could bounce on, great big oil paintings with lights over them. She was a slim little thing, late to develop, with neat features and long dark hair. She made a very good doll. She was biddable and appreciative. She learned fast.

She learned everything.

She learned about the feel of tufted carpets in the bathroom under your wet bare feet, after a huge bath in softened water with Floris bath essence; she learned about Elizabeth Arden and Helena Rubinstein; she learned how to mix champagne cocktails, how to buy a bra, and how to dance. Everything the Mackays knew she learned. Anything they did not know she did not learn.

She became a beauty. Uncle Gordon and Aunt Marigold said so; all their friends said so. It was the fashion among the Mackays' friends to flatter and cosset Victoria.

A teenage beauty, expensively dressed by Aunt Marigold, she dutifully visited her parents. She really had nothing to say to them. She was a stranger in their country. They made noises and gestures at one another, without any communication at all. She came out of duty, stayed with resignation, and left with relief. Aunt Marigold was very insistent that Victoria should not lose touch with her parents. That was well meant but silly. When Victoria came home to Ascot, Aunt Marigold always gave her a welcome-home present. That was well meant and sensible.

Victoria's mother died, in a boarding house in Rottingdean. They went to the funeral. Victoria's father was a scruffy little man with dribbles of soup on his black tie. Marigold wept, but Victoria was dry-eyed. She was commended for her courage. What she felt was a gigantic boredom. She wanted the next party to begin immediately and to last all night. She was fifteen and she knew how to make dry martinis for Uncle Gordon's friends. She was their doll, too. She was special. Everybody said so.

All the austerities of the beginning of the decade had been swept away. A rich man could live openly as he wanted to, instead of furtively. The Mackays took Victoria to Nice in the spring and Biarritz in the autumn.

Uncle Gordon loved Aunt Marigold in his way, but he had a roving eye. Possibly his eye would have roved to Victoria, if she had been a bit older: other eyes were already roving in her direction. She put cotton-wool in her bra, because the idols of the time had high, pointed breasts. But Uncle Gordon's eye roved to maturer beauties, bosomy ladies in cashmere cardigans at the golf club.

Victoria caught Uncle Gordon out. She listened on an extension to furtive telephone calls. She knew about midweek meetings in weekend cottages. She was torn. Uncle Gordon had been kind to her, but of course her first loyalty was to Aunt Marigold. Woman was the bearer of children (though it happened that Aunt Marigold wasn't), the sufferer, the provider, the comforter, the martyr, the one that mattered to home and children and the future of mankind. Man was a biological necessity, and carried suitcases. Victoria knew all about the biology involved.

Aunt Marigold would have sat and suffered. Victoria could not let her sacrifice herself. It was wrong, immoral, disgusting. Aunt Marigold herself was wrong to condone what could not be condoned. Victoria was in the middle of the situation, staying with the Mackays in their house, shocked and puzzled and powerless.

God took a hand, as Victoria had prayed he would.

Victoria was in her bedroom (it had been her bedroom for six years, gradually furnished and decorated round her); the door was open onto the broad landing and the head of the main stairs; she was only in her room to slip on a couple of bracelets before going out with Aunt Marigold. Marigold was downstairs, in the gigantic drawing room which opened on to the hall, waiting for Victoria. They were going out to tea in Winkfield. Marigold heard, but did not see, what happened.

Of course Uncle Gordon was overweight. Brandy and golf had put a strain on his heart. Aunt Marigold tried to look after him, she really did, but he was impatient of being looked after; besides, there were those mid-week days in weekend cottages when he was out of her ken, and probably putting an extra strain on his heart.

He came out of his dressing room and went to the top of the stairs. He would have been waddling a little, blowing a little, purplish, thin-haired, expensively dressed and beautifully shod, smelling subtly of Trumper's Coronis, smoking a Turkish cigarette. He started downstairs. He went downstairs much faster than he meant. He went down over and over, like a tubby cartwheel, like a tractor tyre, giving one shout at the top but otherwise only thunderously bumping.

There were a lot of stairs, because the ground-floor ceilings were high. They divided halfway, grandly, into symmetrical descending quadrants, with a baroque balustrade at the mezzanine. The balustrade looked solid, but it could not withstand the impact of Uncle Gordon's cartwheeling eighteen stone. He nosedived the rest of the way, landing on his head on the reconstituted marble of the hall.

Victoria was braver than Aunt Marigold was. Everybody said so. But of course she had not been married to Uncle Gordon for twelve happy years.

The circumstances required autopsy and inquest. With all her strength, Victoria supported Aunt Marigold through these ordeals. It was established that the deceased had drunk two glasses of brandy after lunch. The Coroner sucked in breath. He had never drunk even one glass of brandy after lunch. Victoria looked stunning in black, with cotton-wool in her bra.

Victoria's father came to the funeral, a little, perky, seedy outsider in the front pew of the church with his sister and daughter. Behind them sat the heir to the title, Uncle Gordon's brother, who had flown over from Canada for the funeral. The title was all he was heir to. The church was quite full of Uncle Gordon's friends, from school, regiment, City and clubs. Many came back to the house for drinks after the ceremony. Uncle Gordon's brother, now Sir Alan, went alone with the parson to the crematorium.

Victoria really acted as hostess, to make things easier for Aunt Marigold. She pretended as far as possible that her father was not there. The silly little man looked about him as though he had never seen a gentleman's house before. Victoria warned the servants not to give him too much to drink. Aunt Marigold asked him to stay, but he said he had to get back for the show in the evening.

Victoria was surprised to see the blackface banjoist talking with apparent ease to quite grand people. They pretended to like him, to enjoy his company. Victoria realised with a sick feeling that they would realise who he was, who she was. There was nothing she could do about it, so she put a good face on things.

Uncle Gordon's betrayal was greater than Victoria had supposed. It turned out he was not as rich as he seemed: at least, that he was rich in a different way. What he had bought himself was a massive annuity, and he had bought Aunt Marigold another annuity, not quite so massive. The effect was that he had a lovely income while he lived, and she had a pretty decent income while she lived, and there was no capital to speak of outside the house and land, its contents, jewellery, cars and so forth.

Aunt Marigold had known all about this arrangement. Victoria had known nothing about it. It put a different complexion on everything. Victoria had thought her fortune was made; she now found that she had to make it.

At the age of seventeen, in 1960, she took the cotton-wool out of her bra and became a model. She was the right shape for the times. She enrolled with a small agency; when they had taught her all that they could teach her, she allowed herself to be pirated by a larger one. She was one of the new faces, and she could wear a miniskirt. She was not photographed by the very biggest names; she did not appear in the pages of *Vogue*; she became an intermittently familiar face in the lesser-known, middle-of-the-market women's magazines. She was never asked to do nude or topless work; she would have refused if asked, probably, because this was only a phase of her life, and she was not about to do anything to threaten the long-range future.

Aunt Marigold sold the Ascot house for a good deal less than the asking price. She bought a flat near the Albert Hall. There was always a bedroom for Victoria, and Victoria was nearly always in it. Aunt Marigold did most of her shopping at Harrods. She was still only forty-five; she was overweight but otherwise young for her age; though sociable and popular, she would have been lonely

without Victoria. There was an obvious chance that she
would marry again.

Aunt Marigold continued the remittances to her brother.
She continued her remittances to Victoria. Even with what
she was earning, Victoria was not able to save; though her
life would have seemed pretty glamorous, to herself of a
few years earlier, she was not a Jean Shrimpton or paid
like one, owing to jealousy, treachery and so forth.

Aunt Marigold was not saving anything, either. She had
no need to: the annuity was perfectly safe. If inflation made
things too expensive, she bought cheaper things.

There were few unattached men in Aunt Marigold's
life, though there were a good many unattached women.
There was always the chance that a man would appear;
there was always the chance that she would unattach one
who was attached. Everything might then be different:
better or, equally likely, much worse. It was not yet a
race against time, with Victoria beautiful and often photographed and only eighteen and nineteen, but she began to
feel a nagging sense of urgency.

The flat near the Albert Hall was absurdly large and lavish
for the two of them. The heating bills became impossible.
They must cut their coats according to the cloth. Victoria
was contributing her mite to the housekeeping, and it just
about kept them in Vim.

Marigold disposed of the lease, and moved to a smaller
flat, further west.

It was cramped and inconvenient. The ceilings were
low. The address did not sound so good to people Victoria
met; it did not look so good to people who came for
drinks. Victoria did not cut loose and find a flat of her
own, because Aunt Marigold would have been so lonely.
1962 began badly.

Aunt Marigold went away for several weekends during
the summer, often taking Victoria with her when there

was room, when there was any young company for her. Victoria did not demand young company, but Aunt Marigold demanded it for her. Victoria went away on her own less often. She had had some bad experiences with young married couples, and older ones too, who 'camped' in cottages on clifftops or among fields. It meant sharing a bathroom with babies, pumping water, helping with the washing-up, carrying in firewood, and sitting on chairs with broken springs. It was difficult to predict exactly what people were asking you to do, but Victoria became expert. Her refusals were therefore more numerous than her acceptances. The loneliness of Aunt Marigold was always her excuse.

There was a sense of overcrowding and frustration in the West Kensington flat. Aunt Marigold showed a patience with the flat and with Victoria which ought to have been better hidden.

They were asked for a weekend in May by some people called Bramall. Gerald and Mary Rose Bramall. He had a lot of money and a lot of medals, and they lived in a beautiful place near Abingdon. They had a daughter of almost exactly Victoria's age, and a son three or four years younger. They were old friends, latterly out of touch; Gerald Bramall and Gordon Mackay had sailed together at Cowes before the war. This was as much as Victoria knew when they climbed into the hired car on Friday afternoon; it was enough to get her into the car.

Her first sight of Court Farm was a revelation, a personal arrival as momentous as tea in the lounge of the Grand Hotel in Eastbourne, as her entry into the house near Ascot. She remembered it with joy and thankfulness, twenty-five years later, lying in the dark in the scent of roses, starlight at her feet and her husband sleeping at her side.

She was coming home.

Emmee had a difficult time with Lottie, after the calamitous twenty-first birthday party.

Emmee had herself been in and out of love. She had been happy and unhappy, and she had believed her heart broken. She had never felt the apathetic, frozen misery of Lottie all that July.

Emmee hated Lottie's mother with a venom utterly unknown to her.

And they were still guessing. Nobody knew exactly what had happened.

For Emmee, perhaps for Lottie, the exemplar, diagram, shorthand, symbol of the affair was the Georgian wig-stand. It had gone off with the chauffeur from Marcus's flat, with the single suitcase of Giles's belongings. Lottie had never seen it. She wanted it described, by Emmee and Marcus, the only people who had seen it. Neither was competent to describe it in technical or aesthetic terms; neither wanted to talk to Lottie about it; her mind nagged at the thought of the wig-stand as a man with toothache nags with his tongue at the painful tooth. She made them tell her about it, the rimmed lip, the pomander, the little triangular drawer, the beautifully curved and splayed legs. Somehow the little wig-stand seemed to be Giles. With his departure it departed; and with its disappearance he dropped off the face of the earth. It was to be assumed that her mother had gobbled both.

Emmee and her friends had to subsidise Lottie, all that July and August. She was too shattered to go out and work. It was no good saying to her: 'He's not worth it.' For one thing, she knew that at least as well as they did; for another thing, they all knew that in a sense—in many important senses—it simply was not true.

Even Emmee's mother, beigely arriving from Princes Risborough, came all the way to Peckham to try and help.

Emmee needed a prop in the middle of all this. Marcus Hills might have been a prop, of a flexible kind, but Elmer had come out of prison and Marcus had his hands full with rehabilitation. A prop marched disjointedly into

Emmee's life: Thurber, reassuringly eight years older, showing reassuring signs of adoration. Thurber helped to shoulder the burden.

Lottie liked Thurber.

Lottie gradually returned to life.

At the beginning of August Felicity rang up the flat—Felicity Henderson, née Bramall, Lottie's half sister. The call was a great surprise, because Felicity had not been in touch for a long time; there had seemed no profit in contact, or much joy.

Emmee had met Felicity, with Lottie, and liked her well enough. Lottie liked her well enough, but it was not likely that the half-sisters would become close because there were twenty-plus years difference in their ages, and because Felicity lived with a husband and four children in Pembrokeshire, immersed in her family and garden and good works.

Emmee knew that at some date, by some means, Felicity and her brother had been ejected from their home near Abingdon. She knew no details. Lottie knew nothing about it at all.

Felicity was glad to be speaking to Emmee, not Lottie. Emmee could deal with the news as she thought fit. Felicity said, 'Have you seen today's *Times*?'

Of course Emmee had not.

Felicity read out an item on the Court Page under the heading 'Marriages':

The Hon. G. Lambert and Mrs V. Bramall.

The marriage took place quietly abroad on Tuesday, July 15, between Giles, younger son of Lord Enniscorthy and the late Lady Enniscorthy and Victoria, daughter of Mr Charles Courtenay and the late Mrs Courtenay, and widow of the late Lieutenant-Commander Gerald Bramall R.N.V.R.

'Oh,' said Emmee. 'Oh.'

'Whoever he is,' said Felicity, 'she's eaten him.'

'Oh.'

'I thought Charlotte ought to know.'

'I don't know if she ought to know.'

'Why not? Well, that's your business. You're on the spot. I've done my bit.'

'Yes. Thank you.'

Their father Gerald Bramall, by all accounts a decent man, struggling against odds to behave decently, had made Charlotte and Felicity known to one another when they had both, a generation apart, had wedges driven between themselves and their father. That was how Emmee had come to meet Felicity, just before Gerald Bramall died in the autumn of 1984. Emmee remembered a sandy lady in her early forties, busy and practical and sane, a little bossy, kind to Lottie, scarcely sane on the subject of her stepmother. The meeting was quite brief, in the Great Western Hotel at Paddington Station: Felicity had had to catch a train back to her children and cherry trees.

Emmee hung up the telephone supposing that she would have to tell Lottie.

Felicity hung up the telephone remembering also that meeting in the Great Western Hotel. She remembered carrying to her train a load of hatred that gnawed at her soul like a cancer. She struggled not to hate her half-sister, fair fattish Lottie, who was a victim like herself. She struggled not to hate her father, who had been an old fool like whom there was no fool, who was a brave man turned lapdog, who was the Knight at Arms in thrall to the Belle Dame sans Merci, who had been her beloved father until he was bewitched.

By a curious flick, by an effect like the superimposition of compatible though not identical photographic images to give a stereoscopic effect, Felicity's perception of herself was almost identical to Emmee's perception of her. She was sure enough in her forties, sandy with streaks of grey, fully engaged in the life of her family and garden and neighbourhood. In most respects she looked exactly what she was, to everybody. What did not show to a stranger was the hatred.

Tinkertitonk went that train due westwards by Reading and Swindon, while Felicity drank tea. *Tinkertitonk* northwest to Gloucester. Change for Cardiff, Swansea and Carmarthen. Felicity had a miniature White Horse, with ice and soda. The journey took a long time; she had a long time to think.

She pushed the ghosts back into the shadows, most of the time, for almost exactly two years, from the day of her father's funeral. Then she saw the item in *The Times*. She had not seen Charlotte for months. She had not been to London for months. But she knew the new telephone number. Apparently it was a squat in South London. She rang up.

She was glad to be answered by Mary-Emma, the miniature sharp-faced girl that Charlotte lived with (it was comforting that any girls lived with girls, these days). She was pretty sure that girls in a place like that did not see *The Times*. She hoped she was doing the right thing, by sending Charlotte the news. She always tried to do the right thing; she was aware that she sometimes worked too hard at it. She had no idea what basis Charlotte and her mother were on; by the precedent of her own experience, they were on no basis at all.

In telephoning, she might have been doing the right thing by Charlotte, but she was doing the wrong thing by herself. She lay awake most of that night. She lay as wakeful as though she had drunk a pint of black coffee at midnight, hatred being as good a stimulant as caffeine. She remembered the results of a weekend visit of an old friend in the May of 1962.

Victoria remembered it equally well, equally wakeful without hatred.

The big white Ford turned off the road between two squat grey lodges. The drive wound slightly uphill between

trees which were an avenue without the pomposity of
a French or a ducal avenue. At the wheel of the car,
confident and competent about the route, was an oldish
chauffeur much the same shape and colour as the lodges.
To the north rose the Downs, to the east the Chilterns, to
the south the White Horse Hills, to the west, remoter, the
Cotswolds. Court Farm basked in the lush valley which
spread northwards, cradling the Thames, to Oxford. Parts
of the valley were pretty densely populated, but you would
not have guessed it, going up that drive.

From the front, the house was more Court than Farm;
from the back, it was more Farm than Court.

From the gravel sweep where the car stopped, Victoria saw tall windows in two-storey bays each side of an
important portico. In the midst of the semi-circle of gravel
there was a small formal rose garden, its paths paved with
flagstones, a marble *putto* with a birdbath on his head in
the centre. On the edge of the gravel, by the rim of an
illimitable lawn, were parked a Rolls and a Mercedes. The
house was extended to the east by an orangery, a kind
of corridor of round-topped glass windows, ending in an
octagonal pavilion with a dovecote over the pavilion and
a weathervane over the dovecote. The sides of the house
looked aged but in excellent repair, like the manservant
who materialised at the door of the car. On the front of the
house grew roses, wisteria and clematis; through the glass
of the orangery could be seen an enormous grapevine.
There were no weeds on the gravel or in the rose-beds.

Round the corner of the house strolled a tall man of
about Aunt Marigold's age. His hair was of the pleasing
dusty colour that might have been straw when he was
small. He was tanned, slim-hipped, broad-shouldered. He
was wearing blue cotton trousers, a terracotta cotton shirt,
and short gumboots. He was carrying a pair of secateurs.
He tucked the secateurs into the hip pocket of his trousers in order to wave in welcome with both arms above
his head.

He owned *this*. Victoria fell in love when she was half-way out of the car.

Felicity was watching from an upstairs window when the fat white Ford crunched up. Old Dennis trotted to the door of the car the moment it stopped; there was not the slightest need for him to do so, and he should have been doing something quite different, but he loved being the Old Retainer. It was less trouble than cleaning riding-boots, and earned more in tips.

Felicity's father appeared on the gravel, waving like a semaphore as he always did, giving the impression, as he always did, that the arrival of the arrivals was the best thing that had happened to him for years. A stoutish lady got out of the car, officiously helped by Dennis. She was used to being helped out of cars. Felicity's father embraced her. That was no surprise—he was a great one for embracing people, and they were old friends, although Felicity herself until that week had never heard of Lady Mackay. She looked all right—a bit out of place, a bit Londony, but ready to laugh and not nearly as frightening as many of the people Felicity met.

There was a girl coming also. The girl was here also. The first that Felicity saw of her was a pair of long and beautiful legs in dark grey nylons swinging out of the door of the car. Their owner followed: dark hair, jet-black hair with highlights from the afternoon sun, and a tangerine coat and skirt that looked straight out of the Place Vendôme.

They said the girl was just Felicity's age. Felicity glanced with a gulp down at herself. She had been painting a cupboard in her bedroom, and she was dressed for doing so. She wore old trousers, gym shoes, and a moth-eaten sweater. She wondered about changing. No skirt would conceal the fact that her behind was far too big.

She was due back at Girton in the middle of the fol-lowing week. A bit of her wished she had already gone.

But she saw the slim and beautiful girl talking to her father, waving at something, smiling, and she was glad she had not gone back. Felicity met few creatures from other worlds.

As soon as the girl had changed into country clothes, Felicity would show her their magic kingdom. Nobody had ever failed to love it, and Felicity knew it better than anybody else.

Felicity was a tiny bit impatient with the friends she had, who were short on glamour. From home and from Girton she saw worlds which she knew she was born to, but of which she had been too shy (and too conscious of the size of her behind) to take possession. It was high time Felicity went on a diet, found a better sort of girdle, and made a new lot of friends. These were not to replace but to complement the ones that she had. The stunning dark girl who had just gone in to the house—said to be her age exactly, said to be a model—was the nucleus of a new life for Felicity.

Victoria did change. By the time Felicity came downstairs, herself changed into a skirt and scrubbed and wearing lipstick, Victoria had changed into very tight pillar-box red slacks which showed that she had a small behind and that she wore no girdle.

Victoria went round the garden—perhaps even part of the farmyard, too—not with Felicity but with Felicity's father. Lady Mackay went with them a bit of the way.

Today is only Friday. We shall be here until Sunday afternoon. The car is ordered for just after tea on Sunday. We have until then.

Revelation on revelation.

The taste of the Ascot house revealed, by comparison, as vulgar. Uncle Gordon's taste, imposed on a younger wife? To be honest, a bit of both. This garden a fragrant paradise. Great spaces, and bowls of sweet-scented syringa. 'Commander' becomes 'Gerald', by order, within minutes.

The wife solid, sandy, busy, middle-aged. Nobody could possibly want to make love to her. The daughter, called something, approximately, exactly, nothing. Never mind about them or the rest of the world, not in the scent of this blossom in the last of the evening sun.

A long skirt in the evening. A very little cotton-wool. An extra button undone. He pretended his eyes were not flickering. He pretended the touch of our fingers was accidental.

This is love.

His manners are beautiful and he is beautiful. There is no calculation here, no greed, no grabbiness. The invitation is issued out of generosity and love. Never mind the future, live these days, these nights. I ask nothing, nothing, except those embraces. There is no price-tag on the goods; there is no string attached. He knows that.

'Goodnight.'

'Goodnight.'

'See you in the morning.'

'Oh yes.'

The kiss sketched in the air, in the middle of the drawing room.

Her night thoughts. His. No prowling footsteps, furtive returns, 'I thought I heard something'. Time enough, better times, sweet-scented.

'Good morning.'

'Good morning.'

'I hope you slept well?'

'Yes, thank you.'

'I didn't,' he said.

Then somebody else came in to the sun-filled breakfast room.

She wore a grass-green skirt with a white shirt. Her legs were bare. It was hot for the time of year. He wore what he had worn when she first saw him, when she fell in love with him. He would be beautiful in uniform or animal skins or a toga or a clown's baggy trousers.

He was full of plans for Aunt Marigold's day. Aunt Marigold had her own plans. She wanted to sit in the shade on the lawn with her Agatha Christie, and be brought a gin and tonic at twelve-thirty.

The wife had to go shopping, and the daughter had to be busy about a blacksmith.

'Then how are we going to amuse Victoria?' he said.

C·H·A·P·T·E·R

5

No strings attached, nothing. I ask nothing.

Your muscles are like iron. You frighten me. Why is
your face so grim?

Who would have thought, in May, the sun would strike
so warm on bare shoulders, bare breasts?

My love. My love. Oh yes. I know I can't have you, but
you have got me.

No, I will not assent to anyone being hurt.

Yes, I've told you. I've shown you. Haven't I shown
you? I love you, I love you.

Blossom arches above. Dry grass crackles through the
rug from the car. Climax of birdsong. God must be here.

Mary Rose? Who is Mary Rose? Oh, Mary Rose. I am
sorry for Mary Rose.

We will tell nobody and do nothing. Nobody is to be
hurt.

Felicity was aware that evening of something strange and
wrong.

Felicity knew her parents' history. Everybody knew it,
because her father was famous. Her parents were famous

as a couple, because of their popularity and hospitality, because of the beauty of the house and estate they had re-created from decrepitude, because of their happiness. They were pointed out as a fixed point in a rocking world.

All right about the furtive fifties and the swinging sixties. Look at the Bramalls.

Gerald was born the week before the Archduke was murdered at Sarajevo. His father joined the yeomanry, was commissioned in the infantry, and died at Ypres. He was rich. It was all based on biscuits. It was astonishing that so much money could derive from something which played so small a part in life: but there it was: biscuits.

Felicity grew up with the unashamed knowledge that the ponies she rode, the porcelain the servants dusted, came from biscuits. Everybody knew it. Her name was synonymous with biscuits. Good for biscuits.

Gerald's mother never remarried. With the best professional help, she managed the fortune sensibly and frugally all the years of Gerald's minority. They lived in a small, decent house near Newbury. Gerald went to Eton in 1927 and Oxford in 1932. His coming-of-age in 1935 was the family's first major extravagance since the beginning of the war. The party lasted for days and was talked about for years. It was not really any more characteristic of Gerald than it was of his mother.

Gerald became a yachtsman. He sailed, as he did everything, with efficiency rather than brilliance, and entirely without display. He was elected to all the clubs all the quicker because of his lack of showiness.

From 1937 to 1939 he was Honorary Attaché at an embassy in Africa and one in South America. He never learned the languages of those countries, but he had a lot of shooting, sailing and polo.

As a yachtsman and certified navigator he was scooped up at the beginning of the war into the R.N.V.R., like most of the other yachtsmen in Britain. He was promoted, decorated, and twice torpedoed.

In 1942 he married Mary Rose Stagg, a Junior Officer in the Wrens, then twenty-two. It was a marriage planned impetuously and carried out with dangerous haste—a typical short-leave wartime marriage. Gerald's mother was aghast. It was a triumphant and enduring success. Amongst all the stories and hearsay, the success of her parents' marriage was a thing Felicity could testify to, from her own experience and observation.

Felicity was born the year after the wedding, her brother Robert in 1945.

After the war, with two babies, Mary Rose wanted to live in the country. They started house-hunting, using as a base Gerald's mother's house near Newbury. Gerald bought a small motorcycle, and with Mary Rose on the pillion they puttered through Berkshire and Oxfordshire. This was because of the stringent rationing of petrol. They could always leave the children with Gerald's mother, who loved having them, who was entirely reconciled to Gerald's hasty marriage and who joyfully approved his choice. All this Felicity had heard from both her parents and from her grandmother. She heard what fun her parents had on the motorcycle, exploring lovely countryside, looking at houses, lunching in pubs.

When they steered between the potholes of the drive of Court Farm, they discovered a ruin and a promise. They got it for a song—decrepit rural properties were very cheap in 1947—and began the long and absorbing process of restoring it. There was no risk of their leaping to ill-considered decisions, of doing anything in too much of a hurry. There was tight control on all building materials then; it was impossible to spend more than a tiny annual sum on plumbing and wiring. Very slowly the phoenix emerged from the dry-rot and wet-rot and cobwebs, the dirty chocolate-brown paint and the tumbled roofs of the farm buildings. The land was derequisitioned, ploughed, reseeded. While hot-water pipes were being led to the bedrooms of the house, rafters and joists were being renewed in the barn and hedges were being cut and laid. It all happened together, gradually, a labour of love; it was still happening within Felicity's memory, at the end of the forties, in Coronation year and for years after that. It could hardly be said to be finished, in the early summer of 1962. It never would be finished: it was like painting the Forth Bridge—before you got to the end the beginning had to be done again. It had been her father's full-time job since Felicity's earliest memories; he adored it, not least as a setting for her mother and Robert and herself.

For a child, it should have been very heaven. It was. When Felicity and Robert asked school friends to stay, they always, always wanted to come again.

Robert was just seventeen, in his last year at Eton. He would have fancied Victoria, if he had been at home. He liked the model type, skinny and leggy, perhaps because his sister was the opposite type; he liked girls a bit older than himself, too, because he felt relieved of responsibility. It was just as well Robert was safely thirty miles away in Windsor.

Before lunch on Sunday, on the lawn, Felicity heard Lady Mackay talking to her father about her late husband, Felicity's father's old sailing friend. She talked about his kindness and generosity, how hard he pretended not to mind not having children, how frightful a shock his sudden death had been, how empty her life was without him. She was not being self-pitying, but answering Felicity's father's questions.

The details were different, the words chosen probably different, but it might have been Felicity's mother talking, if her husband had suddenly died.

What do you do, when your life revolves round a hub, and the hub disappears? Spin on? Lie down? Keep rolling, for the look of the thing, in no direction? Felicity did not suppose her mother had ever asked herself this question.

• • •

After lunch on Sunday, a big lunch, another hot day, a time for somnolence and separateness. The crackling of newspapers could be heard from deck chairs. Nobody knew where anybody was.

'Now I've found you I can't let you go.'
   'No. Don't let me go. How could I go?'
   'I'll come to London.'
   'Come to London. Yes. Come to London.'
   'But I love you here.'
   'I love you here.'

On Sunday evening, after their guests had gone, Felicity saw her mother crying.

Felicity went back to Cambridge, for the last term of her freshman year. Her father took her in the car, because she had different clothes for the summer, because she was going to parties and May Balls. She asked him in to tea, but he would not stay. He left by the London road.

'Yes, but I like you best in the country. I like you best under the sky.'

It took him ten hours to get home, Felicity's mother said, poor Daddy, exhausted. Of course he had rung, from a call-box. He didn't even know where he was, the name of the place where he had broken down. Some navigator! How did he steer a corvette in the war? It was the carburettor. They had to get a part from another garage. All well in the end. Love from everybody.

Did she believe it or was she pretending? Was it better to pretend? Was it cowardly or actually brave? Was she pretending for their sakes, hers and Robert's? Could it be right to do that? Could there be a future in that?

Felicity tried to bend her mind to her books and boy-friends.

Victoria was already starting to ruin her life.

'I can't go on with these lies.'

'If you throw me out of your life I shall die.'

It was true. She would die. He could keep her or kill her.

He paid for her to come to the country in hired cars. He did not pay for her, but only for the cars. She was not for sale. She did not want to receive but to give. Everything she could give him she gave. There was not much of her, but what there was she gave him. If she had owned anything else, she would have given it to him, but all she had was herself, so she gave him that. She was no longer hers to give, because she was his.

They met in the most extraordinary places.

Twenty-five years on, Victoria smiled in the dark at the memory of some of those meetings.

Usually they met on the estate, or very near it. This was so that he could steal the time to be with her without spending too much of it on the road.

She much preferred meeting him on ground which was his property. She was his property. She was as much his as the fence-posts and pheasant coverts. It gave her special joy to be possessed on his possessions.

Love made her shameless, with her own person and with his. When you belong overwhelmingly body and soul, you do not bother with modesty. She did not have to prove the completeness of her love for him, but she did so just the same, by word and with every part of herself.

He said that she made him happy, and she knew it was true. She had faith in the future. She trusted him. He knew that was true.

Felicity heard from Robert, back at school after a weekend at home. He did not often write, but when he did his letters were good. This letter was not good. He would have rung, but in the college it was impossible to reach her by telephone. It might have been impossible to ring from home anyway, because there were always people about and what he wanted to say didn't bear overhearing.

Did Felicity know what was wrong? Something was, but there was a conspiracy at home to pretend there wasn't.

Robert didn't credit himself with telepathy or uncanny sensitivity. He reckoned a blind and deaf-mute rhinoceros would have been aware that there was something wrong at home. But the rhino wouldn't have known what it was, and Robert didn't either.

Their ma's forced gaiety had been more than Robert could take.

Felicity cried when she read the letter. Robert was much softer-hearted than his act suggested. Felicity had caught him crying at books and at old movies on television. He had been furious, wiping his eyes with the back of his hand and pretending he had had a sneezing fit. Robert was easily upset, like all really nice people, and his mother's visible misery and her efforts to hide it would have upset him terribly.

Felicity could offer him no comfort. Academically, they both had calamitous summers.

The summer vacation was more than either Felicity or Robert could bear. They both went away, which—all summer—they could never have imagined wanting to do before. Their father looked awful, and their mother worse.

Robert now knew as well as Felicity what was wrong in the house. They discussed it. They felt guilty, disloyal, doing so. They tried to direct their anger at its proper target, not at their father, who was Merlin in the insidious clutches of Morgan le Fay.

The summer was a time of consolidation. Little and lithe and young as she was, Victoria took nothing for granted.

She gave and gave, taking nothing.

She became experimental, inventive, audacious, in the secret places of that summer. She would do anything for him. They got into some peculiar positions.

None of them ever really got over Mary Rose's suicide, which took place on a weeping afternoon in early October. She went about it in the simplest, most painless, most planned and deliberate way: she ran a plastic hosepipe from the exhaust of her little car into the interior of the car.

The Coroner was able to say that she did it 'while the balance of her mind was disturbed'. She had had the sense, the consideration, to leave no note to make it clear that she was quite sane but mad with misery.

Felicity knew that her mother took things too hard, like Robert. She was too soft-hearted. She minded too much. She had been too happy. She had seen the happy structure of her life filled as though by syringes with lies and betrayal. The labour of pretending, Felicity thought, had become too great; the burden of false gaiety had become intolerable.

Felicity was in Cambridge, Robert abroad. A gardener found the body.

Gerald was ashen and shaky at the inquest and at the funeral. His friends grieved with him and worried about him.

His mother, who had loved Mary Rose, was mercifully unable to understand the news.

Gerald disappeared for a fortnight after the burial. He was believed to have gone into some kind of retreat, an abbey, a place of quiet and physical austerity and spiritual comfort. He had asked both the doctor and the parson what he should do, to stay sane and useful; concerned, the two had conferred, and joined in giving the advice that such a place would help him. They told Felicity so.

He never afterwards spoke about that fortnight. When his advice was tactfully sought by the worried relatives of the deeply distressed—what abbey? Could they be reached by telephone?—he turned away the questions.

He came back something like the man he had been. He got on with his life. Only close friends, his children, people who deeply loved him, saw the emptiness behind his eyes.

Victoria was prouder of those two weeks than of any achievement of her life. She laboured night and day to save a soul from despair.

They went to a private hotel in Breconshire. They had a suite; they could spend whole days undisturbed. Victoria arranged flowers in the nude. She mixed drinks in the nude. She sat at the table in the sitting room, eating the dinner they had brought, in the nude. She quite liked doing that, because of the good she was doing, and because the room was warm, and because she caught glimpses of herself in the mirror over the fireplace in the sitting room.

Sometimes she treated Gerald like a baby, cradling his head between her little breasts. Sometimes she was the slave-girl in an erotic fantasy.

She used the word 'therapy' to herself, the first time she had ever done so.

Felicity had expected the effect on Robert to be bad. It was worse than she expected. He got drunk at noon and in the evening. His father, returned from his retreat, looked at him with empty eyes and went off into his study to turn the pages of photograph albums.

Robert said the verdict of the Coroner's inquest was wrong. They should have said 'murder'.

Robert was supposed to be going to a crammer for his Oxbridge entrance. He was not interested. He sat in his bedroom with his record-player, and came downstairs to get drunk.

Felicity went back to Cambridge, uselessly. The study of literature seemed supremely useless. If she wanted to read books she could read them. She did not want to read any books, or to go to parties or to talk to anybody. She thought she was needed at home, so she went home.

Hunting had started, but she could not be bothered with dressing up and going to the meet and having people either speaking kindly about her mother or kindly not speaking about her. She told herself that her mother would have wanted her to get on with her life, so she tried taking the dogs for walks. She went a little way. At every turn she was overwhelmed by memories. She came back into the house, where she was overwhelmed by memories. There was then nothing for her to do except sit about, so she did nothing except sit about.

All three of them sat about, in different parts of the house. The only one of them doing anything positive was Robert, and what he was doing was getting drunk. Felicity thought they should all be showing more guts, but she could not blame the others for not having guts since she found that she had none herself.

Felicity's father hired a farm manager, a man of thirty with a young family and all the proper qualifications. Felicity's father had never employed a manager before— he had been his own manager, he had turned himself into a successful practical farmer by doing the job. The farm manager's house had been a weekend retreat for a London solicitor and his wife, the lease renewable annually because the house might be needed by the estate. There was a spot of unpleasantness from the solicitor's wife, understandable after more than ten years. But the solicitor had always recognised that possibility would become probability with the passage of years, and he had restricted both emotional and financial investment in the house.

People said that Gerald might have sought distraction, a kind of comfort, even temporary oblivion, by burying himself in the work he had done since the end of the war, in the meticulous personal management of everything that was his. But he sought distraction elsewhere. Presumably he found his comfort and his oblivion, because he kept going back there.

His speech was rational but his eyes were empty. He was an addict, a junkie.

Aunt Marigold took a ridiculous line. She was nosey and hostile. She began making disapproving noises as early as June. She somehow found out who was paying for the cars that came for Victoria, and she found out where they went. She was snooping and spying. The noises of the summer were nothing to the recriminations when she got back from Wales, in late October.

She made Victoria cry. Victoria was always upset by unfairness and cruelty, and Aunt Marigold was cruel and unfair.

Aunt Marigold owed Victoria so much, in the way of comfort and company and spiritual strength. Aunt Marigold, in point of fact, owed Victoria more than she realised, more than she would ever realise. What Victoria had done for Aunt Marigold was actually heroic—it had taken strength and resolution, a strength far beyond her little slim body because she was driven by a sense of justice. She was an instrument, like Gideon and so forth. Now Aunt Marigold, for whose sake it was done, was talking horrible nonsense, using words like 'greed' and 'treachery'.

Aunt Marigold was a complete hypocrite. Victoria knew enough about her life to know she was the last person who could throw any stones. All her life she'd been a tart, opening her legs to anyone with the money. She'd only stopped because she was too old. Victoria was a one-man girl, faithful unto death.

Victoria did not reply to Aunt Marigold as she might have done. She did not stoop to answering cruel insult with just accusation. She was too kind and too civilised. She took her wounded feelings out of the room, her head bowed to hide the contempt in her face.

Troubles never came singly. That was the autumn that Victoria's father had to be put in the nursing home. Aunt Marigold naturally paid the bills, for her own brother.

Victoria became more discreet. Messages came and went circuitously. The meetings were as magical and almost as frequent, but modelling assignments had to be cunningly invented in order to explain days in the country, even afternoons in London hotel rooms. Fibbing was intensely distasteful to Victoria, but she did it for her father's sake.

She never accepted any present, although he wanted to shower her with presents. She never accepted a penny or so much as a pin.

'Do you think *that's* why I'm here?'

She was there because she lived by love for him, and would have died of love for him.

Christmas at Court Farm was like a wake. It was a wake. Felicity's mother was everywhere. When they drank it was to her memory. When Robert got drunk it was in his mother's memory.

People did not know whether to ask them to parties. They were asked to some parties. Felicity thought they should have gone, but her father and Robert did not want to go, and she did not have the energy to go on her own.

They had always had a lawn meet soon after Christmas, not on Boxing Day but during the following week. The Master changed the meet, out of respect; hounds met on a different lawn.

• • •

Felicity made a New Year resolution: she would pull herself together and get on with her life. She did not want to go back to Cambridge. She would have herself taught to type, or something.

She started this new, this virtuously energetic phase by attacking the muddle of her mother's desk. It was in the small, sunny room where she had written letters. Felicity thought it would have been called a 'morning room', but the phrase had apparently gone out of use: perhaps nowadays not many people lived in houses so large that there was a special room with morning sun where the mistress wrote her letters. Felicity's mother had called it sometimes her 'office' and sometimes the 'pigsty'. It was usually rather a mess. It had one of the sofas on which the dogs slept, and there were always bones or chewed-up toys on the sofa and on the floor. Felicity's mother shoved things into drawers in her desk, so that she could get on with something more interesting.

The desk itself was beautiful, mid-Georgian walnut with the original brass and the 'secret' compartment behind the top pair of drawers, which were dummies. There were little drawers in the top and big drawers below, and they would all be stuffed with papers. It might be heartrending going through some of it; some of it would be very dull; it ought to be done: it ought to have been done long before, because of unpaid bills and unanswered invitations.

Perhaps once Felicity's mother had had notions about putting certain sorts of papers in particular drawers or pigeon-holes—bank statements here, receipted bills there, the children's letters in another place. The system had broken down in floods of papers and because there was a horse to exercise or a rose to prune.

Felicity began at the top. Almost immediately she went off to fetch a large waste-paper basket. She was not going to throw anything away that might be of interest or value to somebody: but nobody was ever going to want envelopes from which the letters had been abstracted five years before, or price-lists or garden tools long out of date.

The job was going to take a long time, not only because of the sheer numbers of papers that had at least to be glanced at, but also because some of the oddments were irresistible.

She put things into piles or into the waste-paper basket. There were a lot of piles because there were a lot of categories. Some grew faster than others.

Felicity found letters of her own, from school. She read some with awakened, sharp-focus memory, some with complete surprise. Some of Robert's school letters were a complete surprise. There were old race-cards and theatre programmes. There were photographs that had escaped the albums, shooting parties, people on horseback, herself and Robert at the seaside, yachts, men smoking pipes. There were letters from people saying 'thank you' for dinner or for a weekend. There were postcards with illegible signatures from the South of France and the North of Scotland.

The sun wheeled. It left the east-facing windows of the room.

Felicity stopped for lunch. Robert already had a drink. Felicity told her father what she was doing. He nodded. He did not seem to be interested. She thought he might have been amused by some of the old photographs, but when she told him about them he nodded, polite, uninterested.

After lunch she needed a light over the desk. The days were lengthening but still very short. From mid-afternoon, she was sitting in a pool of light in surrounding darkness. The room was cold. She drew the curtains, and switched on the electric fire. A proper fire was laid, but Felicity thought it would be silly to light it for just herself.

She worked through the autumn list, ten years old, of a London publisher, wondering what item in it had caused her mother to preserve it: guessing that there was no such item, that her mother had tucked it away in a hurry to get on with something more important. There were invitations to ancient parties, and service-sheets of the weddings of people Felicity had never heard of, and calendars of departed years from local tradesmen.

In the second drawer, at the back, there were the letters. There were fifteen of them. The earliest was dated June 23, 1962, and the latest September 27. The letters were inaccurately typed—not illiterately, but with unintended gaps and corrections made with the typewriter. Several different typewriters had been used, but there was no doubting that the writer was the same. There was no address on any of them, and no signature. These were what was meant by anonymous letters.

The envelopes were all there, too. 'Mrs Bramall', the address correct. All the postmarks were London, but different parts of London.

Felicity felt her face grow hot when she read the letters. She was disgusted and appalled. She wanted to stop but she could not stop. She had read books that she thought were pornographic, and even some which everybody knew to be pornographic, but the intimate, lewdly explicit descriptions of sex in the letters was completely outside her experience.

The descriptions were in the third person: 'He did so and so, she did so and so', but the point of view was the woman's. It was always the same woman, unnamed. It was always the same man, named. His point of view was only revealed by what he said, quoted in the letters: how much he loved her, how much more exciting he found her than any other woman he had known, how moved he was by her youth, how greatly aroused he was by her young slenderness, how, now that he had had her so often, and in so many different ways, he knew that it was impossible for him to be aroused by any other woman. That was the sort of thing he was quoted as saying. There was no hint of the woman's name; there was no description of her by which she could be identified, except that she was young and slim. The uses to which she put her mouth, tongue, teeth and body were described in lavish and loving detail, and so was the man's reaction.

Felicity made it to the sink in the flower-room next door, where she vomited. She thought she would not have done so, if the man had been anyone but her father.

She thought, hanging wretchedly over the stoneware sink, that it would be impossible to prove where the letters had come from. The police would not be interested. Felicity had an idea that it was criminal to send obscene material through the post, but the acts described were not precisely unnatural, and the words used were clinically precise rather than gross. In any case, there could never be the slightest question of showing these letters to anybody.

It was obvious to Felicity that her father had never seen them. He must never see them. Clinging to the sink, Felicity changed her mind about the fire.

Clinging there, she understood that the letters had driven her mother to suicide.

Felicity was not particularly squeamish, priggish or over-protected. She was a country girl. She had lived all her life in the presence of death and copulation. She had seen foxes dismembered by the pack, hand-reared pheasants flying into expanding jets of lead pellets from the twelve-bores, and rabbits dead of gangrene after getting out of snares. She had seen the farmyard bantams climbing onto one another's backs, and the Friesian bull with the cows. The facts of life, the sight of death, were perfectly well known to her.

But as a family, they were easily stunned, as though their skulls were too thin. Stunned, Felicity burned the letters in the grate in her mother's room. Their destruction did not destroy them. The phrases volleyed inside her skull like golfballs shot from a mortar in a squash court. The phrases conjured unspeakable images.

He said. She did. He did. She did.

Felicity could not face her father over the dinner table; she could not stomach the white flesh of the chicken they were eating.

When she touched her mother's desk, the aged beautiful walnut, her hand recoiled because the wood was red hot. The piles of papers remained where she had put them, until somebody dusting the room put them back into the drawers.

Later all the papers, all the photographs and postcards and theatre-programmes, all the letters from Felicity and Robert, all the fragmentary souvenirs of a lifetime and of a marriage, were put into a sack which was put on the incinerator. By that time somebody else was using the desk, and wanted the drawers for new papers.

Felicity wondered if the fire inside her father, which had been put out, could be rekindled by his old love of sailing. Moving to an inland countryside after the war, he had needlessly cut sailing out of his life. He was at that time a man who got on with things, who joyfully tackled the present and the future without regret for the past.

Felicity talked to him about sailing. She said she wanted to be taken sailing; she wanted to go to Cowes, and have tea on the Squadron lawn, and be taken out in a beautiful yacht on the Solent.

Her father listened politely, nodded, signified that it would indeed be nice for her to have tea with friends on the Squadron lawn. He looked at her with eyes that had no fire behind them.

The fire Felicity had made in the grate in her mother's room, which failed to consume the things it consumed, had more warmth and vigour than the life behind her father's eyes.

By the end of March, things seemed to have improved. Felicity was learning typing and shorthand. She was doing something. Robert was working on the farm, earning wages. He was doing something. The new farm manager had settled in and taken the reins. There was nothing to stop Gerald Bramall from going abroad, if he wanted to. His friends told him he ought to.

He went to America. He had been there once before, in 1942, the corvette in which he served sent to convoy oil-tankers through the Battle of the Atlantic. He was torpedoed on the way back, the first of the times he was torpedoed. He had happy memories of the hospitality of Americans, and he decided it was the place he wanted to revisit. Felicity—Robert, too, as far as she could tell—was delighted, thankful, hopeful.

He was there for a long time. He was there for four months, until the end of July. He travelled widely. Postcards came.

He took her with him, or caused her to join him. They came back married.

They had a honeymoon in the Bahamas. Felicity knew the physical details of the honeymoon, because she had read the anonymous letters.

Their father spoke quietly, almost in a monotone. He had never been a garrulous man, a fiery or impulsive speaker, but he had never spoken in this flat robot style. He seemed to be reciting words he had been taught. He did not look either Robert or Felicity in the face.

He said, 'I am trying not to accuse either of you of selfishness or thoughtlessness. I am trying not to accuse you of living self-indulgently in the past, or of wanting to sacrifice my happiness to your own emotions. I force myself to speak only with regret. Is my life nothing to you? Is it nothing to you that I have now been given the courage to live again? You were not brought up to egocentricity, or to wallowing in nostalgia. Would you wish me to keep myself under dust-sheets, to live in silence in a darkened shrine, never for the rest of my days to go out into the sunlight? How can you be so blind, so blinkered, so uncaring? Are you deliberately setting out to make us unhappy? Would you prefer me lonely and miserable? Is that what you would choose for me? How can you be so selfish?'

The voice was not his voice. The words were not his words, but he thought they were.

Robert was pale, in spite of working out of doors in midsummer. He was lanky and rather clumsy. He looked younger than his age. He stood staring at his father with a shocked face. Felicity was staring at him too, as though at a stranger who was speaking Hungarian. She thought she was not pale. She felt fat and frumpish. She felt a sick anger which she tried to aim in the right direction.

Robert suddenly blundered to the door and out of the room, as though, like Felicity on New Year's Day, he knew he was going to vomit. Beyond the open doorway stood Victoria, in a cotton dress, barelegged. In silhouette she was very slim. It was darker in the hall. Her face was in shadow, framed by the heavy dark hair. Robert went past her. He gave no sign of seeing her, though he must have done so. He went not to the flower-room, or any sink or lavatory, but out of the front door. He went away down the drive, and none of them ever saw him again.

Felicity went away later the same day. She packed some of her things, and telephoned for a taxi. She went to London. Though her speeds were not wonderful, she got a secretarial job. She slept for a time on the sofa of a girl she had known at Cambridge.

She hated living in London.

Her father continued the allowance he had given her at Cambridge.

Victoria looked at his monthly bank statement, and saw the Standing Order in favour of Felicity. She stopped it.

C·H·A·P·T·E·R

6

Victoria was at pains to make her peace with Aunt Marigold. This was completely unselfish. Aunt Marigold needed Victoria, not the other way about. An effort had to be made not to forget, exactly—that would have been impossible—but to forgive the wounding and unfair things Aunt Marigold had said in October. The effort was required by Christian charity. Victoria asked Aunt Marigold for weekends at Court Farm; the old thing never came, which was a relief, but she was repeatedly asked.

Aunt Marigold seemed to regret, to be repenting, her cruelty and unfairness. She did not actually see Gerald, but she heard how happy and revitalised he was. She heard from Victoria. She heard that Gerald was truly happy for the first time in his life. At last he had a wife he truly loved, who was exciting and comforting and looked after him properly.

Gerald had been betrayed by his children. When he wanted them to share his new happiness, they packed up and ran away. Victoria had done her very best to make friends with them, to get them to accept her, but they were too selfish. They were hard and cynical. Victoria could quote many well-attested examples of the heartless way they behaved. They were notorious for their nastiness in the neighbourhood and at their schools. Aunt Marigold could ask anybody, she did not have to take Victoria's word for it. Aunt Marigold could not, in practice, ask anybody: she did not know any boys at Eton or any neighbours of the Bramalls.

The children had not inherited anything in their characters from Gerald, that was quite certain. As Aunt Marigold knew, he was gentle and a gentleman. Where could they have got it from? Let's think. What other genes had they?

The girl was living like a slut somewhere in London. The boy was said to be abroad. Victoria hoped he was in Australia, too far away to hurt his father's feelings.

When you only hear one side of a story, you find yourself believing it. You find yourself repeating it.

You had to be sorry for anybody who suffered from what they called a black night of the soul. That being said, wasn't there something irresponsibly selfish about suicide? It was a sin not only because you were playing God with your own sacred life, but also because of the unhappiness you were selfishly giving. You were being a coward in the face of the sort of problems everybody faced. Charity could be taken too far, into tolerance of the sinful. It was all too easy to indulge a soft attitude—it was less trouble, less painful, less honest.

There was a reconciliation between Victoria and Aunt Marigold, which was really more than Aunt Marigold deserved, but which represented charity and loving-kindness on the part of Victoria. Aunt Marigold came to believe everything Victoria told her, because nobody else could tell her anything. Aunt Marigold had had ideas about changing her will, but she left it as it was.

Victoria knew she had conceived, the moment she had done so. God stood at the foot of the bed, blessing that midnight coupling, giving her a son. That was a year after they were married; the magic night was in the late September of 1964. Gerald was transformed with happiness when

Victoria was able to tell him the news. A son at last who would love him as he deserved, whom he could be proud of. Victoria took things quietly, the following winter and spring, inward-looking and looking at the future. The boy would have dark hair, grey eyes, narrow hips. He would be a sportsman but not obsessed by sport; he would be as brave as his father but more cultured; he would be as beautiful as his mother but taller and stronger. He would one day tower over his slender little mother, teasing her affectionately and making her laugh. He would not want to be king of the world, because of his innate modesty, but he would be king of the world because of his beauty and intelligence.

The birth of a daughter in June was a disagreeable shock. Gerald seemed to be pleased. He wanted it called Charlotte, after somebody. Victoria let him get on with it. There was a nurse, who dealt with the mess. Victoria's priorities were to get her figure back and to get a tan. This was for Gerald's sake. He had been deprived of her body for too long. She sunbathed by the pool which she had got him to have made during the winter. It was a very splendid pool, with comfortable recliners on the flagstones surrounding it. Gardeners with noisy mowers had to wait until she was somewhere else.

The baby was presumably perfectly all right, in the care of a competent nurse.

The baby showed early signs that she had inherited her father's sturdy bone-structure and his fair colouring. It sometimes made a lot of noise. It began crawling, and pulling itself up by things, and knocking drinks off tables. Victoria had to remind the nurse to keep it out of the way. This was for Gerald's sake. He was her priority. She lived for his comfort and happiness. She protected him against exploitation by a noisy, messy, active child.

It started to kiss Victoria, wetly, dribbling. That was surely not hygienic. Victoria had a word with the nurse.

Gerald seemed to like being slobbered over. Victoria let him get on with it.

Once Gerald made an incautious, a really thoughtless remark, comparing this little Charlotte with his other daughter Felicity. He did not make that mistake twice.

Victoria, studying his bank-statements, found that Gerald was being absurdly, dangerously irresponsible with money. Something like the pool was an investment, substantially increasing the value of the property. His subscriptions to his clubs, though he used them so seldom, were justified because those clubs were part of the person he was. But the blind, the deaf, cancer research, mentally handicapped children—all those things were the responsibility of society as a whole, of the government, not of individuals whose instinctive generosity was exploited. All the Chancellor of the Exchequer had to do was divert some of the money he got from their income tax into things like Oxfam, instead of wasting it by paying so many unnecessary bureaucrats. Gerald had a young family. His first responsibility was to his family. Charity begins at home.

In order to look after him properly, in order to protect him from himself, Victoria acquainted herself with all his investments, insurances and the rest. She spent many boring hours, but it was her duty. Gradually, tactfully, firmly, she took control of his finances. He was grateful to be saved the trouble and the head-scratching. He was all the better for it, mentally and physically. It was a sacrifice she was proud to make.

They cancelled most of the Standing Orders. They called in some personal loans. It was vexing to find that they could not cancel charitable endowments, but they were only for seven years, and some of them had nearly run out, and none of them would be renewed.

And in order to look after him properly, in order to protect him from other people, Victoria looked through his letters before he saw them. It was important for his health and happiness that he should not be bothered by charitable appeals (he who had been such a soft touch) or by business matters until she had had time to decide what was best to be done.

A letter came for him, the address hand written, with an Australian stamp. This could easily be something that would upset him, give him indigestion, keep him awake. Victoria steamed the envelope open, using the electric kettle in her office. This was more trouble than simply using a paper-knife, but it was worth it on account of Gerald's feelings.

Victoria was thankful she had intercepted the Australian letter. It was about the uncouth lout they called Robert, the ungrateful yob who had run away when his father needed him. It was from a friend of Robert's. It said that Robert had been drowned, sailing in a small boat off Fremantle, in Western Australia.

Gerald's heart had been mercifully hardened, by her healing touch, towards those detestable children; but this news might distress him. He might, ridiculously, in some way blame himself—he had that sort of Quixotic mind. Another thing he might easily do was to get in touch with that stodgy, boring Felicity. That would be thoroughly bad for him. It would not really be a kindness to her, either. She could do nothing about the boy's death, and she was not coming to Court Farm.

Victoria burnt the letter, in the grate where letters had been burnt before.

As soon as Lottie was aware of anything, she was aware that she was two people. She even had two names. One name was one person, and the other was a separate and different person. It was confusing for a young child to be two people.

To her father and her nanny and the servants indoors and out, and to most visitors and to other children and their families, she was Lottie. Lottie was really quite good, most of the time. People seemed to like her and some of them seemed to love her. She got through life pretty easily and pretty cheerfully. She overheard nice things said about herself.

With her mother she was Charlotte, and she knocked things over. She was nervous and clumsy and she had nothing to say.

Lottie noticed this more and more, at a time when her Mama's tummy was mysteriously getting bigger and bigger.

God would not do it to her twice, He could not. He did not. Victoria's son was born in the middle of June, not quite two years since the other child's birth.

Lottie's second birthday went almost unnoticed.

He was to be called Terence, after Gerald's father. Victoria did not much like the name, and did not use it. She called him Rienzo, the name, she thought, of a hero. Everybody else, in the end, called him Rienzo, and he would not answer to Terence. The dashing name suited him, because he was a dashing man from birth. His eyes were grey. His hair would be dark and straight, and his hips narrow. He might not want to be king of the world, but he would be king of the world.

He was king of Court Farm.

Victoria experienced true motherhood, for which the other child had only been a kind of rehearsal.

This one could knock over what drinks he wanted. His kisses, wet or dry, were bliss to Victoria.

She said that he must grow up to be self-reliant. This of course meant self-discipline rather than the external discipline of adults. He must learn from experience— even painful experience—what things were wise to do and what foolish. Old-fashioned nursery rules imposed arbitrary limits, arbitrary time-tables, arbitrary rules about the handling of spoons and the throwing of bowls of broth into people's laps; they were an evasion, an abdication of true responsibility: a child brought up like that was sheeplike, unable to think for himself, drearily conformist, doomed to be a second-rater.

Nurses came and went a little rapidly, because they could not adjust their stupid minds to this enlightened philosophy of education.

Rienzo's burgeoning self-reliance did not, of course, mean that people were not to pick him up and comfort and coddle him when he fell: that they were not to give him anything he screamed for. He was precociously intelligent. You could almost see his brain working; you could see him learning from experience. He learned that if he screamed and screamed, he would be given anything he wanted.

If he broke Charlotte's toys it was because they were shabby, fragile foreign toys, unsafe, things the child should never have been given, things she was safer without.

If he threw his food across the nursery, it was because it was the wrong food. Even dogs had the sense not to eat food that was wrong.

Victoria saw one of Gerald's dogs licking Rienzo's face. No dogs were thereafter allowed in the house.

Victoria took many, many photographs of Rienzo, using with skill and originality the cameras Gerald had given her. Some of the prints were enlarged and put in frames in various rooms of the house. Whatever had previously been in the frames went, of course, on the fire. Many of Rienzo's photographs she stuck into albums. There were also photographs of herself, taken by Gerald. She stuck in the best of these, some hundreds. She did this helot work herself, wearisome and tiring though it was, because it gave Gerald such joy and pride, and because nobody else could be trusted to compose the different pictures on a page.

The photographic record of Rienzo's life merited solid, expensive, leather-bound albums. It happened that there

were a lot of them at Court Farm, some in a drawer in
a tallboy in Gerald's study, some on tables in the drawing
room. They were in excellent condition, tooled leather
unscuffed, unflaking, the bindings secure, the pages large
and of proper heavy cardboard. The old photographs in the
books had to be removed, of course. This task also Victoria
set herself, without flinching. She used steam, solvent and
a Stanley knife. The old photographs she threw away,
because they were not interesting to anybody any more.
She burned them in the grate in her office.

There was a symbolism in this which was mythic, religious. Victoria was destroying, by purifying fire, the rec-
ords of Gerald's previous unhappy life, so that the new
life he had generated could flourish in the nutritious ashes.
The images of a new, and holier faith now blazed from the
altar-pieces once occupied by the debased and irrelevant
idols of a pagan, peasant era.

The old photographs curled madly before they caught
fire and whispered into limbo. Victoria knew that she was
exorcising boring old ghosts; it was a kind of spiritual
spring-cleaning.

The new photographs looked very fine in the old albums.
They were already a kind of heirloom.

Victoria carried out regular inspections of Gerald's desk.
She still took not quite everything for granted. She had
made herself responsible for Gerald, and she was responsible for Rienzo. Gerald had still to be protected from
himself, and Rienzo had to be protected from infection.

One drawer was locked. That posed only a temporary
problem. Victoria was conscientious, utterly committed,
in her performance of her duties; consequently she knew
where Gerald's key-ring was, and which key was which.
There were keys to the various doors of the house, spare
keys for the cars, keys to some of the farm buildings and
to the cellars. He did not carry the big bunch of keys about
wherever he went, like a Victorian housekeeper; he left

them in a drawer in his dressing-table.

Gerald went off to see the farm manager; he was going on to look at some sheep. There was no real need for him to look at any sheep, since he had the manager, but Victoria encouraged him to keep up an interest in the estate. It interfered with her performance of her duties, to have him under her feet all day.

There was a letter in the drawer, long, four close-written pages in a neat, rather schoolmarmy handwriting. At the top was a London address and a telephone number.

The letter began 'Darling Daddy', and ended 'Masses of love, Felicity'.

Stodge. In her mind Victoria called her Stodge. There was deceitful communication, behind her back, between Gerald and that treacherous bitch.

Victoria read the whole letter quickly, looking for references to herself. There were none, so it was a boring letter.

It conveyed the barely-credible news that Stodge was going to get married. The man was a solicitor, admitted and with a degree. His father, also a lawyer, was senior partner in a firm in South-West Wales; David was to join the firm and expected to be a partner soon. Stodge had been there, and liked the place. She had met the family, and they were sweet. David and she knew one another really well and they were very certain. She was looking forward passionately to having her own home, and in the country. There was more about her plans. Victoria scarcely took it in.

Victoria was not angry but deeply saddened. She had failed. She did not know what more she could have done, but she had not done enough.

She heard the car on the gravel. She put the letter away, exactly as she had found it, locked the drawer, and returned the keys to Gerald's dressing-table.

She wore a bright mask at lunch. She searched Gerald's face for signs of sickness and treachery, but he looked the same as usual.

The lesson of this was that the treachery was no new thing.

The telephone number on the letter. The obvious implication was that she expected him to ring her up. He had done so, presumably, from the farm manager's office or a pub or the call-box in the village.

Where had she sent the letter? How had he received it? The farm manager also, perhaps, the landlord of the pub, a neighbour who had distorted, sick ideas about loyalty. There was a conspiracy, there had to be, to make possible letters and telephone calls.

The thing to remember was that it was not really Gerald's fault. He had got into bad habits over the years, and he was too weak to break them. Justice required some punishment, yes, but he should not be punished as though he were the mastermind, the spider at the centre of the web.

Rienzo told her, as clearly as though he had spoken the words, that she must forgive Gerald, but that her forgiveness must be conditional on his future honesty; this was for Gerald's own sake as well as for Rienzo's.

Victoria was still only twenty-six. She was only now approaching her best. She was supple and slender, with a golden all-over tan. She looked wonderful dressed and undressed.

She set herself that evening to be kind to Gerald. He was only in his middle fifties. He was most certainly not an old man, at least not when aroused by her. Out of kindness and forgiveness, and with arts that she had taught herself, she was at her most submissive and exciting, at her most innocent and audacious, at her youngest and freshest and most shameless.

'No,' said Victoria.

She drew away from him in the semi-darkness, in the soft light from the half-open door of his dressing-room. She stood dimly visible, dim golden light on her breast and thigh.

'Never again,' she said, 'until you make me a promise.'

Gerald sat up and stretched out his arms to her. He made a noise that was like a sob.

'You must swear on Rienzo's head,' said Victoria.

Gerald groaned that he would.

She made him swear to do nothing slyly and deceitfully behind her back, to have no secret contact with his ungrateful older children.

He swore: and she came like a blessing to lie beside him.

Only later, when he had fallen asleep to the trumpet-calls of angels, did she smile to remember that Gerald would have no contact with Robert anyway.

Felicity had renewed contact with her father within six months of his return from America. There was a kind of bashfulness on both sides. Neither ever alluded to Victoria. In order to avoid doing so, Felicity forbore to ask any questions about the house or the farm or his holiday plans— about four-fifths of the things they might normally have discussed. It was strange to have these enormous no-go areas with a father you had adored. No doubt it was strange and tense for him, too, but it made it possible for them to meet amicably and to love one another.

Felicity had had a card from Robert, from Hong Kong. He had not written to Court Farm.

It was difficult for father and daughter to communicate. She could often not be reached on the telephone at work, and he could not ring up from home in the evening. It was virtually impossible for her to telephone him, unless they had agreed, by letter, beforehand, a time and place for him to take the call; and even then he could never be certain of being there. He could write to her, to her London flat, as long as he wrote in somebody else's house, and gave the letter to somebody to post. This looked distinctly odd, to the people in whose houses he wrote to her: and they saw her name on the envelope. She could write only to an accommodation address; this, near Court Farm, was difficult to find; it had to be somebody absolutely trust-worthy, and somebody who was prepared to lie to Victoria. Felicity understood that it was difficult to ask neighbours to do that.

Although they never spoke about it—never, never came within a mile of the subject—Felicity began to understand, at least suppose that she was somewhere near correctly imagining, the thraldom of her father. After two years, she could think of the anonymous letters without hot shame and hatred and nausea, and in their monstrous fashion they went some way to explaining it. She understood better when she herself fell in love, happily and then unhappily.

In intimate moments with her lover, she found phrases from the anonymous letters, read once and rapidly, invad-ing her head like ants the skull of a dead animal. After it was all over, she wondered in dismay if she had uncon-sciously learned from the letters. Certainly she startled her lover. This may have been one of the reasons why he beat an embarrassed retreat.

She was never, in the first four years of this adjusted relationship, able to ask her father about his younger chil-dren. They were well inside forbidden territory, taboo, deep in a country seeded with landmines.

She had hoped that his enslavement was purely physi-cal—that there was no dimension, no magical magnetism, beyond that spelled out in the anonymous letters. She had herself, under the circumstances, embarked on adult life with a deep distrust of sex. Her early experiences were not encouraging, but she came to see that it could be, as the newspapers said of a summit meeting, 'a frank and free exchange'. She began to put a moderate value on it. She could imagine being committed, but not enslaved. She nei-ther wanted to enslave anybody, nor thought she could.

So probably there was more to it. The serpent's poison reached other parts, brain and heart as well as crotch.

There were precedents. Felicity had seen *Der Blau Engel*, and read Theodore Dreiser and Somerset Maugham. She could not easily fit her father into the leading male roles in these works, nor into *Antony and Cleopatra*, *Carmen* or *Tristan*.

She fell in and out of love, got better jobs, went often into the country to stay with friends, and then met David.

She knew that her father would be happy for her, that he would keep mouse-quiet about it at home, and that he would find it difficult to give her anything and impossible to give her much.

Her father telephoned in the early evening, ten days after she had written to him. He was in a hurry; he was furtive and he spoke softly. Felicity understood that he was at home. She assumed that Victoria was having a bath, or was somewhere in the garden where he could see her.

Felicity felt a surge of anger, at having her father ashamed to talk to her.

He said: 'Great news. I hope you'll be very happy. But I've got to be extra careful. I don't know when I'll be in touch.'

He hung up. Furiously Felicity pictured him hanging up softly, looking round guiltily, ready with a lie.

He was her father, the father of the bride. Why the hell couldn't he say: 'My eldest child is getting married. I'm bloody well going to be there. If you don't like it you can stuff it.'

He didn't because he didn't dare.

Felicity was brought face to face with the fact of her own father's essential moral weakness. He had allowed his wife to destroy herself; he had allowed his son and daughter to walk away from their home. He was as much a slave as he was in the awful summer of 1962, when Felicity found her mother crying, when everything in their lives was poisoned.

He was a slave who lied to his owner.

He was not getting the best of both worlds. He had not the excuse of successful intrigue. Felicity knew he was naturally unselfish, generous, charitable, trusting. He was no good at this kind of thing. He should not have gone in for this kind of thing, for ringing up his daughter furtively when his wife was having a bath. He should have taken a firm line, master in his own house. 'I shall go to my daughter's wedding. If I wish to invite her here, she will be made welcome.' Other men Felicity knew would have said that. David would have said it, if it could be imagined that David could ever be in a comparable situation. Legally, professionally, perhaps he might be, any lawyer might be. He would act with honesty and moral courage. Felicity began to think she had these qualities, too—not in comparison with the best and bravest people she knew, not in comparison with David, but in comparison with her father.

Looking at the silent telephone, she was brought face to face with contempt for her father. It did not send her to a washbasin to vomit, but it was a bad moment.

To David, when he came to take her out to dinner, she was laconic on the subject. She had no secrets from him, but she did not want to be a bore.

Lottie only heard long afterwards about Felicity's marriage. She only heard long afterwards about Felicity. When she knew, to her astonishment, that she had a sister, she was careful who she talked to about it.

She had learned to be wary.

She approached grown ups and other children, teachers at her first little school, friends, the postman, gardeners, all with wariness. Only after she was certain of their goodwill did she relax. She could often be sure, almost at once, that everything was all right, if she knew the people really well: but until that happened, or if she suspected boredom, contempt, enmity behind the smiles, she stood apart in silence, so as not to risk rebuff and humiliation.

That was when she was Lottie. When she was Charlotte she was silent so as not to be snubbed, and motionless so as not to knock things over.

It seemed to Lottie that Rienzo, although he only had one name, was two people also, but in exactly the opposite way to herself. He was voluble and confident only in the one situation where she tried to be a piece of furniture. In the places where, after a cautious beginning, she could relax and talk and listen and learn and run about, he was silent and indifferent, as though the people were unreal and unimportant.

When they tried to take Rienzo to the nursery school for the first time, he kicked and screamed and struggled and bit his nanny. Mama had to get up out of bed and come downstairs; she had to get dressed quickly and go with them to the school, which was in the next village. It was embarrassing for Lottie. Lottie did not see what happened afterwards, because she was in a different class, but it seemed they had rung up Mama and told her that somebody must come to take Rienzo away. Lottie heard about it at break, from children in the kindergarten class.

Mama was angry, not with Rienzo but with the school. They tried to take him again; twice they tried. Exactly the same thing happened. Lottie heard about it afterwards, from the youngest children.

Mama got somebody to come in three mornings a week to teach Rienzo. He was a retired schoolmaster. Lottie met him warily, and relaxed with him surprisingly quickly. Of course he was not teaching her, but only Rienzo. He was called Mr Matthews. Rienzo did not relax with him. He said that if other people could read, they could read to him, and there was no need for him to learn. He said that when he was grown up he would be rich, much richer than Mr Matthews. He would not work. He would pay people to read and write for him, and to count and add up and tell the time. He had no need to learn any of those things, and he refused to do so.

Lottie heard this afterwards, from the nice old man who tried to teach Rienzo. He was talking not to Lottie, of course, but to Papa, but Lottie was listening. Mr Matthews said that if he had been allowed to punish Rienzo, they might have got somewhere. Since this was forbidden, they were wasting their time. Papa went *hrum-hrum*, coughing instead of replying.

Lottie could read easily by this time; she became one of the people who read to Rienzo.

Lottie was sent away to boarding school when she was nine. This made her one of the youngest girls in her new school, a friendly little place in Dorset with an excellent record in Common Entrance results. Papa heard about it from friends. He went to see it, and spoke to the Headmistress. He took Lottie to see it. An older girl showed Lottie round while the Headmistress showed Papa round. The girl said Lottie would like it, and she was right.

Lottie was homesick, but Charlotte was not.

This was odd, because it was Lottie who went to boarding school, leaving Charlotte behind at home. Lottie made friends, after she had overcome her wariness. She was a bit below average in the classroom, but above on the playing-fields, in the swimming pool, and on the school's own shaggy little ponies.

During her first term, there were half a dozen cheerful, encouraging letters from Papa, and he twice came to take her out. The first time he said that Rienzo had a new tutor, who lived in the house almost as a member of the family. He was a young man, Dutch, who wanted to make his English absolutely perfect so that he could be an actor in England. It was pretty good already. He was a great success and Rienzo seemed to trust him. The second time Papa came, he said that the new tutor had left. It was not clear to Lottie whether Mama had sent him away or he had taken himself away; Lottie had the feeling that Papa was not clear about this, either. It was a blow. They were wondering what to do next. Lottie must help Rienzo during the holidays—get him to see that life would be much more fun if he could read and write, and do sums and speak French.

Doing sums and speaking French were not important to Lottie, and she was not very good at them, but she tried because they encouraged her and were kind to her.

She had no success with Rienzo in the Christmas holidays. Mama was cross with Charlotte for failing to make Rienzo want to read. Rienzo started calling Lottie 'Charlotte' whenever he was angry with her; this was whenever she tried to teach him to read.

Suddenly, during Lottie's first summer at boarding school, Rienzo learned to read. It was his eighth birthday, apparently: he was suddenly ashamed, angry, that children younger than himself could do things he could not. He set out to prove that he was cleverer than anyone else, as well as handsomer and a faster runner and a better swimmer. Lottie came home to find that Rienzo was going to be cleverer than she was. She knew that did not take much doing.

It improved the atmosphere in the house. Mama purred when she saw Rienzo reading a comic.

Rienzo had a lot of catching up to do if he was going to get into Eton. He consented to being taught for two hours every morning, even in midsummer, by yet another tutor.

It became obvious to everybody, in the course of that summer, that Rienzo was potentially much cleverer than Lottie. Mama said so, to visitors. She said it was lucky. She said, 'If I have to have one child who's as thick as I am, I'm thankful it's the girl, not the boy.' She did not really think she was thick herself, but Lottie understood that it was the sort of thing to say if you wanted to be popular.

Rienzo never, except to Lottie, boasted about being cleverer than Lottie.

• • •

Lottie wanted to have school-friends to stay during the holidays, people who would have appreciated the pool and the ponies. This was not possible. The very suggestion was inconsiderate. She was, however, encouraged to stay with other people herself.

She began to go away as often as she could, and to stay as long as she could. Charlotte was left behind; Lottie was made welcome.

Lottie became aware that her family was peculiar. She had been in the way, like nearly all children, of accepting her environment as the natural order—households which were different were the ones which were eccentric, as when daughters were happy and confident in the company of their mothers, as when a son and daughter were treated as of equal importance. Such things when encountered were bizarre, until she met them so often she began to think they were normal.

She also became aware that her father was two people, as she was. There was one person called Gerald, Mr Bramall, Commander, Sir, Papa. There was another person, quite different, called Darling. The difference about Darling was simply that he was much smaller.

Lottie went on to her proper school, her main school, for which her father had entered her years before. Rienzo was now going without complaint to a day-school, which meant a great deal of driving for somebody. He still had special coaching as well. His mother had the highest hopes for him.

Lottie was sturdy and sandy, Rienzo slim and dark. She looked a little like her father, he very much like his mother. This seemed to suit all parties.

At her new school, as at her old, she was always called Lottie. She might not have had another name. People even wrote 'L. Bramall'. Lottie treated her new school with wariness, until she settled down.

She came home from school to find Charlotte waiting for her, invading Lottie's skull and skin the moment she arrived. Charlotte was fat and plain and clumsy, though Lottie was a normal, active twelve-year-old. Lottie was growing up, but Charlotte remained a baby. Charlotte was tongue-tied, and knocked things over. Her elbows and hair were out of her control. Lottie was good at tennis and swimming and riding, and sang in the choir at school. She was not academic but she was an enthusiast. When she made a friend, that friend was a great friend. Charlotte could never make any friends at all.

Rienzo was never angry with Lottie nowadays, because he never noticed her. He called her neither Lottie nor Charlotte, because he never spoke to her.

Felicity had her first baby. Victoria did not see the announcement in *The Times*, because she did not know the name of Felicity's husband. They did not, in the announcement, commit the solecism of including the wife's maiden name.

Felicity knew they had been right to use *The Times* and to play safe, because her father wrote to her from a friend's house. His letter was full of love and joy in his grandchild.

Felicity was pleased by the letter and appalled by it. It was written in somebody else's house, on the paper embossed with the name of that house. Any reply was to be directed there.

What kind of a man was that?

The letter told Felicity where Lottie was at school. Felicity knew that Lottie existed, and nothing else about her at all. She wrote to Lottie.

Dear Lottie (this is what Daddy told me to call you) . . .

Thus Lottie knew she had a half-sister.

She could not understand why nobody had told her.

She could understand, unfortunately, why her father had not told her: but what about neighbours, servants, the people on the farm? The fact was that nobody had taken it upon themselves to tell her.

Lottie replied to Felicity's letter, but as Felicity was in West Wales with a new baby there was no likelihood of an early meeting.

A voice with an Australian accent telephoned for Mr Gerald Bramall at Court Farm. A cool female voice answered. Jim McCready and Brenda his wife, from Perth, Western Australia, had known Robert Bramall. This was the reason for a call out of the blue. The McCreadys were in London. They wanted to get in touch with Robert's father and his sister.

Jim McCready was surprised to hear that there was not and never had been such a person as Robert Bramall, and if there was he had no sister.

They remembered that Robert had told them a little about his stepmother—she was his reason, incredibly enough, for being in Australia. They began to believe a little of what he told them. They found out the name of the local vicar, and telephoned him. He was new to the parish; he had heard various stories, more or less contradictory, but Mr Bramall's older family was long before his time. He referred them to a doctor, now retired but until recently senior member of the local partnership, who had known that family all their lives.

Doctor Charles had Felicity's married name and her address. He and his wife had been asked to the wedding, and they exchanged Christmas cards. Doctor Charles knew the situation, more or less, and refused on professional grounds to discuss it with strangers. But he felt justified in referring them to Felicity.

The McCreadys had time on their hands. He had just retired from his insurance company, which as a farewell present had given them this trip to Europe. They telephoned Felicity; they hired a car, and drove to Pembrokeshire.

They told Felicity about Robert's life and death. He had been a sailing mate of Jim's in Fremantle, a good bloke though inclined to be moody when he hit the sauce. He had given them his family's address, because he knew that they planned to visit the land of their fathers when Jim retired. He had given them a good deal of information besides this, but they did not know how much of it to believe.

Felicity was not deeply grief-stricken. She had loved Robert dearly, but she had been morally certain for a long time that he was dead. He was not a great correspondent, but he would have written—he would have wanted her to know where he was, that he was all right, because he knew she cared about him.

Felicity confirmed to the McCreadys everything that Robert had said and hinted to them about the stepmother. They did not know how much of this to believe, either. They realised there was something in it all—that cool voice on the telephone, flatly denying what they knew to be the truth, proved of itself that there was something in it. But although Felicity was happily married and mother of two, it was clear that she was too embittered to be believed literally.

Felicity wrote to her father with the news about Robert. She was sure he did not know it, because he would have told her. She addressed the letter to the Safe House three villages away.

Lottie had been at home for ten days of the summer holidays.

Suddenly, for no new reason that she could see, her father began to die in front of her eyes.

C·H·A·P·T·E·R

7

Rienzo got into Eton. By this time, though everyone was pleased, no one was surprised. There was a celebration.

Lottie's fifteenth birthday, towards the end of her third summer term at her school. For most of her contemporaries, the O Level examinations loomed the following summer. Her teachers advised Lottie to wait, with most of her subjects, until the year after that. She saw their point.

Lottie had grown into a big, strong girl. Her figure was good, but like many girls of her age she was overweight. Her hair was still very fair. Her features were strong. She would be handsome, probably attractive, never beautiful.

She took a great deal of exercise, but it was still difficult to lose weight. She wondered about going on a diet, until a girl she knew became so obsessed with being fat that she developed anorexia and nearly died. This frightened Lottie and all her friends.

Besides being excessively weight-conscious, the anorexic girl came from a broken home. Lottie wished her home would break.

At the end of the term she discovered in herself a violent desire not to go home.

Mama would greet her with a remark about her weight, and Lottie would discover that she had become Charlotte.

She went home because she was only just fifteen and she
had nowhere else to go, until the first of her invitations to
stay with schoolfriends.

Rienzo was full of Eton. He gave the impression that
Eton was full of Rienzo.

Their father continued gradually dying, as he had been
doing for almost exactly a year. He was sixty-six. He was
far too young to be dying. It was painful for Lottie to see
death growing over him like a fungus.

Rienzo that summer was continuously on display, all the
time that Charlotte was at home and, presumably, all the
time that Lottie was away. If his mother were not by to
show him off, he showed himself off. He learned to drive a
tractor, and drove it over the lawn; he did fancy dives from
the springboard; he sulked when he was beaten at tennis.
After a time he would not play against Lottie because
she beat him. Sometimes Charlotte played against him
(depending who was watching) and then she made so
many mis-hits, and served so many double faults, that
Rienzo managed to win.

It was a strange summer, Lottie's periods of happiness punctuated by Charlotte's spells of apathetic misery.

During the course of it she became aware of the existence, and condition, of her two surviving grandparents.
She had never seen either; neither was ever mentioned.
Mama's father was in a home for helpless elderly people
on the South Coast; Papa's mother was in another home,
of the same sort, in the West. She came to the family's
attention by dying. She had been very old indeed, in her
middle nineties. It was a great tribute to the nursing in
the place where she lived. Mama said that if you were
completely mad you lived longer, because you were not
faced with the ordinary worries. That was, said Mama,
if you had a foolishly generous son who kept you in a
luxurious nursing home for more than twenty years. At

lunchtime the day the news came Mama calculated aloud
how much it had cost.

Felicity told Lottie that Granny had loved her mother,
Papa's first wife. That was why she was no longer mentioned at Court Farm.

A person called Great Aunt Marigold was paying the
bills for Mama's father, her older brother. Lottie had always
known about Great Aunt Marigold, but had never met her
or spoken to her. Lottie had seen Christmas cards, and
received presents for which she wrote correct letters of
thanks. Great Aunt Marigold was the same age as Papa.
There was no reason, as far as Lottie knew, why she
did not come to Court Farm, but she never did. Mama
sometimes spoke to her for a long time on the telephone.
Mama's voice in these conversations was one that Charlotte had become used to—a kindly warmth overlaying a
killing cold.

Victoria, that summer, reminded herself that the Emperor
Napoleon was small. A small, elegant man, neat-featured,
adored by women and idolised by men. She imagined
Mozart as small (she did not threaten her image of the
porcelain, miniature master by much listening to his music)
and Leonardo, and Alan Ladd. There was something vulgar about being a big man. Sir Gordon Mackay, Uncle
Gordon, had been a big man; Aunt Marigold was a big
woman. Vulgar.

Certainly Rienzo was small. He was only thirteen, and
obviously still growing, but unless he shot up in a gawky
way quite unlike him, he would be a small man. Victoria,
at five foot four, looked down at him, or would have, if
they had stood face to face: but usually he sat at her feet,
or she at his feet. Placed so, they formed a picture which
should have been caught by the brush of a master. Victoria
considered the idea of commissioning a pair of paintings,
not so very large, one of Rienzo at her feet and one of her
at his feet. But since the death of Sir Alfred Munnings

there was no painter to whom this commission could be entrusted.

Victoria was sure that Rienzo's plumpness was a sign of health, that it was puppy-fat, that he would lose it.

Lottie was at home for the last three weeks of the summer holidays. She had used up all the welcomes elsewhere. It was not convenient for people to have her to stay at the end of the holidays, when they were buying clothes and marking them and pulling school trunks out of attics. Lottie suspected that she had outstayed a number of welcomes already.

She was wary when she went to a new place, but she was more wary when she went to what they said was home.

Her father, dying, poured drinks in the evening for neighbours. Charlotte shuffled in a corner, watching Rienzo plugged into his Walkman in the midst of the guests. Mama said that, like herself, Rienzo was passionately fond of music. Major Henderson stared at Rienzo, who stared back, insulated by earphones. Major Henderson's son was Rienzo's age, at Wellington; he was a boy with whom Rienzo did not wish to play tennis.

Rienzo knew many young lords, but he had not gone away to stay with any of them during the summer. Rienzo said he had been asked, but had refused. He had too much consideration for Mama to spend half the holidays away from home. Mama said the same. It was not clear to Lottie how many invitations to the castles of dukes Rienzo had actually received.

Lottie went back to school without wariness.

In that November of 1980 Aunt Marigold was killed in a car-smash. It was an ironic way for the old thing to die, because for the previous two or three years she had hardly gone anywhere. She was arthritic and fat, and travelling was more trouble than it was worth. She was killed on the Hog's Back, an articulated lorry having skidded on black

ice and sideswiped the car she was travelling in. She had
been on her way to spend a weekend with friends near
Farnham, a project which was evidently more attractive
to her than staying at Court Farm.

Victoria allowed herself a private smile, that the Hog's
Back should have been the name of the road where Aunt
Marigold was killed. She was greedy and lazy, and she
had been cruel and unfair to Victoria.

There were a number of beneficiaries of the will—her
furs, most of the jewellery, some of the silver and the pictures went to various old friends and to more or less remote
Mackay relations. The lawyer, who was the executor, was
unfortunately in touch with them all. Victoria was, as she
expected, residuary legatee.

Capital? There were a few holdings of shares, valued
for probate at not quite £4000. There was about the same
sum on deposit. The rest had gone on the sizeable annuity
which Gordon had bought before his death.

Furniture? All the fine big pieces from the Ascot house
had long gone under the hammer. There were only the
contents of a two-bedroom flat. The pair of Tiffany lamps
were fakes. The Persian rugs were full of cigarette burns.

By the terms of the will, Victoria had to pay out of
her inheritance the Capital Transfer Tax on the furs and
jewellery and silver. There was no way she could get round
this. Her visit to London, her meeting with the lawyer,
were absolutely infuriating. The cheque she finally got
from the lawyer was for only a few hundred pounds.

Victoria had not attended the cremation, because she
was worried at the time about Gerald's health, and the
living had greater need of her than the dead. She was
glad she had not troubled to go all the way to London,
when she got the paltry cheque from the lawyer. She
decided against a memorial service. Nobody would have
come. There was something absurd about spending a lot of
money on somebody who was no longer there. There was
something hypocritical about singing hymns and saying

prayers in memory of a fat, lazy, self-indulgent woman, who in her youth had been a tart and in her prime a vulgar nobody.

The will directed that Victoria assume responsibility for her father; the assumption made was that Victoria would pay the bills of the nursing home. Considering the uselessness of her father to herself, considering the irresponsible folly of his whole life, Victoria found this idea preposterous. She could not immediately move her father without the lawyer knowing about it; but as soon as she could she did. He went into the geriatric ward of a National Health hospital, where probably he was happier because he had company.

It was kinder not to worry Gerald with any of this.

At Christmas Rienzo was given too much to drink. He was sick on the drawing room carpet. Mama said it was something he had eaten: his digestion was delicate, as was that of many high-bred people, and it had rejected something not good for it.

This tremendous rubbish enabled Lottie to distance herself from the whole business, to observe it objectively, to retain her identity. She successfully repelled Charlotte. Meanwhile the sight and smell were disgusting. It was ridiculous that something unimportant and revolting should be the agent for pushing her to independence.

She was able to be amused by the implication of what her mother said—that to have a good digestion was a sign of vulgarity, of grossness. If the Princess had not felt the pea under the mattress she would have been less royal. If Rienzo could drink a few glasses of wine without being sick, he was less a gentleman. Lottie thought being sick in the drawing room was gross.

Lottie thought that her father, looking greyly at the mess, was not only gradually dying but in some ways already dead. She did not want to be separate from him, or independent of him, but the situation was beginning to arise in which she had no choice. It was no good being dependent on a dead man.

Lottie thought that, with her father already dead, there was no longer anything for her at Court Farm.

She stuck out the Christmas holidays by dint of going away for half the time. She went back to school with relief and faced Easter with wariness.

At the end of the spring term she climbed into the car they had sent; she could not stay in the school, and there was no other car to climb into.

The sight of her mother at prayer on Easter Day put Lottie off religion.

Rienzo did not come to church. He said he had become a Buddhist. His religion required him to stay in bed all morning. If he was meditating, the stereo in his bedroom must have made it difficult to concentrate.

Lottie looked at her father, and he looked back at her. He looked an old man, much older than the fathers of her schoolfriends. He looked back at her sometimes with what she thought was recognition: at other times not. He sometimes returned her look with the eyes of a dead man.

Though he was dead, he was still sane. He could talk rationally to neighbours, and do the crossword puzzle in *The Times*. He transacted no business not because he was incapable of it, but because his toys had been taken away from him.

Felicity told Lottie, during one of their telephone conversations when Lottie was at school, that she had seen the fire go out. Lottie wondered if she had ever seen any fire. There was no fire at Christmas or Easter.

Mama tried to put Rienzo on a diet, but he continued to eat a great deal of chocolate, which he bought on credit at the village shop.

The memory of Rienzo being sick at Christmas enabled Lottie to retain her sense of detachment. This sense, in

turn, enabled her to contemplate her mother, dispassionately, for the first time. Lottie knew that it was difficult
and unusual for a fifteen-year-old girl to be dispassionately
critical about her own mother. None of her friends had
reason, need or power for this sort of appraisal. Their
relationships with their mothers were not always easy
or tranquil—often tortured and stormy—but they were
basically loving and explicable. Lottie realised that it was
also her age that made appraisal possible—she was nearly
sixteen, she was old enough to judge adults, she was old
enough to judge her mother.

Lottie had realised the previous summer that her home
was peculiar, being given eyes by her experience of other
families. Now, growing up, she was able to identify the
reason. It was odd and upsetting and filled her with a desire
to be elsewhere.

Looking at her mother, Lottie saw that she lived for herself and for Rienzo, usually in that order but sometimes in
the reverse order. Court Farm was a frame for her mother
and Rienzo. Her father was a part of the frame, or of the
easel on which the gilded frame rested. Lottie herself was
outside the frame, seen in a blur, peripherally, at the corner
of the eye, an irritant which you could live with if you
managed to forget it.

Lottie saw that her mother was only half a person, but
at the same time two people. She had the feelings of a half
but the strength of two. She was a kind of Grand Prix car,
supercharged, with none of the comfortable amenities of
a family saloon but with incomparably more power, with
performance and durability which took her into a different
league where ordinary people were obstructions, were kept
for their safety behind chain-link fences.

Later, four and five years later, Lottie tried to explain
herself to Emmee, to Felicity, to fellow-tenants of the
Council block in Peckham, many of whom had satisfactory relationships with their families. Felicity was the

only one who completely understood, and there was a difficulty even there, because Felicity could not outgrow an
instinctive resentment of Lottie. This derived from dislike
not of Lottie's personality but of her existence: at the age
of fifteen and at the age of twenty Lottie realised this.
At her father's funeral, Lottie kept out of Felicity's way,
because Felicity thought their father was more Felicity's
property than Lottie's. Felicity had not, of course, come
to Rienzo's funeral.

Rienzo's fourteenth birthday was celebrated at Eton.
It was a party that Lottie could have attended but did
not attend. Rienzo's voice was breaking, but he had not
grown much. He was plump because of the chocolate to
which he was addicted, the creamy and sugary desserts
which were set before him at home, the gin-and-tonics
to which his mother urged him to help himself during the
holidays, and the wine which his father silently poured.
He had given up playing tennis, or striking attitudes on
the springboard, owing to self-consciousness about being
fat. He was always pale, and lived an indoor life with
earphones.

Lottie did not see his reports from school, nor hear them
commented on. Her mother, as far as she knew, did not see
her reports from school.

Lottie's sixteenth birthday was a happy, uncomplicated,
girlish party in which she felt surrounded by goodwill.

It made her wonder what would have happened if she
had been born to a poor family, or at least one less rich than
hers—if she had gone to a day-school, and lived all the
time at home. In that case, presumably, the house would
have been smaller, and the inhabitants forced into living
cheek by jowl. Her mother and Rienzo, her father and
herself, all using one little sitting room? Lottie realised
that she would have run away years before. Having a rich
father, hospitable friends, had postponed her departure.
Otherwise they made no difference at all.

• • •

As the end of term approached, immediately after her birthday, Lottie was in a proper muddle. A part of her wanted the pool and the ponies, her comfortable familiar room, regular meals, perhaps her father's grey unassertive presence. Most of her wanted nothing more to do with any of it. As far as she could see, only two routes faced her. The road forked: both roads foreseeably ran pretty straight—no doubt there were turnings off both, but they were invisible and should not be counted on. No maps were available. To swan off into the blue, without money, resources, skills, qualifications, anywhere to live, any visible means of support, was a frightening prospect. You saw them in the newspapers—they came from all over the place, from northern cities in the grip of recession, from broken homes and 'fancy men' and the yap of the telly, from lack of hope, from rebellion and boredom, and they hung about under Waterloo Bridge or in the amusement arcades, purposeless and hopeless, unemployed and unemployable, fed intermittently by the Salvation Army, mucked about by pimps and pushers . . . was that a defeated army she wanted to join?

Yes.

If it meant not going home, yes.

If she had just the two options, one of them intolerable, then she was obliged to take the other.

There were friends she could have appealed to: take me in. It would have worked for days rather than weeks. The parents would have contacted her parents. Well-meaning, they would have joined the enemy. The whole establishment, seeing the surface and the glittering reflection off the surface, would have sent her home. Consult the other child. Is Rienzo happy at home? Rienzo is happy, indulged, emotionally secure. We have a girl here who is suffering from the typical, reasonless, rejection of the values of her upbringing. She will grow out of it. There was no help to be got in the adult world.

Her heroic project was a bit of a fraud, really. She knew very well that if she could contrive to make contact with her father, secretly, she would not starve. Felicity had told her so; Felicity had been through the same thing.

A friend asked her to stay, most of the summer, in a farmhouse in Tuscany. To a modest extent she would be expected to earn her keep. She wavered. Everything could be postponed; nothing would be changed, but it could all lie in the pending tray. She would be that much older when she got back from Italy; she might have added to her qualifications by speaking some Italian; on the other hand she would face a homeless winter. She wavered and wavered, the lure of the Tuscan farmhouse confusing an otherwise clear decision. The invitation fell through: the farmhouse was sold to somebody who wanted a farmhouse and who cut through the knot of Lottie's indecision.

A man paid in dollars for the farmhouse. Lottie's friend's father had been unable to refuse so many dollars. Sometimes Lottie thought that the man had unwittingly changed her life; sometimes she thought he had made no long-term difference at all. There was no way she was going back to Court Farm.

When the car came for her, on the last day of term, she had her trunk put into it. She told the driver that she was coming separately, later, in another car, with a friend. Probably the driver thought this was strange.

Lottie would have liked to give the driver a message for her father—a note, or by word of mouth. It was not how things were.

Lottie thought that her mother would hardly notice, and Rienzo would not notice at all, that she was not there in the summer. Her father would know she was all right, if she was all right, because she would find a way of telling him.

The bulk of her possessions having gone off in her father's car, Lottie felt almost weightless. She had a small suitcase and three plastic carrier-bags from shops. With this inconvenient baggage, she was given a lift to London by the family of a friend. They believed her story that she was staying for a couple of nights with a cousin before going home. Why not? It was perfectly normal and credible. Lottie's friend scented amorous intrigue, to be kept from a disapproving family. Lottie did not squash this suspicion, because it also was normal and credible, and fully explained her wanting a lift in the opposite direction from home.

Lottie had in fact, at that point of her life, never had an amorous intrigue, her hesitant flirtations with the sons of neighbours never having come to anything. She expected to have one very soon after arriving in London: but in that, as in much else, she was largely disappointed.

The hobbledehoy reported that Miss Charlotte was coming later, in another car; meanwhile, here was her trunk. Victoria noted this as evidence of something, and assumed that somebody would do something about the trunk. Rienzo was expected home.

Lying wakeful in bed with her husband sleeping beside her, starlight and the scent of roses touching the soul of her unborn son, Victoria remembered with a diminishing pang the last years of Rienzo's life.

Her new son would be taller and slimmer.

Her new son would be utterly unlike Rienzo, because he had a different set of genes and would be differently brought up. Her new son was the descendant of aristocrats, people of culture, easy manners and startling beauty. Rienzo on his father's side had been the descendant of tradesmen, bakers, biscuit-makers who had become rich. The Bramalls were not people of culture or personal beauty—how could they be? The cards—though Victoria had loyally struggled to hide the fact from herself—were genetically stacked against Rienzo. And Gerald had not been clever about bringing him up. It was not perhaps Gerald's fault—he could not be expected to have vision or wisdom beyond his spiritual capacity—but lumbered by such a partner even Victoria's efforts were foredoomed. She could not have done more than she did.

With hindsight, she knew that Rienzo was bound to disappoint her. She had never expected anything of the girl, and she had been proved right.

A distraction in their lives was removed by the unexplained disappearance of the girl. Victoria was hurt and sad when she simply failed to come home from school, even though she was another Bramall, another Stodge. Gerald made various enquiries. It was important not to have two people making enquiries about the same thing, or wires got crossed.

The puppy-fat did not roll away from Rienzo, as Victoria had been sure it would. He almost had breasts, like a girl, and his knees were dimpled like those of an overweight nymph in a baroque painting. It was something chemical.

The girl should have helped, instead of selfishly and treacherously disappearing off the face of the earth; she went to an insanely expensive school, so she knew the girls who were sent to that school, and she should have brought them home to dance round Rienzo. Then he would have switched off that noise and taken an interest. By running off as she did, the girl had betrayed her brother as well as her parents.

Gerald seemed reconciled to the girl's absence, though previously he had seemed to like her. Gerald had by that time outlived his usefulness. He would not sire another child, whatever delicious audacities Victoria allowed herself. But Victoria was fond of him, and they lived comfortably together. Rienzo was the justification for everything, although it was a pity he did not lose weight.

Victoria was aware that Rienzo had a difficulty—a difficulty, about which nobody had warned her, special to men with bewitching mothers. All his life, Rienzo would compare the girls that he met with his mother, and of course they would suffer by comparison. Victoria did not see at the time how she could do anything about that; looking back at that time, she did not see what she could have done. When her new son was born, would she do anything differently? She pondered, looking at the lovely rectangle of starlight. She stroked her own nakedness, thinking of the future of the new life she carried. She searched her soul, her conscience. Most devoutly she wanted to do her very best for her new son, but she could not change herself, make herself ugly and frumpish and matronly and dull. It would be a crime against the Holy Ghost to conceal or distort her own beauty, a betrayal of the God who had formed her, of herself, her husband, her son, her friends. 'To thine own self be true. Thou canst not then be false to any man.' Apollinaris, or some such. Why did a man call himself after mineral water? Scotch and Polly. Uncle Gordon used to drink that mixture in theatre bars in the interval. It was doggish; it sounded good when you called it out to the elderly barmaid; it evoked all kinds of Edwardian images with which Uncle Gordon liked to associate himself.

Amused but self-reproving, Victoria accused herself of wool-gathering. She had set herself to ponder the future of her unborn son, and here she was thinking about white hats and clouded canes.

It did not matter what her son was called. Probably the aristocratic Lambert tradition would suggest something. Victoria would find her own name for him; he would choose his own name for himself. It was a pity he would not be Lord Enniscorthy, but Giles's older brother had three sons. Something might have been done about that, but they were all in New Zealand.

Although she had decided not to choose names, she found herself choosing them. She liked alliteration. Louis Lambert (like Lord Mountbatten). Laurence Lambert, or possibly Lawrence (like Lord Olivier). Ludovic Lambert (like the man on television, somebody's husband). She fixed on that. Ludo. Her Ludo. She stroked him through the velvet skin of her stomach, communicating that name to him, which was accompanied by starlight and the scent of roses.

Because of her age, there had been a scan of the unborn baby. The doctors were subject to rules. It was perfectly unnecessary, but Victoria consented to the rigmarole without fuss because they were obliged to obey the rules.

The doctor was also obliged to ask her if she wanted to be told the sex of her child. He did not have to tell her, but he had to offer to tell her. She laughed. She did not want to be told. She knew already.

Although Victoria's sleep had been interrupted by wakefulness, by thought and prayer, she awoke almost at once when Giles brought her a cup of China tea at nine-thirty. She sat up in bed to drink her tea, still naked, the covers slipping down from her lovely shoulders and breasts. Giles knelt by the bedside to kiss her. His hands felt for her breasts. She pushed him away, gently, because she wanted her tea. He submitted, as he always did. He was her good boy.

Victoria put on a silk peignoir for breakfast, which Giles as usual brought her in bed. She had fresh fruit juice, coffee, and a wholemeal biscuit with honey. She looked at the papers, upset by the dreadful things that were going on all over the world. They ran her bath at ten forty-five—it was to be a bright and early day because they were going to a private view before luncheon. She was half dressed by eleven-fifteen, and Cosette did her hair. Cosette exclaimed as always in her amusing fractured English about the raven-black silkiness of Victoria's curtain of hair. Cosette helped Victoria to finish dressing, and between them they chose undemonstrative morning jewellery. By eleven forty-five Victoria was strolling out into her garden, into the fragrance of her beloved roses.

Giles jumped to his feet from a teak-wood chair where he had been doing a crossword puzzle. He was wearing a dove-grey lightweight flannel suit, a Turnbull and Asser shirt of pink and white stripes, black shoes from Tricker, and a Countess Mara tie which lent a touch of discreet exoticism to the sober correctness of his turn-out.

Victoria had taken him to Gerald's tailor and shirtmaker and shoemaker. She had given him a manly Rolex watch so that he would never keep her waiting. She loved giving him presents. He loved giving her presents, too, but his allowance ran only to trifles. He saved up his allowance to buy her flowers, because he knew how much she loved flowers.

The car was waiting to take them to the gallery, with Dagobert at the wheel. Dagobert was Victoria's private name for her chauffeur; she had private names for almost everybody, because of her irrepressible sense of humour. Dagobert took them to Bloomsbury. The artist was a friend of Giles, a young man of good family who had cut loose to be a Bohemian. Victoria admired that. She kept an open mind about whether to buy any of the pictures, until she had seen them. She did not in the event see any of the pictures, because there was such a crowd. She congratulated the artist on the success of his one-man show, only it turned out that the man she talked to was not the artist at all, but somebody who worked for the gallery. She had quite a laugh with herself about that, and made a story of it, against herself, at lunch in the River Room of the Savoy.

Giles said he liked the artist and admired the pictures. There was a picture in the exhibition he wanted to buy. But it cost £600, so for Giles that was pie in the sky. He was a baby about money. In many ways he was a big baby. That was one of the things Victoria loved about him. He was tall and slim, with aquiline features and grey eyes and chestnut hair and a fine brain and a great love and knowledge of the arts, and he was her baby, depending on her for everything.

She paid for lunch with her American Express gold card, and then Dagobert took them home for their naps.

After her nap she was busy in the garden, pointing out to Mr Childers, who came three times a week, weeds among the roses that he had overlooked. Left to himself, he would have let the place become a jungle.

It was Victoria's fancy that the roses reserved their greatest beauty, their sweetest perfume, for her alone, in recognition of the loving care she bestowed on them. She laughed at herself for this vanity. She was forever laughing at herself.

'A woman who can't laugh at herself,' she said, 'has begun to die.'

Gerald stopped laughing at anything, and he began to die.

Victoria tried: God knew she tried. Even she was helpless in the face of senility. He was not seventy. He had no business to be senile. He doddered. It was irritating, humiliating, for a young girl to have a doddering husband.

She was fairly sure he had some money she did not know about, which he spent in ways she did not know about. She did her very best to protect him from himself, but she had the infuriating suspicion that in some way she was being outwitted.

It was like looking after an alcoholic, who somehow bribes a servant to smuggle in bottles of whisky. Victoria felt the sting of ingratitude; it filled her not with anger but a great sadness. She did not know all at once how to put a stop to it.

Victoria and Giles were giving one of their dinner parties. These parties had become quietly famous, although they were not reported in the gossip columns. There were no pop musicians or television personalities. Photographs were sometimes taken by guests, who brought little cameras with flash attachments. Often they sent enlarged prints to Victoria, with their thank-you notes. The best of these were put in frames, to add to the beauty of the rooms.

Victoria's idea was to mix people who would interest one another but who might not otherwise have met. She described herself as a catalyst; she said that the best parties were the ones at which she felt no need to speak at all. She chose her guests as carefully as she chose her menus. Giles was responsible for the wine. She gave him *carte blanche* in that department, since a marriage without complete mutual trust is a mockery.

The ideal number was ten, so that Victoria and Giles could sit at the head and foot of the table.

Like all good hostesses, Victoria kept a careful record of all her parties, who sat next to whom during dinner and after it, everything that they ate and drank, the clothes and jewellery that she wore. Her aim was to surprise people and to make them happy. She forbade any kind of game after dinner, because what was important was conversation; if people wanted to play bridge or Trivial Pursuits they could do it at other parties. Sometimes Giles played the piano. They usually dressed. Victoria had given Giles a rifle-green velvet smoking jacket for the winter and a white sharkskin for the summer. For the buttonhole of the sharkskin she picked from her garden a flower that went with whatever she was wearing. On summer evenings she wore filmy, romantic gowns, often backless. Giles said that her back was like a young boy's, and that her bones were like a bird's. He said that she was the only woman in the world whose back was as beautiful as her front.

Before she went up to change she checked that the dining table had been correctly laid, with the silver all polished, that there were four glasses, innocent of sticky fingerprints, by each place, that there were new candles in

the George II candlesticks, fresh-mixed mustard, pepper-
corns in the mills, salt in the blue glass liners of the salt-
cellars, rock-salt in its mill, the claret and port decanted
(Giles could be trusted about that, but Victoria checked
anyway). She moved some of the glass and silver on
the Empire sideboard, shifting decanters and salvers and
wine-coasters left and right, back and front, until the effect
was harmoniously lavish. Even with the best servants, the
mistress's last little touches made the difference between
the humdrum and the magical.

Still on her way upstairs, she pondered once more the
aged leather-bound seating-plan, the cards with the names
of her guests rimming it like the petals of a stylised flower.
On one of those madcap impulses which were central to
her character (which had sent her out into her garden,
naked under the starlight at three in the morning) she
changed the cards. She moved old Lord Hazelhurst from
her right to the middle of the table, and put in his place
Charles Varley, a young Conservative M.P. with a rich
wife. The wife was a flamboyant and rather slapdash
dresser, with the freely expressed views of those who
have been brought up with a lot of money. Neither her
bosom nor her opinions were likely to be of interest to
Giles, for whom as always Victoria was really giving the
party, and who had in any case sat next to Miranda Varley
at a lunch party before the races at Newmarket only a year
before. Victoria moved Miranda to the middle of the table,
and put beside Giles old Lady Hazelhurst, who had been
in embassies all over the world and would amuse him with
her stories of diplomatic life.

Victoria took upstairs with her a small glass of La Ina
sherry. Aunt Marigold had preferred medium, which was,
as a matter of fact, all you needed to know about Aunt
Marigold.

Victoria had been wearing a bra. She would not be
wearing one with the backless grass-green silk she had
chosen for the evening, a dress none of those to be present

except Giles had ever seen before. She unhooked the bra and slid the straps off her shoulders. In the full-length triple mirror she contemplated herself half naked and then naked. In some ways it was a pity that she lived in a civilisation whose conventions required the covering of nakedness at dinner parties. She giggled to imagine herself greeting her guests with nothing on but a tiara. It would suit Giles, too, with his broad shoulders, narrow hips and flat stomach. Only the sight of her would have the effect on him it always had, which would not do in front of Lady Hazelhurst or Miranda Varley . . .

Giles came in, in the dressing gown she had given him in Rome.

As so often, he expressed her exact thoughts, as though they were telepathic, as though where she led he was certain to follow. 'What a pity we're not nudists,' he said. 'It's such a waste to cover you up.'

Victoria smiled at him. There really wasn't time. She had to get dressed.

He went back into his dressing room to tie his tie and put on his embroidered evening slippers.

Victoria was proud of Giles that evening. He looked old-fashioned; he looked an aristocrat. He bent to listen to smaller people, smiling with warmth and interest. He stood, sat, turned, made all his movements with unselfconscious elegance. You could never in a million years imagine him standing with his toes turned inwards. He poured out some of the drinks with his own hands, although Dagobert was there to do it (Dagobert became a butler when they entertained). He was solicitous without being obsequious. He was most truly a gentleman. She had never regretted for a second the decision she had made the very first moment she saw him. It was the end of a search which had lasted for nearly two years.

It was a race against time, and she had won it.

At his end of the dinner-table there was much laughter. At her end there was rather a monologue from Charles Varley.

Giles and Dagobert between them kept the glasses filled with a two-year-old Pouilly Fumé, a 1978 claret, and a luscious white dessert wine which Giles had discovered and which they all said was bottled sunshine. Giles answered questions about the wine with fluent affability, but without being a bore or a wine-snob. Charles Varley was a wine-snob, but he couldn't fault Giles. The silver gleamed in the midsummer sunset. Warm air and compliments caressed Victoria's shoulders.

Giles played for a little after dinner, because it was the only way Victoria could think of to stop Miranda Varley talking about herself. Miranda fancied Giles, so she was showing off to him. Giles pretended not to notice, which ought to have shown the bitch where to get off, but she had been so rich all her life that she thought she only had to say 'I want' to get anything. If she thought she could have Giles she had another think coming. She was going in for sidelong glances and speaking looks, but Giles pretended not to notice.

Gerald was rich all his life, and he remained rich because Victoria protected him against himself. She prayed that it might be complete protection, but she knew it was not quite complete. She was sad because she was used to having her prayers granted, owing to the steadfastness of her faith. She was sad because Gerald was being got at, and he was too kind for his own good.

There were stupid reports from Eton about Rienzo. Victoria did not distress Gerald with them. The masters were silly little men, out of touch with life.

People sometimes asked Victoria if Rienzo had any sense of direction. The question was stupid. He did not need a sense of direction because he was not going anywhere. He would be master of a house and an estate which he would manage with firmness, humanity, vision, and her help. The future was perfectly clear. There were a few slight problems about the present, but there were no problems about the future.

Not long before Rienzo's seventeenth birthday, something went wrong with the car in the middle of the night. The mechanic who had serviced it had left something loose that should have been tight.

The future was in ruins. Victoria was brave. She had to start again, so she started again. She was forty-one. Nobody would have guessed it. She was as slim and fit as a young girl. She was a young girl. Her life was before her. She was custodian of the future. She was a priestess. She had a mission and a duty.

She had as clear a sense of her duty as when she was the instrument of God's justice, punishing Uncle Gordon for his betrayal of Aunt Marigold. It had worked once, and it worked again, though not so well, because this one was a week dying. He did not fall as far, and he landed partly on a rug near the foot of the stairs. He died knowing why he was dying, but fortunately he did not tell anybody. He seemed to want to die in the end, so the outcome was best for all concerned.

With the body and soul of a young girl, Victoria began her search, knowing that it was a race against time which it was her duty to win.

C·H·A·P·T·E·R

8

Certain decisions made themselves immediately.

Berkshire and its neighbouring counties were not her hunting ground. She had lived there for twenty-one years, social, hospitable, asked everywhere, extravagantly admired, and she had a thick address-book of close friends. She flipped through it, as a pointer will quarter a root-field conscientiously but without really expecting any partridges. Names triggered images, memories, circumstances, and were instantly discarded. A few names made her pause, as a question mark hangs almost visibly in the air over a gundog wondering whether to point. But these names too were discarded—some with reluctance—in the light of other decisions that were making themselves.

Court Farm was therefore put on the market. This was readily to be explained. After all those happy years, all those throngs of memories . . . and it was a ridiculously big house for a lonely widow . . . if Rienzo had lived . . . Everybody understood, or thought they did.

A second decision was based on experience. As the breeder of thoroughbred racehorses consults bloodlines, evidence of speed and honesty, transmitted qualities of conformation, so Victoria knew what she was looking for. She had not, before, sufficiently reduced the margin of error. She required to be more certain of height and slimness. She could afford to be very, very choosy, as long as she was quick about it.

And this was her third decision. She would know what was right when she saw it, since her blueprint was so exact. When she saw it she must take it, bam. The chosen must not get away, or be fenced or hobbled or locked against her. Bam, before anybody else knew what was happening. Instant and audacious action won battles through history. The folly, the disaster, would be to give the enemy time to regroup. The one she wanted other people would want; other people would think they already had him. But they would be taken utterly by surprise, by boldness and brilliance, and Victoria would win.

What she had she would keep. She was good at keeping things.

The Battersea house was horribly expensive. Victoria knew she was being cheated. She got the price down a little by means of a surveyor's report which she influenced. The house was still far too expensive, but she had fallen in love with the garden. It was right to come to London, but she could not live without a garden.

She brought Huxtable with her from Court Farm, having privately renamed him Dagobert. There was no reason for this amusing nickname, but it somehow fitted him. He did not live in the house, but over the garage two streets away where the car was kept. It was the car Gerald had bought to replace the one destroyed by Rienzo; it was still only a few months old. Victoria went everywhere by car, with Dagobert at the wheel. This was not a luxury but a necessity. Dagobert was also a butler when she needed a butler, and he did odd jobs in house and garden.

Cosette, who did live in, was a success after a series of short-lived failures. A caring, skilful lady's maid-cum-parlourmaid was indeed a treasure. Cosette's loyalty was unswerving. She idolised Victoria. She was clever with Victoria's clothes, and with her hair. If Victoria depended on Cosette, Cosette also depended on Victoria, because she had a retarded illegitimate daughter in a home in Haslemere that her family knew nothing about.

Mrs Mollam came in four mornings a week, which was almost enough for the cleaning. She needed watching: she had a great dislike of cleaning the oven, and where cobwebs were concerned she seemed to be deliberately blind. She would have been absurdly lavish with cleaning materials, bleach and detergent and the like, so Victoria kept a delicately restraining hand on the reins. But she was a great character, was Ivy Mollam, a real old-time Cockney with a fund of traditional, pawky humour, and for her the sun set round Victoria's shoulders.

Mrs Calloway came in daily to do the cooking. She arrived in the middle of the morning. Sometimes she brought in dishes already made in her own or somebody else's kitchen, and put them in Victoria's oven. This was in many ways convenient—there was less smell of cooking and less noise. Mrs Calloway could quite well carry the dishes on the bus. To a qualified extent Victoria had to trust her about the cost of the dishes she made at home, but without trust how could there be a household?

Mr Childers came in three times a week to do the garden. He was a countryman born and bred, and for him Victoria's garden was an oasis of delight in the concrete desert. Victoria was able to teach him a lot about gardening, which was for him also great good fortune.

It was a lively and bustling household, often full of laughter. Loyalty and love for Victoria kept the ship sailing smoothly over untroubled seas.

This allowed Victoria to pursue the serious business of her life.

She was sometimes frightened that she was running out of time.

To her married life with Gerald, Victoria had brought few friends of her own generation. Of course she had known the model-girls, photographers, men from the newspapers and advertising agencies. No member of these overlapping circles would have looked or felt at home at Court Farm. In the country, she had of course entertained, and been entertained by, Gerald's friends. It was her clear duty to be as nice to them as patience permitted.

Some of Gerald's friends had been, from the moment of her marriage, so jealous that they did not ask her to their parties. Of course Gerald did not go to those parties either. He was better for losing touch with such envious and small-minded people.

As well as neighbours, Gerald had many friends from the old days, from Oxford, yachting, the Diplomatic Service, the war; some were quite interesting. But many lost touch. They used the excuse of Gerald's marriage to Victoria to lose touch. They would have been the pompous and boring ones. They were no loss.

Gerald had been a London clubman as well as a country gentleman. No doubt they called themselves lifelong friends, those elderly members of White's and the Beefsteak. But they did nothing for Gerald's widow when she moved to London. That showed how much their self-styled friendship for Gerald was worth.

Victoria found herself obliged to form a new circle of friends when she set up house in Battersea. It was a thing to go carefully with. If you burdened yourself with embarrassing friends, you could have difficulty getting rid of them. In a way Aunt Marigold had been an embarrassment that Victoria had contrived to get rid of.

Victoria looked about her in London, and began in a very discriminating way to join things. She had never had cause to be a joiner before, or a supporter or a donor of anything but her love and loyalty and devotion (given freely and with joy), but now she carefully became a Friend of Covent Garden and the Royal Academy, a member of the National Trust and the National Art Collections Fund. She tried to become a member of the Glyndebourne Festival

Society, but they told her she must go to the back of the queue. So much for Glyndebourne.

The Committees of the bodies she did join, listed in their copious literature, were studded with people whom she identified as her new circle of friends. There were many Events, of a cultural kind. She sent for tickets for the Events, with cheques and stamped self-addressed envelopes. Lectures, exhibitions, concerts, tours of places not open to the public. It was very cultural. It was, of course, the ambrosial food on which Victoria's spirit fed (it fed also on flowers and all forms of natural beauty, such as her own) and she expected to meet kindred spirits—tall, slim, good-looking young men of ancient family whose eyes would light up when they saw her. They would be full of culture but not boring about it. She was always, at those Events, on the lookout.

There were such people, but they talked to one another, or to overdressed girls, or to old ladies. They all had their own friends. Victoria stood looking serious, and nobody came and talked to her. She looked alert, receptive, whimsical, vulnerable, all of which she was, and still people introduced other people to still others, because they all knew somebody.

The ones she talked to were exactly the ones she did not want to talk to. They were the ones who did not know anybody. They were quiet old couples up from the suburbs.

After one conversation with an elderly couple during the interval of a concert, Victoria had a sickening revelation. The old bores thought they were being kind to her.

That was in the spring of 1986, after the hardest and most miserable February anybody could remember. Even Victoria's indomitable spirit drooped in those iron weeks. She did her exercises, to keep her bosom young and firm and her tummy flat. It hurt to breathe in the open air. It would have been irresponsible to allow her cheeks to be

chapped by the harsh east wind. Victoria supervised Mr
Childers in the garden through the misted French windows.
The house was warm before she got out of bed. There were
some Events that she missed, even though she had bought
tickets for them. There was that one that she attended,
when the weather relaxed in March: and then she had the
horrible idea (later dismissed) that the old couple were
being kind to her; and then she remembered that it was
the year of her forty-third birthday; and then she felt a
sense of urgency that was almost panic.

She had by now made some friends, of the best sort.
They were nearly all people whom she had met 'by
chance', known to Gerald, known in some cases to herself
in Gerald's lifetime. She had remembered the names, or
found them in Gerald's address-book, previously put aside.
She had looked them up in Who's Who and Debrett. Telephone calls in funny voices. All quite amusing and quite
easy. 'Chance' meetings in shops and hairdressers. Great
care thereafter, and one thing led to another. She conjured
pity for her loneliness, laughing internally. This circle did
not come to include any friends who became close, nor
any slender young men.

Victoria could give parties and go to them. She could
go to Events for which she paid. It was the year of her
forty-third birthday.

Somebody (an old man) quoted lines of poetry to her
about Time's winged chariot hurrying near. It was an
ill-natured thing to do. The lines might have haunted her,
if she had remembered them correctly. She kept her breasts
firm and her stomach flat, and her skin as creamily flawless
as the petal of a magnolia. She kept her eyes peeled.

March wheeled into April. Flowers opened to the sun
in Victoria's garden. Mr Childers cut the grass, and she
walked across it, drawn like a bee to the scent of blossom,
drawn like a thirsty nymph to the wellsprings of beauty.
She had a hat that it pleased her to wear in the garden:

broad-brimmed, tied with a muslin scarf under her little chin. Nobody saw it except the servants. She felt as one of her flowers would have felt if no bee had visited it: unappreciated, unpollinated, wasted.

The flowers bared themselves with innocent shamelessness to the sun. They opened the arms they had crossed over their shadowed breasts, and gave themselves luxuriously to heat and light, to healing and loving, to hope and life. Victoria opened her arms to welcome the occasional April sun.

As she stood arms wide, palms spread to the sun, she heard the telephone. Mrs Mollam answered it. It was a creature called Mary-Emma Black, who began talking about somebody called Charlotte. Charlotte? Oh yes. Charlotte had cut herself out of Victoria's life; Victoria, in emotional self-defence, had cut Charlotte out of hers. Twenty-first? Could the girl really be almost twenty-one?

A party?

Victoria spoke noncommittally to the girl Mary-Emma, to give herself time to think. She thought that Charlotte's father had sent her to a very good and expensive school. She therefore had, or had had, the right sort of friends, girls from homes like her own. Such girls had brothers and boyfriends, a few years older than themselves, taller and slimmer than Rienzo.

There was here a possibility. But Victoria was not to be stampeded into reviving a relationship which had made her sad, owing to treachery, owing to the girl having played her an underhand trick by being born female. It was no better than an outside chance. There were nearly two months until the birthday, of the date of which Mary-Emma reminded Victoria.

Victoria adroitly invented a trip abroad to which she was utterly committed. She remembered the name Biarritz from holidays with Uncle Gordon and Aunt Marigold. There would be time enough to organise a party when she 'got back'. She promised herself a final few weeks of freedom from the child: a period which she would spend in a last, intensive effort to find what she was looking for. If she succeeded, she would not bother with Charlotte.

She succeeded at the end of May.

It was the original plan that succeeded, the one involving Events. She went one weeping evening to a private view, for which she had paid £4, of an important exhibition. She found herself talking not to a miffy little couple up for the evening from the suburbs, but to a tall and slender man perhaps nearly thirty. His hair was thick and fair and brushed in shiny wings over his ears. He wore a very dark grey suit with narrow trousers, and good shoes. Victoria recognised the very light whiff of expensive hair-oil: she thought it was Trumper's stuff, which Gerald had used. He knew about the paintings. He did not try to patronise Victoria, but assumed in her as much knowledge as he had. He was an expert, a specialist; his field was ceramics, but he knew a lot about painting too.

Victoria was dressed in a severely simple (French) silk suit in cherry-red, relieved by a ruffle of white lace at the throat. The suit was cut to display the subtle elegance of her figure. Her lovely legs looked their best in dove-grey tights; on her little feet were black Gucci shoes. Her jewellery was chosen with taste and tact, because at these cultural Events there were often people who were not rich. Her lipstick matched the silk of her suit. Her scent was Joy.

They smiled and talked, softly, in front of a lovely picture of something. Introductions were needless at such functions, because you were all Members, as it were colleagues, there for no other reason than to indulge a love of beauty.

In spirit Victoria detached herself from them, and observed them from a little distance. My God, what a handsome couple. He so tall, almost glossy, speaking with a graceful eloquence of gesticulation. She like a glorious girl, beautiful beyond words, beyond tears, bearing herself with a dignity which was not stiff, smiling with a warmth which was not coquettish . . .

Victoria rejoined herself, in order not to miss what he was saying. But as she did so she envied the people who were still looking at them.

He was talking not about the picture but about herself, using such terms as he had used about the angel in the painting. On any other occasion these words, used at a first meeting, would not have done. From anybody else they would have been impertinent; to anybody else they would have been ridiculous.

His name was Graham Whittingham-Barnes, and he lived in Mayfair in what he called Chambers. They were not in Albany but they were that sort of thing.

She told him her name. It was new to him. There was no need for him to write it down—he would not forget it.

They withdrew from the press of people, talking, talking. He said it was not important that he saw all the pictures, because he would come to the exhibition again, probably many times. It was much more important that he talk to Victoria. His manners were gentle, amusingly self-deprecating. He was tall and slim, sufficiently handsome, with glossy buttercup hair. He would strip well unless he was, perhaps, a little too slim. He could be fed rich stews (Mrs Calloway could bring the casseroles on the bus) and given tonics. His eye for beauty had singled her out. It was not by chance that they had met and talked—it was because he had seen her in the distance and made very certain that he talked to her. It was not impertinent of him to say so, even at a first meeting, because they were who they were.

Hearing that his special field was oriental ceramics, Victoria mentioned her own collection from the Imperial Palace. He was keenly interested. He asked her to describe them.

'I am at a loss for words,' she said.

She gestured with enchanting helplessness, as one who

had seen a marvel beyond description. The collection had been valued for probate and for insurance (quite different valuations) but the figures were tentative because objects of such *vertu* came seldom on the market.

His invitation to dinner, at a private club near the gallery, was made diffidently, not as though he thought he were being brash or premature, but as though he were sure she must have a previous engagement.

She refused on the grounds that they had only just met, that they did not know one another. Her 'no' was expressed without outrage and without finality.

'Our not knowing one another can be put right if you accept my suggestion,' he said, 'and if you don't, how can it ever be put right?'

She laughed, and touched his sleeve.

The private club had Italian waiters. Guests were given menus without prices. Dagobert could have his supper and come for her at eleven.

Over dinner they talked about a thousand things.

Victoria learned a great deal about Graham; he responded shyly at first and then more confidently to her questions. Charterhouse, Bristol University, the Courtauld Institute, the job with the Fine Art dealers which had recently become a junior partnership. He had been an athlete (a hurdler) though not of championship class. His principal motivation was love of beauty, but he admitted he was not averse to earning money. He made a joke of that, using his forefinger as a pistol to shoot himself through the head, self-convicted of the crime of not being entirely indifferent to security and the trappings of success.

There was absolutely nothing wrong with any of that.

Graham learned the essential things, the central soul-things, about Victoria. Her twin gods of loyalty and beauty. Her abiding and childlike sense of wonder. The great heart within the supple little body which had given her courage to survive repeated personal tragedy. Her ability to laugh at herself. Her hatred of greed, pomposity, snobbery, cruelty, unfairness. It was of these things that she told him, because he asked.

Having found exactly what she was looking for, Victoria was ready to reach out, to give all of herself and to have and to hold. It was not possible that evening. Graham kissed her hand as Dagobert held open the door of the car.

He exclaimed at the porcelain. He made notes in a little book. He said he thought it was whatever he said it was. He would not give a firm opinion until he had consulted the authorities; Victoria at first thought he meant the government or the police, but he meant books.

He exclaimed at the lovely things in the house and at the tranquil beauty of the garden. He had time only for a brief visit. The servants could not be sent out, without explanation or with too much tacit explanation, suddenly in the middle of the day. Victoria was confirmed in her certainty, and he looked at her with open adoration. He pressed her hand.

They would be in touch soon and often.

Really it was just in time.

He said the porcelain was beautiful and quite unusual. He did not want to say any more about it. Victoria pressed him, because of her duty as custodian of such a treasure. He said you could hardly tell that it was not the real thing.

She accepted his invitation to luncheon in his Chambers.

She wore no bra. When she opened her coat, as its designer had intended her to do, the sheer and clinging silk of her blouse revealed while concealing, like the translucent mists on the flanks of a magic mountain.

The apartment had the appearance of a small flat in

a building of such flats. Graham's wife was cooking the lunch, in an apron with a polka-dot design. He was a German boy of about twenty-three, who kissed Victoria's hand.

Rudi was not jealous of Graham's admiration of Victoria. They gave one another space. It was essentially an old-fashioned marriage, but a civilised one. Rudi did not feel threatened.

It had only recently become possible, Graham said, to be open and honest about such a marriage. Victoria felt sophisticated, having luncheon with the two of them.

She rang up the girl Mary-Emma, whose number she had kept. She got hold of her in the end.

Time's damned winged chariot. It was worth a try. Nothing would come of it. It would be interesting to see the girl's friends. The day you lost curiosity about people was the day you began to die.

The party was to be a modest little affair. It was planned quite quickly and easily. The girl Mary-Emma was tiresome to deal with, but of course it was worth a little effort, a little patience. Firm guide-lines had to be laid down. Victoria was not about to allow an army of Peckham layabouts into her treasure-house. That settled, there were no problems that could not be solved on the telephone, or by a commitment to writing cheques.

Victoria understood from Mary-Emma that the Peckham contingent would be sober and shaven, not wearing jeans or boots, not smoking pot or disappearing into the loo to give themselves injections. They would include attractive men in their twenties: some would be approaching, might even have passed, the age of thirty.

Victoria did not really want a nineteen-year-old, much as many a nineteen-year-old would have wanted her.

During June, she made a good story of the fact that she was giving a birthday party for her rediscovered baby. It might have seemed to her listeners that she had employed teams of private investigators to trace her missing child. The story promised the happiest of endings. Victoria laughed at herself, as always—it was one of the characteristics that made her so much loved. Old, old friends of Gerald—rediscovered, like her child— warmed to Victoria when she told them about the party she was giving.

Graham Whittingham-Barnes was quite a help in orga- nising the party, which was not unlike parties he was accus- tomed to arranging for his firm. He and Rudi promised to come, though Graham privately warned Victoria that Rudi could not be relied on—he might be overcome at the last moment by shyness or petulance. Victoria, who was their Mother Confessor, smiled indulgently, and Graham kissed the rosy tips of her fingers.

Giles knew of (had heard about) a really clever man, a literary critic of the scholarly sort, a man of serious reputation and solid achievement, who once turned up at a country house party, at which the entertainments were to include a wedding reception, a dinner party and a dance, with a suitcase found strangely light by the person who carried it upstairs; it contained a single tennis shoe.

Giles was consoled by contemplation of that man.

Giles prided himself on several qualities (not on others) one of which was self-knowledge. He did not fool anybody for long; he did not fool himself for a second. He did not trust himself to pack for a weekend in a country house, though he thought he would have done better than a single tennis-shoe. He did not trust himself, when he had come down out of a house and set off in a certain direction, to remember where he was going. He did not trust himself with money, his own or anybody else's. He did not trust himself at the wheel of a car, to sit alone with a bottle of whisky, or to be let loose in the Food Halls at Harrods.

For Lottie Giles felt warm affection, bottomless grati- tude, and simple lust. She was a great girl, a girl in a million. Giles liked Emmee and admired her guts. She was twice the man Giles was. But there were aspects of life in the Council block in Peckham which depressed him. He told himself at first that he could ignore them—that in so much love and friendship and supportiveness and sexual satisfaction he could rise above the graffiti on the concrete stairway, the machine-age squalor of the surroundings. He should be like Diogenes, or a Zen Master, whose richness of inner life and intimate relationships made unimportant the surrounding squalor.

He should be, but he was not. He had been brought up among servants and Georgian furniture.

When he went back to Peckham in the evening, most of his heart ran gladly before him, rejoicing at reunion with Lottie and the fun they would have, and a little growing part sank at the thought of the concrete stairs and the pop-music, the callow political outpourings and the varnished plywood furniture.

He was a bit old for it all.

He knew that Lottie's background, considered objectively, was richer than his own; but she had cancelled her membership of the world into which she was born, while his was only in suspension. Living in the Peckham block, eating spaghetti on the floor with a bunch of twenty-year-olds, he was acting a role which was economically required of him. He was too old to sit on the floor and eat pasta, with or without red plonk full of unthinkable additives. Memories of his Irish childhood, of Winchester and New College, never obtruded so strongly (all unbidden) as when he began to get backache from sitting on linoleum to eat spaghetti.

The sort of job he was having during this current phase (the details changed more often than was revealed in Peckham) reminded him of the things he knew and loved—of the club from which he had not resigned, but his membership of which had been temporarily suspended owing to non-payment of subscription—of pictures displayed in frames instead of posters stuck up with Blu-Tack.

He would have liked to throw a fly over a trout-stream again, to go to the races with a badge for the Members' Enclosure, to drink good claret from a Waterford wineglass. The language to describe these things was not spoken in Peckham.

Graham Whittingham-Barnes was only a part-time predator.

What with his job and his domestic responsibilities, he had neither time nor nervous energy to spare for preying on people, except as a hobby activity.

When he encountered a full-time professional like Victoria, he regarded her with awe. He was thrilled to show her, as a specimen, to Rudi, who was perhaps even better equipped than Graham to appreciate her. They laughed about her very much after the luncheon Rudi had prepared, but it was awestruck laughter; and they felt a little guilty about laughing, because she was in some ways pitiable.

Neither of them was going to take on Victoria, in any area. The thing to be, was an ally. Being an ally would not be quite safe—it might be exciting—but being an enemy would be perilous.

Graham was shading it a bit, in the matter of Victoria's porcelain. It could easily have been a trap, to test his knowledge or his honesty. He boxed clever, reserving judgement. He went away and found out if pieces like that had ever been successfully imitated. It was *possible* that they had, though the copies, not being very precious, were long lost or broken if they had existed. But it was *possible*. Graham felt safe enough, therefore, in telling Victoria that it was copies she had—French, late nineteenth century, curiosities but not treasures.

There was no immediate benefit in this ploy, not one that sat up and begged. It was a bit of harmless fun, really. Victoria kept the stuff in a glass-fronted case in a darkish

hall. There was no way she was *feeding her soul* on the
things, as she said she did on other things. There were
several possibilities, more or less long-term. It might be
possible to *buy the things* at a knockdown price (generous
if they were copies) and export them privately for auction
in Hong Kong. Or *substitute copies of other china* for
the genuine stuff she had there. She'd never notice the
difference.

It would be fun simply to hug the knowledge.

It would be fun to give it one day to Victoria, as a
lovely lovely present—your porcelain does come from the
Forbidden City, darling, and it's *perfectly genuine*.

This last was probably what they would do, because
they were both sorry for Victoria; she was formidable but
she was also lonely and directionless. They had *hosts* of
friends, but there was always room for another as beautiful
and rich as that.

The party, in prospect, filled Graham with a sense of
déjà vu. A caterer's buffet supper, a non-vintage champagne giving way, the moment you started eating, to over-
chilled white rubbish. Graham had been to hundreds of
such parties, and had organised dozens. He would probably
know the caterers and their wine-merchant. At Victoria's
party, the old would be too old for Graham, and the young
too young for him. When he wanted a puppy-dog he had
one at home, and very nice too. The Bohemian birds—
plump Mimis with classless voices, with tatty second-
hand or home-made clothes, with terrible opinions about
government funding of the arts—were evidently what the
Bohemian lads liked: but if Graham had had the taste and
hormones for that sort of thing he would have preferred
Victoria.

Meanwhile Graham and Rudi agreed that they were *so
very sorry* for Victoria, being all alone and not liking it,
and if they could help her to even a bit of a happiness
such as theirs, why, they'd do it!

• • •

The party was *exactly and precisely* as Graham had predicted.

Two age-groups. Ill-assorted. Not much mix, though some of them tried. It was like a *mayonnaise* or a *maître-d'hôtel* where something has gone wrong, where the ingredients don't blend. The old looked askance at the young; the young looked at one another. The old were dressed in the manner of Graham and Rudi, the young were well-scrubbed but spike-haired.

Graham thought they would only stay long enough not to show discourtesy to Victoria.

Rudi, at his elbow, twitched. Graham followed his eye. Graham twitched, too, but with the objective admiration with which he regarded Victoria or Marlene or a piece of Sèvres. The man was about Graham's age, and similarly dressed although his suit did not fit as well as Graham's. His hair was chestnut, worn a little long—not as glossy as Graham's nor a boyish shock like Rudi's, but as though he had pushed his fingers through it in a moment of bafflement. The wind-blown, casual look suited the stranger, actually: he looked the things which Graham had no wish to be, such as a sportsman. Graham's admiration was objective because his instinct told him that there was nothing there for them to get twitchy about. Somebody, General Sir Somebody, told Graham that it was Enniscorthy's boy he was looking at, but as he had never heard of Enniscorthy he could not place this information in any useful context.

It was not a big party, so quite soon Graham and Rudi met this Giles Lambert, who was charming to them. He was charming to the old bores and the young bores, all of whom seemed to like him. The children seemed to know him. He had come with them; he was theirs. This was completely surprising. It was obvious to Graham that Giles Lambert belonged in this milieu, among these objects, with people like Victoria and himself and the General.

Graham saw that Victoria's eyes were wide and her

mouth a little open. She was looking her very best. It was hard to believe that she had a grown-up child, unless you looked closely at the skin round her eyes, and something could be done about that. Victoria looked as though it was her twenty-first birthday, and she was being shown the present she most wanted in the world.

Graham understood that Giles was the present. Whoever had brought Giles to the party was giving Victoria what she most wanted. Graham understood and sympathised, and so did Rudi. Though they laughed at Victoria they respected her, and they were a little frightened of her and quite sorry for her; if they could help they would. Graham decided they would not leave the party as early as he had expected, in case Victoria needed help.

To Giles the party smelled of home. It smelled of good scent, Havana, Trumper's *Coronis*, flowers and beeswax furniture polish—

> *. . . That softly o'er the perfumed sea*
> *The weary, way-worn traveller bore*
> *To his own native shore.*

To Odysseus the smell of home would have been aromatic herbs crushed dryly underfoot, the scent of herbs from a cooking-pot hanging from a tripod over the aromatic smoke of burning olive-roots.

To Giles it was the scent that came from the cleavage of this slim woman with long hair who was holding his hand in the semi-darkness.

Candlelight on polished walnut, on Waterford and de Lamerie. The voices were sober and civilised. Nobody preached. There were chuckles but no screams. Somewhere outside there was more noise, as of another party with different people at it. Giles did not want to go to that other party. He had been to too many such parties, and he had outgrown them.

The piano was a Blüthner, in beautiful condition. She leaned on the piano. She was called Victoria. She was in beautiful condition. He played Schubert and Cole Porter. From somewhere a special bottle appeared, and they drank vintage champagne.

Peckham was far away.

'Darling,' said Victoria softly to Graham, 'you know travel-agents, don't you?'

'One in particular. He always *says* he'll do anything for me.'

'Is it possible that you could ring him up now?'

'Only just after eleven. Oh yes. He won't be in bed.'

'We can cash a cheque and get some currency at Heathrow . . . He'll need his passport.'

'He can get a temporary passport over the counter at any main Post Office. Unless you're going to America?'

'Not this time. And perhaps when you know the time of the flight you'd very sweetly ring up my chauffeur?'

'But where are you taking him?'

'I simply don't care. I want two first-class tickets not too early in the morning.'

In Peckham a room had a light on or it didn't. Most lights dangled from ceilings.

Indirect light, low and amber-coloured, turning her skin to gold. The sheets were scented with lavender. Giles did not understand how any of this had happened. He was not drunk. He might have supposed that he was dead, but he knew he was not entitled to this kind of heaven.

In Peckham there were no *en-suite* bathrooms with deep pile carpets.

Nobody he ever heard of could have resisted that invitation, the flattery of it, the softly-expressed need. Giles had never been needed, and he liked it. He had never before met this mixture of gentleness and ferocity, of shyness and audacity.

He was too old for romps on lumpy mattresses, on the twanging of cheap bedsprings.

He was tired of wearing second-hand clothes and cheap shoes. He was tired of travelling by bus and pretending to earn a living. He was tired of living in squalor among garish colours and uneducated voices. He was tired of being lectured and patronised, and he was tired of being broke.

Her fingers were like moths. He was bewitched by moth-soft fingers and husky words in broken sentences. Nobody he ever heard of could have resisted that magic. He was wrapped in a magic cobweb and he had neither strength nor any wish to struggle free.

He felt big and strong and rich and properly admired for the very first time. He was not slave but master: she said so. It was obviously true. She would not have done what she did if she had not been his slave.

A piece of paper was pushed under the door. Naked, she took it to the lamp on the dressing-table.

'We're going to Lausanne,' she said.

C·H·A·P·T·E·R

9

Graham's friend was very efficient, and so was Graham, and so was Dagobert, and so was Victoria. A girl met them at Heathrow with their tickets. Dagobert carried Victoria's bags, which Cosette had packed, to the check-in. Giles had no luggage, although Dagobert had already collected his things from wherever he had been living. They were not worth taking. Cosette would get rid of them. Victoria bought dollars, Swiss francs and traveller's cheques with her American Express gold card. Giles had not actually, at the time, got a bank account, though there had been periods of his life when he had had one. Victoria paid for his temporary passport, to which was affixed a lurid coloured photograph taken by a DIY machine in the concourse. Victoria made Giles laugh while he was photographing himself, so that, with his unruly hair and crumpled collar, he looked pretty raffish. They laughed about the photograph. They foresaw laughing about so many things.

They flew to Geneva, drinking wine that was not as good as the wine they had drunk the previous evening. Giles became more crumpled, in his best dark suit. He was dazed. Victoria was bridal. She travelled in a beige trouser-suit of uncrushable cotton-synthetic; she looked as fresh as a dewdrop on a cobweb, as wholesome as a

Cox's Orange Pippin. To Her Man her manner was pliant
and tender and hesitant. The cabin-staff in the first-class
section, which was almost empty, made special pets of the
couple.

They lost an hour, owing to the time difference, but
still they were in time for a late lunch, which they had
in the open air close to the lake. The restaurant was full,
but room was found for so eye-catching a couple. They
took a taxi to Lausanne, where their suite was waiting for
them. Giles had seen hotel rooms before, though not many
(since Oxford, he had spent most of his sleeping hours
on people's sofas) but he had never seen a suite. It was
Victoria's joy and privilege to introduce him to civilised
things.

Giles was in urgent need of many other civilised things,
but most of them would have to wait because the shops
were shut. He could wait until next day for dressing-
gown, slippers, casual shirts and trousers, a lightweight
suit. Razor and toothbrush could be procured in the hotel.
Of pyjamas he had no immediate need at all.

Morning and early evening were sweetest. At ten he
would brush the crumbs of a croissant from her breasts.
At six there would be glasses of *kir royale* on their bedside
tables, and then a bath deliriously shared. Giles bought
one thing out of his pocket-money, which symbolically
outweighed all the things Victoria bought: on Tuesday he
bought a celluloid duck for their bath.

'Her name is Hildegarde,' said Victoria, blowing it
towards him over the surface of the bathwater.

'I think he's a drake,' said Giles.

'He's a drake called Hildegarde. I've already got a little
duck. I've got a little duck called Giles.'

They soapily massaged one another in the scent of clove
carnations.

Nothing in Giles's past had prepared him for living in a
suite in an hotel, for being a whimsical millionaire, for

owning a slave like Victoria. But he became adjusted quickly. By Wednesday he might have been doing these things all his life.

Victoria telephoned Graham Whittingham-Barnes, most supportive and understanding of all her friends, and asked him to put the marriage announcement in *The Times*. It would have to be sent to them in writing. He knew she would pay him back.

Ivy Mollam polished the wig-stand, wondering whatever it could be. She put it in the sitting room, in the absence of instructions about where to put it.

Graham realised that Victoria had not said where she was calling from, and he had been too excited to ask. They might still be in Switzerland, or have gone from there in any direction. It was not clear where, by whom, under what code of Civil Law the marriage had been conducted. Presumably they would bring back some kind of evidence of the legality of their status, to satisfy Her Majesty's Representative at Ascot, the Inland Revenue, and so forth.

Without ever having had occasion to study the matter, Graham supposed that most countries required a residential qualification of at least one of the parties before they let you get married. July 15th? They had not been abroad for as much as three weeks. Would anybody let you charge in and get married after only a fortnight?

Anyway Graham did as he was told, in good faith, and when the bill came he paid it.

Cosette kept a few flowers in the house while She was away. There would have been a frightful fuss if She had come back suddenly and found no flowers. Cosette put a vase of white roses on a peculiar and unfamiliar bit of furniture in the drawing room. It seemed the only thing the bit of furniture was any use for.

● ● ●

The announcement in *The Times* caused widespread comment. Who on earth is he? Who is she?

Few of Victoria's old friends or her new ones had heard of Lord Enniscorthy, and only those who had been to the birthday party had clapped eyes on Giles Lambert.

People who remembered Giles from school and university did not know Mrs Bramall.

Graham Whittingham-Barnes said, 'I forbid anyone to use the word "toy boy".' But he used it himself.

'How on earth did you manage their disappearance?' somebody asked.

'I managed nothing, darling,' said Graham. 'When Victoria locked her door, that was a locked door.'

'But there were reports of a dragon, guarding the mouth of the shrine.'

'I did find her. She was a sort of backstage *obergruppenführer* belonging to the caterers. I don't think she had any idea there was anybody else in the room with Victoria. If she'd known, I daresay she'd have been on to William Hickey first thing in the morning.'

'No. The next morning was Sunday.'

'That wouldn't weigh with a creature like her.'

Victoria was sure she had conceived her son, if not that first night then during the first week. She was proved wrong. She tried and tried. Giles was wonderful. Of course it was wonderful for him. He had never experienced such lyrical excitement so very often. Practically nobody ever had.

They slipped back into England in September.

Letters had piled up addressed to 'The Hon. Mrs Giles Lambert', as well as some to 'Mrs Gerald Bramall'. There were a few for Giles also. Victoria made sure she saw all the letters that had come for Giles; it was another hard lesson which the knocks of life had taught her. Cosette knew what to do with the post the moment it arrived. If she thought it was strange she had the sense not to say so. There were a great many bills to pay, including the caterers for the party, and Graham's note of what the announcement in *The Times* had cost.

They were married quite secretly, quite legally. Victoria had not really fibbed to Graham Whittingham-Barnes: she was simply reporting the future instead of the past. Her son could have been conceived in wedlock as recognised by God and herself; in the event he would be conceived in wedlock as acknowledged by the law.

Victoria had waited two-and-a-half months because experience had taught her caution.

She knew from Giles that his father, though now bent and shrunken, had been a tall, spare man, and that Giles's brother in New Zealand had the same build. His sons were like that—all the Lamberts were. It was aristocratic stock, quite different from the peasant origins of the Bramalls. Giles was as perfect a shape for what he was as Victoria for what she was.

Victoria also learned during those trial weeks that Giles was never going to be silly about money provided he was given very little of it; that he sufficiently liked his new life never to take the slightest risk; that he worshipped her. 'With my body I thee worship.' Victoria realised that she had never before fully understood the meaning of those grand old words, until, with his body, Giles worshipped her.

As soon as she was sure her arrangements were durable, she brought Giles back to England and told him what to do. Then they went on a second honeymoon to Scotland, everything booked by telephone in advance, Dagobert driving them.

Once or twice in Scotland they were able to make love under the arching afternoon sky, something that had never seemed quite safe in Switzerland. Dagobert stood guard a quarter of a mile away, not realising that that was what he was doing. Victoria loved feeling the sun on her naked back while Giles worshipped her: love above and below: God and Giles. Victoria gave God to Giles even as he was giving her his seed. She fully expected to conceive during that Scottish idyll, but she found that she had not.

Giles's chestnut hair might be beginning to get just a little thin on top.

He played the piano wherever there was a piano good enough.

In Scotland as in Switzerland, girls were drawn to him like wasps to a honeypot—older women, too, affecting modesty or shamelessly provocative. It was inevitable. Victoria would never fight a battle because she would never allow one to begin. The greatest leadership was not in winning desperate wars but in bloodless victories. The qualities required were alertness and a good intelligence service. Victoria had been born with the one and had created the other. She needed no bombs or rockets to defend her property, but she had them in case. She believed, with Lady Olga Maitland and President Reagan and so forth, that to be properly armed was to live in peace.

In October, Graham Whittingham-Barnes said, 'Mark my words. This will turn out to be the best thing Victoria ever did. I can make no comment about their *vie intime*, and God forbid that I should be afforded even so much as a *glimpse* of it, but for Victoria's social life this will be a bonanza. People are returning to the metropolis, darling, hostesses seeking whom they may devour. They will gobble up Giles and beg for more. Now that Victoria's fitted him up with proper frocks, he's more beautiful than even I realised. And *funny*. He's wasted on Victoria, really, but he's not wasted on the people she's going to be entertained by. On the people by whom she will, in the coming months, be entertained. Anywhere that Lambert

went, his Vic was sure to go. I hope she has the sense
to keep her lovely trap shut. When she gives an aesthetic
opinion, strong men wince. I am a *very* strong man, and I
wince. Rudi winces. It takes a lot to make Rudi wince.

'Giles has contributed to the *ménage*, you know, by
more than his mere presence, gigantic as that contribution
unquestionably is. He's given her *the prettiest* wig-stand.
He says it's 1790, and I bow to his superior knowledge
in that particular area. Its legs are truly *balletic*, although
there are three of them, which would make a funny danc-
er . . . It's been rather obviously restored, so it's not worth
so terribly much, but it's a most charming little piece.
Never in one million years would Victoria have spotted
that wig-stand in a shop. But now she dotes on it, because
she's been told she should. Do look at it next time you're
there. Look at your fellow-guests, too. I think we're all in
for a surprise. Indian summer of a débutante. Lucky me,
I got in on the ground floor.'

For Victoria, that autumn was a triumph. She was able to
show the world to Giles and Giles to the world. For her
sake, he was made welcome in all kinds of places where
he could never otherwise have gone: he made friends he
would never otherwise have met.

As she dimly remembered having done before, Victoria
found that she had the habit of distancing herself from
herself, and from a distance watching the two of them
entering a room or standing amongst courtiers. The Fairy
Queen and her Consort. They were lucky, those people
who had acquired (been granted) the privilege of greeting
this glorious couple; they were lucky who stared in startled
admiration from the far end of a room.

Victoria launched Giles as though by breaking a bottle
of champagne over his bows. But like a ship on the slipway
he was tethered. He was bound by worship and so forth.

As a compliment to Victoria, older men friends suggested putting Giles up for clubs, since it was discovered

to everybody's surprise that he belonged to none. The Garrick was mentioned, because, it was said, Giles would find kindred spirits there, men of artistic and cultural interests.

'Probably there's an endless waiting-list, darling,' said Victoria.

He joined the club Graham Whittingham-Barnes had taken her to. It was much more stimulating for Giles than a lot of black leather armchairs.

Giles's name was removed from the Candidates' Book at the Garrick 'at the request of the Proposer'.

Giles went shopping with Victoria and Victoria went shopping with Giles. They often went to drinks and dinner parties and sometimes gave them. Giles was an attentive host and an appreciative guest. He behaved as though he had done this kind of thing all his life. Victoria saw that he did not have too much to drink.

Aristocratic Anglo-Irishmen reappeared in his life, and Wykehamists, and people who had known him at Oxford. They made their memories of Giles their excuse to get to know Victoria. She was alert for social climbers, but she detected none among the people who claimed ancient friendship with Giles. Many of them were very busy, in politics or the professions or the City, but they made time to come to Battersea. Victoria had an adoring court of young men who pretended they came because they were friends of Giles.

Other friends, of more recent vintage, reappeared in his life too. They were the more presentable of the friends of his Bohemian days. Some of them were clearly on the make, but some were said to be genuinely talented and to be making reputations. Victoria did not want to deprive any of the future stars of the advantage of her friendship. She would be a Fairy Godmother, even perhaps a patroness, to an élite among the Bohemians. Graham Whittingham-Barnes told her which was which: she allowed him to give her the names of the artists,

musicians and actors who were to be admitted to friendship.

Giles had, of course, to be protected from himself. In
some ways he was a child, innocent and trusting and a
silly-billy. Victoria did not often say this in front of people,
and she tried to stop herself from saying it often even in
private.

There were several mornings and evenings and mid-
nights when Victoria was sure she had conceived her son,
but each time she turned out to be wrong. She knew that
in the end God would compensate her for her unmerit-
ed misfortunes, and reward her for her faith and loyalty.

'One day,' said Cosette to Ivy Mollam, 'I shall kill that
bitch.' Cosette spoke with a French accent only in public.

'Let us know when you decide, dear,' said Ivy. 'We'll
help.'

They went to Jamaica for Christmas, Victoria making the
bookings through Graham Whittingham-Barnes's travel-
agent friend. With his fair skin and chestnut hair, Giles
had to be careful in the tropical sun. It was Victoria's
delight to anoint him with Sea-'n-Ski. When she had done
his back, he was too excited to move from the towel on
which he lay.

Victoria had a new court, although she was alert for
climbers and parasites. Giles took people as they came,
high and low, and he had to be protected against himself.
Friends made in a resort hotel might be acceptable on the
spot, like cheap wine drunk in its place of origin, but, like
such wine, fail to travel. There was a man with a bulbous
nose who always said 'Good morning', whom Victoria
did not encourage because it would be humiliating to
be accosted by him in Piccadilly. After he had left the
hotel, she learned that he was an Earl; she was annoyed,

because it would have been interesting for Giles to have known him.

Giles had saved up his allowance to buy her pearl earrings for Christmas. In the course of her way of thanking him she thought, but wrongly, that she had conceived her son.

Emmee took Lottie to her mother's for Christmas, Thurber having gone to his family in Jersey. Although it was dull at Emmee's mother's house, they were both glad to get out of London for a few days.

They were glad to get back to London again, in time for the New Year, although the flat was chilly and clammy from having been empty.

They were festive on New Year's Eve and on New Year's Day. At a large lunch party on New Year's Day, Lottie met a tall and thin young man who bumped into things. He was not drunk. He was four or five years older than Lottie, so he was not a child. He had yellow hair and a face like a gentle hawk. He was a painter, a working artist, who supplemented his professional income by means of menial jobs in restaurants. He was, in all this, fairly typical of Lottie's friends, and it was not at all surprising to meet him at that party.

He was called James Drummond. It was obvious to Lottie after half an hour of intensive conversation that he could be trusted with a palette-knife but not with a carving-knife. He had, as of that morning, nowhere immediately to live. Marcus Hills had a spare bed, Elmer being unfortunately inside again.

In spite of a number of apparent coincidences, Lottie was quite certain that history was not repeating itself.

Emmee was aghast. Thurber hovered, alert to pick up and brush down anybody who had fallen over and hurt themselves. Even they had to admit after two days that James was poor but not insolvent, that he had neither need nor desire to borrow any money off anybody, that he had his own adequate clothes, and even luggage, that he had actually sold several pictures over the previous three years, and that he had overruled Marcus in the matter of rent, insisting on paying twice what Marcus asked.

There was a wound? James helped to finish its healing. There was a scar? It did not show. Lottie was wary. Lottie had always been wary.

Emmee, Thurber, Marcus and others discussed the matter anxiously. They did not want Lottie hurt again. Marcus swore that James would not hurt a fly; he would have sworn that Giles would not hurt a fly. The terrible thing was that Giles would *not* hurt a fly, any more than would, of its own volition, a fly-swatter.

James was taller than Giles, but they were of similar build. He was less beautiful, but Lottie's friends thought there was more strength in his mouth and chin.

James was not as expensively educated as Giles, and he did not have the same breadth of culture. But he was an authentic creative artist, while Giles was at best a gifted handyman, a fixer.

James had, and had always had, a clear sense of direction. Giles had been born without a compass, a map, or the capacity for buying shoes, and he had never acquired any of these things.

The consensus of her friends was that James needed Lottie less than Giles had, until his circumstances changed; but that Lottie needed James more than she had needed Giles.

James needed marriage as he did a hole in the head. Lottie was far too young to get married. So what? So an 'ongoing situation' normal to that group in that place and time. And hearts could be broken in Peckham as comprehensively as in Gloucestershire or Nice or Los Angeles.

Lottie, once bitten, was one-and-a-quarter times shy. She looked a little bit wary all through January and February.

• • •

Victoria came home in triumph. Their return to London was like a Tiepolo ceiling.

Victoria knew what a Tiepolo ceiling looked like, from a book which she had given Giles. There was a radiant central figure, slender, with a lovely face at once pensive and eager, with a robe of soft silky stuff flowing with her movement, supported by a cloud and by attendant angels, the whole lit with a golden glow.

Victoria laughed at herself, as she so often and so disarmingly did; she laughed at the idea of Cosette and Mrs Mollam and Mrs Calloway and Mr Childers and Dagobert being attendant angels, with the pinions of their gull wings touched to a rosy glow by the radiance of her return. She did not really picture herself as the central figure in a religious painting by Tiepolo, or Michelangelo or Titian, because of course she was not in a strict legal sense a virgin. She was the wrong shape for Tintoretto and Rubens and Renoir. She was more out of Botticelli (Giles said she was by Botticelli) except that his angels all had wavy hair, which was rather a common thing to have. She was a cross between a young child by Romney and Salome by Aubrey Beardsley. Mostly it was the Romney side of herself which people saw.

They were at once caught up in the whirl of social and cultural Events.

She was suspected (by the jealous) of paying a press-agent: but Graham Whittingham-Barnes did it free.

'It hasn't really worked out as I expected,' said Graham. 'They *do* go to *frightfully* grand parties, and their photographs are printed in the very glossiest magazines. But those are the parties in aid of something, which Victoria pays to go to. The ones they go to free are rather on the cosy side. You know—cultured widows and small-time retired generals. Rather a Bayswater emphasis. One enjoys oneself, but it doesn't make William Hickey. I suppose the trouble is Giles, really. One feels that he's let one down. One thought he'd be everybody's darling, but there are people who simply can't be bothered. Don't you have a feeling he's made of caramel?'

'Fondant,' said a sharp woman who knew them all. She supplemented her husband's income by writing clever novels, so she was expected to make sharp remarks.

'You're quite unfair,' said someone. 'I was once sent, from South Africa, by an ill-wisher, what in delight I took to be a large box of crystallised fruit. I was quite wrong. I was deceived by a delusive appearance. These objects had in truth started as fruit, growing properly on trees, vines and the like, but had been pulped, subjected to an assortment of mechanical indignities, extruded like gods from the machines, and only then reconstituted, and artificially coloured, as the simulacra of the natural objects. Giles has been gorged, digested, regurgitated, and presented to the world, elegantly packaged and at a premium price, as though he were alive.'

Graham would not allow this. He reckoned he had invented Victoria, and although he retained the right (often exercised) to be satirical about her, he did not permit anybody else to say anything nasty.

She could still be a Force for Good, helping to bring to public notice young talent which was struggling for recognition.

James Drummond understood, from their friends, that Lottie's background was exotic. He heard barely-credible accounts of chauffeurs, brothers at Eton, Lord Lieutenants coming to lunch. He heard none of this from Lottie herself, who answered questions on the subject with a curtness foreign to her usual manner.

James's own background was not humble but it was certainly not glamorous. His father had been Company Secretary of an organisation which marketed American toiletry products, its headquarters in Tottenham. James's grandfathers, both alive and retired, had been respectively London representative of a Yorkshire firm of printers, and Managing Clerk of a small firm of City solicitors. James had gone as a day-boy to a fee-paying school in Outer London. He felt that he came from the country of Charles Pooter, Candida, Kipps.

That he should turn out artistic was predictable if not welcome. His mother and his paternal grandmother were both talented amateurs (which caused an unseemly rivalry between them) and members of local art clubs. Nobody tried to stop him becoming a painter. Nobody gave him any money, either, because there was no spare money to give him. He was all alone in one sense, though not in another: his father's parents had retired to Pembrokeshire and his mother's to Cornwall, and his father, after his employers' company had been taken over, had found a job in Fife. James was not cut off or thrown out: he was simply left behind in London and told to get on with it. He wrote and received letters, when he had a fixed address, but long-distance telephone calls were regarded in his family as an insane extravagance.

James had inherited, or absorbed, a careful and even reverential attitude to money, and he had been brought up to scrupulous honesty. The slapdash liberality of Lottie and her friends filled him with dismay.

James was supremely lucky, as he knew at the time, in his art master at school, a scratchy little man whose gods were Constable and Turner. He was not so much generally an admirable teacher as specifically one: he was right for James. He understood what James was trying to do before James did, and verbalised and directed it. He sent James to look at pictures and told him what to look for; he set him drawing, with proper materials and paper, and told him what to draw.

James heard his teacher's rare laugh when he showed him a sheaf of *pastiches*. He had a precocious gift of visual mimicry. At the age of sixteen he could do you a John of Dorelia, a Picasso of a bullfight, a Rembrandt canal bridge (in brown pen and wash) and even a Leonardo siege-engine, complete with indecipherable commentary in mirror-writing. This was a dangerous facility, and for years had the effect of obscuring his personal sense of direction.

They were dubious about him at his first art school, suspecting him quite wrongly of frivolity, but they let him in and later gave him a scholarship. He went on to the Royal College. He worked hard, trying not to imitate Matisse or Mondrian or Kitaj.

He knew when he was twenty that he could make a living by painting imitation Georges Braque; he also knew that this would be a life of shame and betrayal. He proposed to make a living painting real James Drummonds, if only he could discover what they were.

It was less a prostitution to work in the kitchen of a restaurant than to sell imitation pictures. James began taking a sketchbook to various places of work, and worked up composites of the sketches into medium-sized paintings, oil on board. He repelled, when he detected them, traces of Goya, Murillo, Hogarth and Toulouse-Lautrec invading his pictures of kitchens, cellars, bars. Some of the pictures were strictly representational (even the dramatic *chiaroscuro* was realistic), some semi-abstract: but they made a coherent sequence. James began to hope that he was finding an authentic and personal voice.

He badly needed a studio. He was bursting with ideas that he could not work on until he had an adequate space, properly lit. He had a lot of studios, but none was satisfactory and he had none for more than a few weeks.

He spent part of a summer with his grandparents in Pembrokeshire; he lived in a tent in their tiny garden, and came in for meals and baths. He went down to the rocks, and painted nearly all of every day. All these paintings needed more work, or to be treated as sketches, for which he needed a studio.

Although the paintings of the Pembrokeshire seashore were as different in subject as could possibly be from the slightly hellish Hogarthian world of the restaurant kitchens, James allowed himself to think that it was the same voice talking.

In a decent studio, that voice could resonate and be refined; it could become more powerful, more distinctive, more elegant.

James found a studio, the top floor of a house in East Dulwich, midway between East Dulwich and Peckham Rye stations. The studio was moderate and the rent immoderate. James put a sleeping-bag on a mattress on the floor, propped his canvases all round the walls, and paid the rent by working 'unsocial hours' in restaurant kitchens. He was sure that he could stay there indefinitely.

Just before Christmas a man came from the property company which owned the house. The company had tenants for the studio. James's landlord had a lease of the rest of the house, but not the top. He had been renting to James something which was not his to rent. The man from the property company was apologetic, understanding and reasonable; he had to have vacant possession on New Year's Day. The new legal tenants were a commercial design partnership who had lost their own premises, who had contracts and deadlines, and who were paying more rent.

James hired a self-drive van, put everything in it, and drove to a party he had been asked to in Peckham High Street.

At the party he met Lottie, and with Lottie he met Emmee and Thurber and Marcus Hills.

Somebody found room to store the canvases; but it was not possible for James to spread himself and his materials in Marcus's flat or in the girls'. He felt like an amputee who has been given an artificial leg and had it taken away again.

Some of the pictures were hung, few finished and none framed, in the flats of various friends. This was the nearest

James had come, since college, to being exhibited.

Within three days of their meeting, and being aware of the developing situation, Emmee told James that if he made Lottie unhappy she would skin him slowly with a blunt knife.

James had already understood that Emmee had made herself responsible for Lottie, as Thurber had made himself responsible for Emmee. James was now brought to realise that Lottie had made herself responsible for him; but he did not need looking after. He needed first a studio and then the backing of a gallery.

James did not know that any of his contemporaries, at school or college, were making a living by painting. They were painting, to be sure, but they were paying the rent by being waiters. Some of his friends had found studios. Some had prosperous and supportive families. Some could not possibly afford to have their pictures framed.

It was said that there had once been limitless jobs in advertising, in commercial studios which produced brochures and showcards and so forth, and on magazines. Such jobs were now, in a time of recession, almost impossible to come by. James thought that he might design television commercials, which he thought he could do better than the people now doing it; thereby, he would earn enough to take Lottie to Italy in May. He hardly even got an interview. In order to take Lottie to Italy, he had to work overtime in kitchens.

Victoria loved to give private nicknames to people—even to things and places—which she used only silently, to herself. She had all kinds of funny names, which she never meant to say aloud, and which almost nobody heard about; sometimes she forgot the names, and then she had to think of new ones.

One person to whom she had never given a nickname was herself.

It came to her one evening, while she was dressing. She was *Debonnaire*. She was allowed to spell it like that—the dictionary said so. *De bon aire*, of good appearance and manner, *aire* being an old masculine word. *De bonne aire*, *aire* now being a feminine word, which was just as it should be. Victoria did not often find time for studying the dictionary, her life being full to bursting with people, the arts, beauty, love and so forth.

My name is *Debonnaire*. I am *Debonnaire Lambert*. Sometimes I might be *Debonnaire Courtenay*.

The room where Cosette slept was one of three at the top of the house. Victoria used the other two for storage of things she might one day need.

There were rooms on the floor below for her son and his nurse.

The two spare attics had a connecting door, and both gave on to the top landing from which Cosette's room was also reached. One gave north, over the street, the other, with two outside walls, north and east. The eastern aspect was an attractive roofscape, which had put Giles in mind of the works of that French painter, briefly fashionable, whose signature was bigger than his pictures.

Giles wanted one of the attic rooms for a workshop. Although it seemed to Victoria that their life together was one long buzz, he sometimes felt that he did not have enough to do—or rather, he corrected himself, that he was not helping enough, contributing enough.

Mr Childers was called in from the garden, therefore, and he and Huxtable (Dagobert) moved a few odds and ends from the north-east room into the north room, including two battered school trunks left over from an earlier period of Victoria's life. They evoked memories in Giles, of prep school and Winchester, but apparently not in Victoria. It was understood that the trunks would one day be useful for packing up and carting away other jumble, when Victoria found time to go through it. Into the north-east

room went the kitchen table from Court Farm, a solid
bit of old pine too big for the Battersea kitchen, and
some beechwood kitchen chairs in case Giles wanted to
sit down in his workshop. A vice was clamped to the
table. Giles himself put up shelves and hooks for the tools
which Victoria bought for him. Giles also fixed up a new
system for lighting the room. It kept him happily busy
for hours while Victoria (Debonnaire) tolerantly watched
some programmes on television.

Lottie continued wary, before, during and after the anniversary of her meeting with Giles on a bus going the wrong
way in Oxford Street.
   Ironically, it was by dint of what she had learned from
Giles, the previous early summer, that she was able to
judge James's work, unfinished and ill-presented as it
was. She thought he had superb technical skill and a
convincing and completely personal vision. She admitted
in private that her view might be prejudiced, but nothing
would have induced her to admit it in public.
   She continued wary.

Graham Whittingham-Barnes carried on a desultory and
intermittent search for outstanding young talent in need of
a patron.
   He was aware of the potential of Victoria's north-facing
attic as a studio, in combination with the other room next
door which the artist would also need. He realised that
something would have to be done with all that furniture
and glass and china. He did not discuss this with Victoria,
in case she and Giles took it into their heads to discover
a deserving young artist of their own, thus cutting out
Graham as middleman and footnote in art history.

On Victoria's instructions, Giles applied to Her Majesty's
Representative for vouchers for the Royal Enclosure at the
Ascot June Meeting, both having been vouchsafed this

honour in previous seasons. Victoria had not actually been
to Ascot since Rienzo's death, Giles not since the summer
of his premature departure from Oxford, but having been
acceptable once they were acceptable again.

Lottie had not been properly away for a year and a half,
except for those few days at Christmas. Emmee agreed
with James that it was high time she had a complete
change.

James told Lottie that he had to go to Italy, to experience
Italian light and Italian art, as had practically every major
British artist for more than two centuries. She was appalled
at the idea of James wandering alone through a strange
country with rapacious inhabitants and incomprehensible
signs. Everybody else might be clear that James did not
need a keeper, but Lottie was clear that he did.

In return for the delight of Lottie's company, James
consented to pretend that he was helpless without her.

They made plans, found out about trains, and assembled
gear. There was a whip-round to buy James a decent
Japanese miniature camera. Everything else he had.

May Day had always been something quite special.

The children dancing round the maypole on the village
green, garlanded, in celebration of innocence and rebirth.

The May Queen. 'I'm to be Queen of the May, Mother,
I'm to be Queen of the May.' Debonnaire Courtenay is
Queen of the May.

James and Lottie had a dusty and crumpled journey in
interminable trains. Being so tall, James found it difficult
to curl into a position that permitted sleep. They went by
Milan and Bologna and Florence. In Tuscany, James was
abashed by what he saw, even though he was familiar
with much of it from illustration and reproduction. There
remained vestiges of Lottie's wariness: she was there to
look after James, not anything else.

They went to Perugia, Assisi, Spoleto, and in the Umbrian air, for some antic or antique reason, Lottie's wariness disappeared.

James filled his sketchbooks, in pencil, pen-and-wash, aquarelle crayons. He photographed what he drew, to trigger memory of colour. When he got back he would need a studio more urgently than ever, desire one more passionately, be as much as ever completely unable to afford one.

Victoria knew, by the Tuesday of Ascot Week, that she had conceived her son.

C·H·A·P·T·E·R

10

Once Lottie was committed she was committed. She was in love as never before. She had supposed her heart broken, eleven months before; it had certainly felt like that, and she did not then suppose she would ever get over it. But in Spoleto in the third week of May she realised that what she had had was a crush, a childish infatuation; she had been beguiled by charm and chestnut hair, by humour and helplessness. Presumably it had been a hard mixture to resist; she had not, in those far off days of her childhood, been able to resist it. She was sure she would react differently now—grown up, nearly twenty-two—and would do so even if she had not met James.

She had to get used to the fact that when he was working he was working, *working working working*, that when he was doing it he was doing nothing else, that he would not look up for a bomb or even the sound of her voice, that it was incomparably the most important thing in his life. Every artist's woman had to get used to that. It gave their relationship an extra value, an extra meaning: it gave it an absolute permanence.

Lottie was not capable of being any kind of artist, but she was capable of helping someone to function as an artist. It was the service of art, even though in practice it was feeding the brute and fetching and carrying. Lottie had

absolute faith in what James was doing, and in the times he
was not actually doing it he was sweet to her, thoughtful
and considerate and patient. He would have indulged her
every whim, when he was not working, but the only whim
she had was to look after him.

'It's a bit depressing,' said James in Spoleto.

'Nothing's depressing at the moment,' said Lottie.

'Yes. I had great hopes for this year. I thought I'd grown
up in the last two years, artistically and possibly in other
ways. I thought I was ready to show that to other people.
I thought this might be the year of sales and galleries and
backing and shows.'

'It will!'

'No. Not possible. Having you is all the luck anybody
could hope for in one year.'

Lottie was pleased by this remark. A smile spread across
her face, as, at sunrise, the golden Umbrian light spread
over the towers of the towns.

At Ascot, a star danced.

It was comical to see how many people peered to read
Victoria's name on her badge.

Only a stupid person could have been unaware of the
breadth and depth of the admiration aroused by Victoria.
She supposed there was envy. Giles said there was. She
was constitutionally incapable of feeling and so of sensing
so small-spirited an emotion.

Nobody asked them to the Jockey Club, and they had
been too late to get a place in the West Car Park.

'The quality of life has deteriorated,' said Victoria to
Giles.

'Up to a point,' said Giles, who looked very well in the
morning-coat Victoria had had made for him. He wore it
as to the manor born because, of course, he was born to
it. He carried Gerald's race-glasses with more of an air
than Gerald had ever managed. His son would look just
so, in twenty years time, but with straight black hair.

Victoria did not open an account for Giles with a credit bookmaker. She gave him a few pounds to bet with, and a few more to buy drinks with. Of course he did not go off on his own, as so many men selfishly did at the races, because he could not have borne to be parted from her. Victoria had heard from friends about a place called the Iron Stand, where men got away from their wives. Looking at some of the wives, and the clothes they wore, Victoria was not surprised. Things were not like that with Giles and herself. He was proud to be seen with her; he was only happy when he was with her.

Girls would have flocked round Giles, given half a chance, but he was not interested in any of them.

By the middle of the second day, he had lost the money Victoria had given him to bet with. She punished him for his folly that night, but she relented next day.

Victoria did not subject herself to undue exertion, because of the precious burden she was carrying. She drank only champagne, because as everybody knew it was best for her. Giles found her places to sit, and fetched her glasses of champagne. He did not do this in a fussy or obsequious way, which would have revolted Victoria, but in a manly way. No man is so much a man, Victoria said to herself, as when he waits on a lovely woman. She laughed at herself, as she so often did, but in her heart she knew it was true.

Just after the running of the Gold Cup, a young girl—a tall awkward creature of about eighteen—pretended to fall over and hurt herself in the grandstand, in order to attract attention. Giles, obedient to the instincts of a gentleman— but a gullible gentleman—was on the point of hurrying forward to help the girl. But Victoria had seen through the ruse, and drew him away. At the races, even more than in the Caribbean, he had to be protected against himself.

Giles massaged Victoria's feet and her shoulders when they got home.

• • •

At the beginning of the week after Ascot, in the middle of Monday afternoon, Giles disappeared upstairs to his workshop. Victoria smiled at his receding back, and reached for the telephone.

Whatever he was doing would be for her.

At five o'clock he was still there. Whatever was the old pudding doing, spending the whole afternoon fustily at his workbench?

Victoria crept mouselike up the stairs. (She could be like a mouse, as well as like a bird and like a panther.) She said 'Boo' as she threw open the door. She was no longer being a mouse; she was being his little girl.

He was sitting on one of the old beechwood kitchen chairs. He was reading. Victoria saw that the book was in Spanish or Italian. She did not know how he had come by such a thing. Victoria knew that people spoke well of reading, but she preferred living. Reading was a thing to do when you got too old to live. God intended you to live, not read, when you were still young and full of energy and curiosity. It was perverse to sit with a dusty book, in an outlandish language, when all the vibrant sunlit world was full of people who were living, walking books, if only you could find the key to reading them. It was perverse to sit in a house where she abode, preferring to stare at a foreign book, to read crabby, uncouth words rather than discourse with her. This was not because she was special, really, but because she was alive and throbbing, and had over the previous week of glamorous encounters recorded thousands more graphic impressions than they had had time to discuss.

There was something deceitful about creeping away into an attic to read.

It would have been all right if he had said, 'I am going to read this book,' like a man, in the drawing room; he would soon have dropped his book into his lap and earned far greater dividends by discussing with her the sights and scenes of the previous week.

Reading books in the attic was not what Giles was *for*.

Oh, he was disarmingly contrite. He had not come upstairs intending to read. But the book had been lying there, God knew why, and he had picked it up, glanced at it . . . She knew how it happened.

Victoria did not know how it happened. It had never happened to her, except with other people's letters and bank statements, which it was her onerous duty to study.

Victoria wondered if it had been a good idea, giving Giles this bolt-hole of his own to hide himself in. He had to be protected from himself in Jamaica and Ascot and Battersea. It was not good for him to crawl away into a hole by himself, like a dying animal; it was morbid and unhealthy; it was not truly a kindness to make such a thing possible.

Victoria might easily find herself needing those attic rooms for something else.

Victoria forgave Giles for being deceitful, because during the week that followed fell the anniversary of their meeting. She saw that he needed freedom to follow his bent, to assert himself, to achieve his potential, to be his own man. As long as it took him no further than the attic, and no longer than two hours at a time, Victoria accorded him absolute liberty.

He had saw and chisels, which he said you needed in a workshop, and of course the predictable happened. It was so predictable it was almost funny, except for the mess. The cut was in the palm of his left hand. He was hacking at a piece of wood in the vice, the chisel held in his right hand. He was a clumsy old silly, and he made a frightful fuss. There was a bit of blood on his shirt-front and on the bench, then he had the sense to wrap it up in his handkerchief and run downstairs. He ran straight past Victoria's room and down to the kitchen, which was unexpectedly thoughtful because Victoria's room had a pale fitted Wilton broadloom overlaid with precious Persian and Turkish rugs, and the kitchen had York stone and rush matting. There was quite a bit more blood there, while Mrs Calloway swabbed the cut with disinfectant in warm water, and then put a dressing and a bandage on it.

Mrs Mollam took one look and said it needed the doctor—it needed stitches. Mrs Calloway thought not. Victoria decided in favour of the doctor, because she did not want the kitchen, still less her bedroom, continually full of the smell of disinfectant. She even, herself, telephoned the doctor to say that Giles was coming and she even, herself, telephoned Dagobert to bring the car round.

Giles reportedly had three stitches and an anti-tetanus jab.

Mrs Mollam scrubbed the stone floor and the matting where the blood had splashed.

Giles had a bandage for a week and sticking-plaster for a week after that. Victoria kissed the scar to make it heal quicker.

Her unborn son touched by starlight and the scent of roses, Debonnaire (Victoria) lay wakeful and wondering. She had not lost her sense of wonder. Sometimes when she glanced at herself in a mirror, a child looked back (framed in the elaborate gilt of the Chinese Chippendale in the drawing room, in the heavier, darker gold of the convex circular glass in the dining room, in the porcelain-framed triple mirror on her dressing table, in the full-length greeny triple mirror beside it, in the three great mirrors in her bathroom). She thanked God that she had remained essentially child-like. She prayed that her son would be like herself a Seeker:

We will go
Beyond that angry or that glimmering sea . . .

Debonnaire had laughed with childish delight as the yacht (on day charter) swooped over the steep ultramarine waves, white crested, under the Caribbean sun. No fair-weather sailor she, with enough barrier-cream to protect her magnolia complexion from the salt-laden tradewind. People laughed with her laughter. She made people see, as they could not otherwise have seen, the beauty of palm-fringed beaches in the evening sun. Giles had to be watched in case he had too many rum punches. Six months later she smiled in the dark at the memory of his excitement. To be lovely you must be loved, and to be loved you must be lovely. Debonnaire in the darkness pitied almost the whole of the rest of the world. She prayed that everyone might find some sort of consolation.

Certain privileged intimates could call her Deb. People hearing this would probably think she was called Deborah. Deborah was a person in the Bible, some kind of heroine. Victoria had a notion that she had driven a nail through somebody's head. Victoria's last waking thought was uncertainty about whether this was a good thing to have done. Victoria came downstairs in the scented morning (it was still just morning) herself scented and silken.

She found the Bible, and looked up her near-namesake in the index of proper names.

Deborah was somebody's nurse. All she did was die and get buried under a tree. That was no person to be named after. Ah, but there was another one. She was a priestess, a prophetess. That was more like it. She did not hammer the nail through the man's head—somebody else did that, but Deborah thought it was a good thing to have done. The Bible said it was a good thing to have done.

Awake, awake, Deb: awake, awake, utter a song.

Debonnaire Courtenay, priestess of the flowers, went out into the garden to be worshipped by her roses.

During that first party Graham immediately, *on the spot*, looked up Giles in Debrett. He suspected that Victoria had already done so. The editors acknowledged Giles's existence, assuming that he was who he said he was, and Graham thought he must be. Somebody had, indeed, spotted a likeness to old Lord Enniscorthy, a name which immediately became Graham's favourite title.

Giles had had—had still—friends of his own, of a kind that might have numbered Graham but had not, in fact, done so. This was not so very surprising, because Graham on the whole moved on a glossier plane than that of spaghetti dinners in Hammersmith attics. Some of Giles's Bohemian friends, re-adopted, became Victoria's Bohemian friends. They liked free meals as well as anyone: Graham did not begrudge them a single sip of Victoria's whisky. They included *soi-disant* painters and such. But there were no discoveries to be made among them. Some of them had already been discovered, to the extent of mixed exhibitions in provincial galleries every couple of years; some of them were really no good. But out there somewhere was the Big Talent, the Shooting Star, the Hockney of the late eighties. Graham Whittingham-Barnes spent quite five minutes a week wondering how to find him.

People said long afterwards that what happened was straight out of Greek tragedy. They meant that the malicious intervention of jealous gods had altered the course of people's lives; they meant that the meeting was a bizarre coincidence. Everybody who knew the people involved accepted that what *followed* the meeting was inevitable; but the meeting itself, they said, was a weird and calamitous chance.

Graham Whittingham-Barnes knew very well that there was no coincidence about it. He found Lottie because he was looking for Lottie, and he found James because he was looking for James. It was true that he did not know that it was James he was looking for until he found him, but he *was* looking for somebody who turned out to be James. It was also true that, after the initial moment of surprise, it was no surprise to find James with Lottie, because Lottie was obviously what James had needed, up to that point, since there was no Graham in his life.

Nor was there, in spite of what people later said, any oddity in Graham going out to find Lottie. Basically it was, he said, his inborn sense of *Fair Play*. In talking about it he capitalised and italicised the words, in order to introduce a note of self-mockery, and thus retain his intellectual and aesthetic (and commercial) credibility: but it was possible that he exactly meant what he said. People got him wrong when they forgot that he was a Public School man. This was much later, when it all came out.

It started, inexorably, with the Chinese porcelain.

Graham had not consciously thought about Victoria's porcelain, more than once a fortnight, during the intervening fifteen months. He concluded that his subconscious had been chewing on the subject.

It came up with the following proposition: Victoria had obviously not bought the stuff. Nobody could have done so; she would not have done so. She had inherited it. From whom? From her own family? No—it was revealing how little was revealed about them. From her late husband. He had certainly inherited it, by way of a chain of three or four generations from the ancestor who looted it from the Imperial Palace. Nobody had thought to bequeath the collection outside the immediate family. They might have given it to the British Museum, but they had not. They might have sent it to Sothebys, but they had not done that, either. The collection did not have—could not have had—the legal status of heirloom; no entail was officially attached to it; but the intention of each generation was to entrust it to the next, keeping it in the family.

The late Gerald Bramall had had children by his first marriage. Victoria did not talk about them; Giles probably did not know about them; Graham was nearly sure there were children, and he thought they included a son. That son was the rightful owner of the porcelain, whatever Gerald Bramall's will said. This would not have been terribly important if the porcelain had been fake. Since it was real, it was important.

The sum of money involved was mind-boggling, unguessable. The amount of beauty involved, of precious and unique art and craftsmanship, was approachable by intimates, with awe, though it was to passers-by in that hall undiscernable, since the collection had been put where it could not be seen. This also was a factor, to which Graham's subconscious mind had given its secret attention over fifteen months.

Graham could not ask Victoria whether her husband had had any children of his first marriage. He could not ask Giles. Since it was clearly a sensitive topic, Graham could not ask those of Victoria's friends who had survived from the first marriage. They were dreary enough. They would regard the question as impertinent. They would, he supposed, be right.

Bramall was not a common name. There were only seven in the 1985 London telephone book, one a building company. None was the son of the late Gerald Bramall of Court Farm. There was a large amount of the world's land surface on which that son could be living; and he might have changed his name; and he might never have existed.

Thinking thus far, Graham thought that his thoughts were like one of those East African rivers which, fed by the rains in the big hills edging the Rift, flow deep and dangerous towards the Indian Ocean . . . and peter out in the sand and lava rock of the eastern desert. Graham's notions did not stick, or strike an obstacle: they simply evaporated.

The notion of pursuing this putative son was too fatiguing to contemplate. Rudi agreed; Rudi did not really understand what Graham was on about. Rudi was in many ways a moralist, but as a younger son he was unimpressed by primogeniture.

And then Graham's subconscious reminded his conscious of something which he had, perhaps, chosen to forget: the circumstances of the strange and rather scrubby little party at which Victoria had met Giles. Graham had been happy to play Fairy Godfather, or conniving Nanny, on that occasion. He was still, on balance, happy that he had done so. Victoria and Giles, all qualifications registered, were among his most congenial friends. What Graham now remembered was that the party had been given for the daughter, and the daughter had been a rebel. Graham could not actually summon a mental picture of the daughter and he had no idea what connection, if any, she had had with Giles.

The girl had rebelled, so much was clear. If against her father only, why had she taken so long before being reunited with her mother? Against her mother? Graham could not imagine rebelling against one's mother; his own had been (remained, when given the rare chance) indulgent and adoring. But *if* it were so, there was a strong possibility that the girl was in touch with Gerald Bramall's older family: to the senior surviving member of which the Chinese porcelain rightly belonged.

What was it to Graham to whom a lot of cups belonged? He was never going to get his own mitts on them. Why should he care? No reason, he later said, except his sense of *Fair Play*. This was not entirely frank. Victoria was entitled to exert visible hegemony over Giles—it might be uncouth, but she could get away with it because she paid the bills. She was *not* entitled to hegemony over Graham, nor yet Rudi. She had perhaps, in the early months of their friendship, shown signs of taking Graham for granted; he rapidly and quite gently made it clear that he was having none of that. But her patronising attitude to Rudi was sometimes *over the edge*. Once it literally gave Graham indigestion; that Rudi did not apparently notice it did not dispel the anger nor the bile in Graham's diaphragm.

Nothing like bile for giving a bit of extra horsepower to *Fair Play*.

What was the girl called? Something predictable; she was called Charlotte. How do you find Charlotte Bramall, not in the book, among London's teeming millions, supposing her even to be in London? Not so very difficult. You enquire among those of Giles's Bohemian friends who have graduated into friendship with Victoria, and from them hear about the friends who have not so graduated. You are beginning to pothole now, to plumb new depths; among stalactites and dripping subterranean pools you find persons increasingly obscure, on the fringes of civilisation (to change the metaphor, which Graham in narration was content to do) who were in touch with Giles in his Peckham period. Among these were some who had known Charlotte. They knew her still. They knew her address and telephone number.

Graham had this information for weeks before he used it. He was busy in the early autumn; his professional and social calendars were full to brimming. He was not sure if he wanted to upset applecarts.

Then there was the episode, after dinner, in Battersea, on 17th October. Rudi passed the port the wrong way, and Victoria called him an 'ignorant little Kraut'.

Next morning, after a night of indigestion, Graham telephoned to Charlotte Bramall.

Before he pushed the buttons, Graham rehearsed his approach.

He hypothesised that the girl rebelled against a stifling and overprotective atmosphere, as it was conceivable that Giles one day would. That would be the direction in which Victoria would err. Graham had seen it in Battersea. It

followed that in order to communicate with her, Graham
should be remotely polite, should treat her as an adult, as
someone with an independence of lifestyle which she probably had, and a sophistication which she probably had not.

If she had rebelled against her mother, for excessive
maternalism or any other reason, she would not at once
willingly co-operate with an intimate of her mother's.
That, then, must be played down. Should Graham repre-
sent himself as a friend of Giles rather than Victoria? The
girl had evidently known Giles during his Peckham period;
perhaps no more than that; perhaps would now barely
remember him. A suggested friendship with Giles, mere
acquaintance with Victoria, was a beguiling but possibly
counter-productive approach.

Graham chewed the knuckle of his thumb, his boyish
habit when thinking deeply. He not only thought through,
but actually wrote down his opening sentences. In front
of a mirror, which always helped, he practised a polite,
adult voice. He arrived at what had first puzzled him—his
declared interest in the matter, his ostensible motivation.

He was taking all this trouble because of *Fair Play*, bile
and the promise of a feeling of power. And it was possible
that he might have the selling of the porcelain.

'May I speak, please, to Miss Charlotte Bramall?' said
Graham in his cool voice.

'Who is that?' said a voice, female, young, which might
have been the girl he wanted or a different girl. Even in
those three clipped syllables there was a note of alarm,
suspicion.

Why?

Graham realised with a shock—though it was something
he ought to have thought of—that in Peckham 'Miss Charlotte Bramall' was not a form of address in common use.
'Miss' was a floater. It would be on a letter, too. He
had made himself sound like a lawyer or an Inspector of
Police.

It was possible that he was already talking to Charlotte Bramall.

He said, 'She won't know my name. I am called Graham Whittingham-Barnes.'

He knew that this, though true, was in Peckham barely credible.

Reading from his script, he said: 'I am bothering Miss Bramall entirely for information which I think she may be able to give me.'

'What information?'

'Am I addressing Miss Bramall?'

'No.'

'May I ask who I am addressing?'

'My name is Black.'

Black. It meant nothing to Graham. The tone sounded blackish, thundery.

'I can of course conduct my enquiry through you,' said Graham, departing from his script. 'But it would be convenient to talk to Miss Bramall.'

'What is this about?'

'It concerns, hum, inheritance. Not hers, I think. Somebody else's. As I say, I am bothering her purely for information. There is, I am afraid, nothing in this as far as I know for her, nor for me, but I believe there is something most notable in it for somebody else.'

Graham had returned to his script. He thought this line would get a reaction. Apparently it did: he heard a muffled exchange of female voices, as though a hand were being held over the mouthpiece of the other telephone.

Emmee had picked up the telephone, but Lottie could equally well have done so. They were sitting side by side on the collapsed and legless travesty they called a sofa, the telephone on the floor between them.

Lottie could thus hear the caller's voice; she heard him announce himself, and she heard the yappy and wah-wah tones of a different world.

Emmee, as she listened, saw the wariness in Lottie's eyes.

'I'd better talk to him,' murmured Lottie.

'You needn't.'

'He knows where I am. Who did he say he was?'

'I can't remember.'

Lottie took the telephone from Emmee.

'Charlotte Bramall speaking,' said a quite different voice, as young or younger but more expensive.

Victoria's daughter. How more than extraordinary. Now that he was having this conversation, Graham could hardly believe that he was having it.

He said, slightly adapting his script: 'Thank you for according me a moment of your time, Miss Bramall. I will state my business as briefly as possible. Please feel free to interrupt me with any questions that occur to you. May I mention first that I devoutly hope that nothing I have to say occasions you either anger or distress.'

There was a kind of grunt at the other end, as of a gentle animal surprised by a predator. The telephone was not hung up. She was still listening.

Graham proceeded: 'I was, in my professional capacity as a supposed expert in certain branches of art, taken by a mutual friend a few days ago to a house in Battersea. I saw there a remarkable collection of Chinese porcelain displayed, as it happened, where it could not possibly be seen, either by visitors or even by residents of the house.'

'Why are you telling me this?'

'It was your mother's house, Miss Bramall,' said Graham, knowing that the girl already knew the answer. He read from his pad: 'I understand that Mrs Lambert inherited the collection, with much else, from her late husband, your father, who had in turn inherited it from generations of his family. I think you will agree that it must have been the intention of his ancestors, who are also your ancestors, that so remarkable a treasure should stay in the family, unless it went to a public collection.'

'Public collection?'

'The British Museum suggests itself.'

'Oh.'

'In default of that, Miss Bramall, this literally invaluable collection should be the property of, or at least held in trust for, descendants of the body of the late Mr Gerald Bramall.'

'Yes.'

'I would not be—harrumph . . .' Graham cleared his throat, having come to a point in his script where he had put an asterisk to indicate the strategic clearing of the throat . . . 'I would not be *stirring things up* except for two unrelated but significant factors.'

'Factors,' echoed the girl, sounding as though she were in danger of losing his drift.

'There are two things that make me feel obliged to *stick my oar in*,' explained Graham, improvising. Returning to his lines, he went on: 'The first factor is that a marvel of oriental art is now condemned to invisibility. They might as well be in a cupboard under the stairs. This is a tragedy and a disgrace.'

'Coo.'

It was not really 'Coo', but it came out awfully like it.

'I do not,' said Graham, 'give a personal *hoot* where the porcelain is displayed, provided that it *is* displayed. This is a matter of responsibility and trusteeship, presently abdicated.'

The soprano grunt again. He might be going too fast. He slowed up.

'I must now,' he said, 'step right out of my ground. But I think this must be said. We agree that the Bramall family would wish the collection to remain in the Bramall family.'

'Yes.'

'As things stand it will probably not do so.'

'Why?'

'Because your mother is pregnant.'

Emmee watched and listened anxiously as Lottie made alternate gurgles of belief and disbelief. Emmee could hear much of what the man was saying. She did not remember the stuff he was talking about; if it had been put, as the man said, where nobody could see it, then obviously she would not remember it.

Lottie's face changed, in response to something Emmee did not hear. There was no knowing what emotion Lottie showed. It might be nausea or anger. If anger, it might be with the speaker or with someone else.

Lottie said, 'There's my half-sister. She may not want to be bothered with any of this. She lives a long way away and she's busy.'

Graham loosed off the bomb because it was high time to do so. He had committed himself to this action, but he was not prepared to spend his life at it. There were other calls on his time, more immediately pressing.

There was a daughter of the first marriage. No son mentioned, so presumably no son.

Graham said: 'I understand you do not wish to give me the name and address of your half-sister. I regret but understand that decision. May I ask you therefore to contact her, give her my name and address, and tell her what I have told you? She can then decide for herself what action to take. I sincerely believe that she should be offered the option. I do not think, with respect, that you have the right to deprive her of the knowledge.'

There was a noise which Graham took to imply assent.

Lottie gestured wildly to pencil and paper, using the hand that held the telephone and thus missing some of what the man was saying.

She wrote down a name and address, and agreed to give them to her half-sister.

'Of course I remember it,' said Lottie. 'Well, I sort of remember it. Things like china don't mean much to a child. It was in a case in the drawing room. People made a fuss of it. Nobody was allowed to touch it. Even if Felicity wants it, I don't see how she can possibly get it.'

'Still, you've said you'll tell her.'

'Oh, I'll tell her.'

'Perhaps Mr Double-Barrel will have some ideas.'

'I don't understand what he's at.'

'You were talking to him.'

'He said it ought to be where people can see it.

'Will it be in Felicity's house?'

'Some people, I suppose. And then I should think she'd leave it to a Museum.'

'Your Ma can't like it very much, if she keeps it in the dark.'

'She likes it all right. She likes anything valuable. I'll ring up Felicity at lunchtime.'

'Mr Whittingham-Barnes? My name is Felicity Lewis. My half-sister rang up at midday. About some china. Yes, of course I remember it. I was twenty when I left home. Of course I remember the china and a lot of other things my parents had. Morally? Morally it'd all belong to my brother, obviously. He's dead. Married? Children? No. He was only a boy when he was drowned. Of course I know the story—I was brought up knowing it. It was my great-grandfather's brother. George Bramall. Captain. He was in the Indian Army. He was in Peking in 1860, at the end of the Opium War. He brought it home. He was married, but he never had any children. It was left to my grandfather, his nephew. There were fifty-two pieces. We remembered that, because it was one for every week of the year. The provenance? Yes, as a matter of fact it is documented. There are letters from George Bramall to his father and to his brother. They were privately printed by his widow.

I'm sure the British Museum has a copy. There's one in a military museum, too, but I forget where. My father's will? Obviously he would have left a thing like that to my brother, if he'd come back and settled down. He might have given his second wife a life interest. I suppose that would be normal. I don't know whether she liked porcelain. I hardly knew her at all. You'd have to ask Charlotte.

'Obviously my father made a new will. He had a new family. We pushed off. I never expected anything.

'Yes, I'd like to have it very much. I haven't got a single thing that belonged to my parents. I left home without anything and I never got anything. Yes, I would put it where people could see it. Of course I would. My parents did. Of course it was never used and hardly ever touched, but people certainly *looked* at it. Ultimately? I don't know. It would depend on where my children live, and how, and who with . . . Not *visible*? Why on earth not? Surely anybody would make room . . .

'I don't in the least mind stirring up trouble, but I can't see that it would do any good . . . Oh. Yes, of course, I understand that if you're a professional . . . Have you? What sort of pressure? *Moral* pressure wouldn't do any . . . Yes, I know, but we simply don't need any more Georgian desks and sideboards . . . Yes, my husband's family had a big . . . As it is, we've got things in store that we can't bring ourselves to . . . No, they're in trust. Not actually by the terms of anybody's will. Yes, we could sell it all and put the money in trust—naturally we've discussed that, but . . . Yes. I don't want to sound unfriendly or ungrateful, but as far as . . . Oh, I see. I've only just seen the point of your question. Yes. Morally I could claim every bloody thing in the house, certainly I could, but I'm not . . . Yes, he is, but it wouldn't look very good if he . . . I agree, much better if it was a complete outsider . . . But what am I supposed to do? How much am I letting myself in for? A caseful of porcelain is only worth . . .

'No, it would never seriously have occurred to us to

contest the will. My brother and I did go away. Nobody threw us out. I don't want to do Charlotte out of . . .

'Oh. Yes, Charlotte told me that her mother . . . It does put a different complexion on . . . She's only just over forty. She can go on for a bit. She's exactly the same age as me.

'I honestly don't know. It never occurred to me to wonder, when I was still at home. There always seemed to be plenty. Looking back on it, we lived very . . . No, not ostentatious, but comfortable, and they entertained . . . And Court Farm sold at a time when . . . On the other hand I suppose she's spent . . .

'He doesn't do anything? Oh, changes fuses. Unless their wiring's pretty crazy that's not exactly a full-time . . . Oh. Yes. She'd like that . . .

'I don't quite see why you're bothering, but I'm not going to look a gift horse . . . Yes, I'll give any number of interviews. Television? Why not? Yes, but truth is a complete defense in a libel action . . . "The greater the truth . . . ?" Yes, but that's only criminal libel, which is an entirely different . . . Safety of the realm, military secrets . . . Yes, I bloody well would. Of course I can prove it, I was there, I was a witness, I was grown up. My mother . . . I'll tell you exactly what happened and I don't care how widely you quote me.'

'From a solicitor *where*?' said Graham to Victoria. 'Good gracious. I wouldn't have thought there *was* a solicitor in . . . It sounds like blackmail to me. A solemn *what*? Let me get this clear. They're offering you a solemn undertaking made in the presence of a solicitor, the signature witnessed . . . No other claims on you at all? Never ever? Fancy. I said, "Fancy". Ejaculation of amazement, if you'll forgive the expression . . . Then I think, dear heart, you'd better . . . Yes, *I've* seen them, because you very sweetly . . . Not much, honestly. Of course if they were real . . . Of course I'm sure, my sweet, I've been studying this subject for . . . Somebody switched them, I suppose, some time in the last 125 years. It's often done with pictures and, as you know, jewellery—you keep the real thing in the bank, and . . . There are lots of convincing copies of Gainsborough and Reynolds, the originals being far away in Gettyland or Yale . . . Stately homes teem with . . . That's what I'd do. Only you can say how nasty they can turn, if they do turn nasty. I don't know the history, do I? Only what you've told me. I'm all for a quiet life, myself, and I'd simply hate some details of my personal history being given headlines in the . . .

'I wonder how she knew the porcelain's in your hall. There is a Judas in your midst. Is someone so very resentful that . . . ? Of course if your conscience is . . . You *could* snap your fingers in their . . . Oh indeed, indeed, I accept whatever you tell me, dear, I accept that there was a will and that nobody disputed it, or if there wasn't a will then the gifts were made in his lifetime . . .

'I'm simply saying that if it was me I'd be bothered about the future. Once they start, there's no knowing how much they might not ask for. Break up your nest about your head. Silver, glass . . . Money as well. But this way, from what you tell me . . .

'It's simply not the sort of publicity which, personally, I . . .

'Yes, take legal advice by all means. But if you go to a lawyer you'll have to be very, very frank. I understand the suicide . . . Darling, *nobody* has nothing to conceal . . . Well, if you don't want my advice, consult someone who . . . But if you start tangling with somebody really bitter, and if this legal solemn undertaking thing goes from their lawyer to your lawyer . . .

'I'm simply telling you what I'd do, if it was something I kept in the hall and that wasn't very valuable, and I was guaranteed the safety of everything else I had . . .'

• • •

'I wouldn't be bothering,' said Felicity to her husband, 'if she didn't keep the whole lot in the dark.'

'But this chap who rang up, that Charlotte put you on to—'

'*He's* only bothering because she keeps it in the dark. She doesn't know about it or care about it at all. He thinks it ought to have a better home.'

'Is that really all?'

'No, of course not. There's a bit of malice, too. She's snubbed him or something. But he wants to stay in with her.'

'Why would anybody want that?'

'I don't know. Business. Perhaps he fancies her toy-boy.'

'And are you honestly only stirring things up because she keeps the china in the dark?'

'Of course not. I'm allowed all the malice I want.'

'I'm damned if Stodge gets my cups,' said Victoria.

'*I am at a loss to understand your letter*,' said Victoria's letter after it had been edited by the woman from the secretarial agency. '*There was a collection of porcelain as described by you, but it suffered an accident. The fragments have been kept, and are in a sack. Your client is welcome to them.*'

Victoria signed the letter. She went out into the garden, although the autumn afternoon was growing chilly, and with the big hammer from Giles's workshop struck a few more satisfying blows at the sack which held the bits of broken china. Stodge could have the sack if she came and got it. Otherwise it would go to the dustmen, who would have to be paid extra for taking it.

C·H·A·P·T·E·R

11

'It was an accident,' said Victoria. 'It's a pity, really. It was a workman. He was supposed to be a builder, but he was just a navvy.'

Graham Whittingham-Barnes felt himself goggling, looking at the empty cabinet. The glass fronting the cabinet was complete, untouched.

'Anybody who likes,' said Victoria, 'can stick it all together again. Giles started to try, but he said it would take a hundred men a hundred years.'

'I don't understand how the glass . . .'

'Nor did we. We weren't here. Cosette and Mrs Mollam were upstairs. Mrs Calloway was in the kitchen.'

'Where were you?'

'Out. The man saw what he'd done, and bolted. Nobody's seen him since. He's disappeared off the face of the earth. He was called Sid. That's all we know. Somebody recommended him.'

'Who?'

'Somebody local. Dagobert might remember, I mean Huxtable.'

'Surely the cabinet was always locked?'

'Yes, of course. I have the key. I've got it still. I'd unlocked it. We were going to wash it all. Lux and warm water, and then rinse in clean water. One by one. That's

why I unlocked the cabinet. It would have been a labour
of love. We think he must have had a brainstorm.'

'And he's run away into the West Highlands?'

'Probably three streets away. He's bolted back into his
warren.'

'Would you recognise him?'

'I suppose so. One doesn't study the faces of builders'
labourers. Yes, of course I'd know him.'

'Would the servants?'

'I don't know. Possibly not. If they saw him at all it
was in the dark, here, in the hall. He didn't go anywhere
else.'

'Why was he here?'

'He came asking for work.'

'And you left him alone in the house?'

'He wasn't alone in the house. It was full of people.'

'He must have made a hell of a noise.'

'Yes, but Mrs Calloway had the mixer on in the kitchen,
and Mrs Mollam was hoovering upstairs, and Cosette was
cleaning my bath. The place was like a factory. That's one
of the reasons I went out.'

'And Giles?'

'He was with me.'

'Yes, of course. Yes, of course.'

'I see it as a howl of impotent rage,' said Victoria. 'This
ape comes straight here from his slum, he sees the way we
live and the things we live among . . .'

'Not so very impotent,' said Graham, 'if he pulverised
fifty-two pieces of Chinese porcelain.'

'They sent me a copy of her letter,' said Felicity. 'If
she couldn't have it, nobody could. I suppose she's now
claiming the insurance.'

'My God,' said Graham. 'I hadn't thought of that.'

'What?'

'I said, I don't know her well enough to guess.'

• • •

'I don't know her well enough to guess,' said Graham to Lottie. 'The only two explanations anybody can think of are both frankly incredible. The vanishing labourer with a violent grudge against wealth and culture? Like Chinese student activists in the Cultural Revolution, bent on destroying all vestiges of civilisation? Why did he stay his hand? Why stop at the porcelain? Why not slash the pictures and smash the Waterford?'

'He was frightened of the noise he'd made.'

'Yes, so would I have been, but he must have been making it for quite a long time. Thank you, most welcome,' said Graham to Emmee, who had come in with instant coffee on a tray. 'Your sister's explanation is probably widely believed amongst your mother's acquaintance,' he said to Lottie, 'but, as I say, I barely know her personally and I can't judge.'

'But did she have to give the china to Lottie's sister?' said Emmee. 'She was the widow. She could say it had either been given to her or left to her.'

'The moral pressure being brought to bear was very nearly irresistible. The threat of publicity.'

'Blackmail,' said Emmee.

'Yes, blackmail.'

'I don't know Felicity very well,' said Lottie, 'but she's never struck me as being capable of blackmail.'

'I don't suppose it was her idea.'

'Whose, then? Yours?' said Emmee.

'No. All I know of the history is what Lottie and her sister have told me. I was taken to the house, just once, by a mutual friend. We went in his car. I couldn't now even tell you the address. I went specifically to look at the porcelain. I barely met the *châtelaine*, although I think I know many people who know her. My eyes were glued to the cabinet. I had to send for lights. I am told that, empty, the shelves are a lugubrious sight. The cabinet itself is late Victorian and without merit. What she'll do with it now I can't imagine. Perhaps fill it with Copenhagen figurines.'

Graham was genuinely appalled at the results of his muck-stirring. As connoisseur and as entrepreneur he was aghast at the destruction; he did not feel guilty, exactly, as nobody could have predicted what happened, but he felt in small measure responsible. He owed the Bramalls something. If he could not repay the older daughter he could perhaps make some reparation, on account, to the younger.

That was his reason for coming all the way to Peckham in which, as far as he knew, he had never set foot before. Emmee thought it was very rum, and Lottie thought it was a bit rum. Neither recognised him from the party of sixteen months before, at which, to be sure, he had kept a low profile.

By this time he had had half a dozen conversations on the telephone with Lottie, and two or three with the other child. Lottie was a bigger girl than he had imagined from her voice: Emmee a much smaller one. As to their lifestyle and dress, he had guessed about right.

He was aware that he was exactly what they expected.

He was perfectly prepared to sit on a cushion on the floor—he had done so at numberless parties in Hampstead and Wandsworth and Putney. He was prepared to drink instant coffee, although Rudi would have refused it. He had come to do penance, but he was moderately enjoying himself. He knew the more affluent fringes of Emmee's street-market world, and he knew one of the wine-bars where Lottie had worked.

The young, Graham found, were more classless than he liked, but they took people as they found them in a refreshingly honest way. These girls undoubtedly had gay friends. There was no need to pretend about anything, except his intimacy with Victoria. He had a second cup of coffee and smoked three cigarettes.

It was because he was sitting near the gas-fire, facing away from the wall, that he did not see the picture over the fire until he got up to leave.

'I say I say I say,' he said, like an old-fashioned stand-up comedian.

'It's not framed and I don't think it's finished,' said Lottie.

'Start telling me about this,' said Graham, 'and don't stop until we both fall down from exhaustion.'

He heard that there were numbers of paintings stacked in various parts of the range of buildings, or barracks, where they were, that few of them were finished and fewer framed, that an exhibition in some remote place was a future possibility, and that the artist would be coming in later, probably, when he got off the work he should not have been doing.

'I can't stay,' said Graham. 'I may not. I must not. You have my telephone number. You will without fail induce or instruct this fellow to get in touch with me. I require your absolute promise. He's not tied up with a gallery? What fools they are. He was evicted from his studio? He must get another. He can't afford framing? He must be helped. If I said I was motivated entirely by generous enthusiasm I would lie. None of this will happen overnight.'

'What are you motivated by?' said Lottie. 'If it's not a rude question.'

'Money and fame,' said Graham. 'Perm any two from two. Bless you for the scrummy coffee. I shall be seriously angry if your friend does not contact me within twenty-four hours.'

'I don't know,' said Lottie. 'He gives me the creeps.'

'Yes, I know,' said Emmee. 'But you've got to tell James. You can't let it go by default. It's James who's got to decide.'

'He's such a child.'

'He's a child without a nursery or any toys. This might be a chance to get them. We can make sure he doesn't sign everything away. You can't just pretend Mr Double-Barrel never happened. He'd be back again. We can't keep giving him coffee, it's too expensive.'

'Oh my oh my oh my,' said Graham Whittingham-Barnes. 'What a clever boy you are. These twelve constitute the Pembrokeshire sequence?'

'When I look at them now I wonder if they're not a bit repetitive.'

'Somebody very ignorant could say the same thing of Monet or Bonnard. Think how many painters have done repeated explorations of the same material. In commercial terms, we might not expect a single collector to buy more than two of these, but even if I took your point, somewhat similar pictures at opposite ends of London are not going to throw the art world into a frenzy of contemptuous boredom. Now *this* one and *this* one are to me full-sized studies on board for finished paintings on canvas, to be executed in the warmth and comfort of the studio.'

'Yes. I haven't got a canvas or a studio.'

'We must do something about that. Mark you, the studies are saleable. Your sketchbooks? What are these? Italy? Tuscany?'

'Tuscany was overcrowded. These are Umbria.'

'Oh yes. The *smell* of Umbria. What a lot of work you've given yourself. I think you're going to need six months before you're ready to show, even if we find you a studio tomorrow, which we won't. And then we have this other distinctive sequence, these visions of hell.'

'Restaurant kitchens.'

'Lurid and seething. Baroque illustrations to the *Inferno*. Not as liveable with as these or these. Not comfortable centrepieces for dainty parlours. But you could say the same about Francis Bacon, couldn't you?'

'I'm not claiming comparison—'

'I know you're not. People will compare you to all sorts of people, and you should ignore them. Influences I do see.'

'I hoped they weren't visible.'

'Influences are indispensable, not only for forming critical judgements, but also as part of an artist's equipment. It would be ludicrous and arrogant to embark on a career or painting without some awareness of the achievements of the past. You don't want to be a modern primitive—at least, I wouldn't advise it. In these Pembrokeshire pictures I see a touch of the benign genius of Turner. In your kitchens I see a handling of light which pays distant and proper respect to the ghost of Rembrandt, even when, as here, you are semi-abstract. And when you work up those Italian sketches, I hope we shall see echoes of the High Renaissance and of the French seventeenth century.'

'Yes,' said James, not knowing how seriously to take any of this.

'He's not exactly my cup of tea,' said James to Lottie, 'since you're exactly my cup of tea. But I think he knows what he's talking about.'

'That's what we thought,' said Emmee.

'He's going to lend me what I need. Money, I mean. At the going bank-rate.'

'Blimey.'

'He says that's what he has to borrow it at. The difference is that his credit's good and mine isn't. He'll accept the work I've done as collateral for up to £10,000. Then he pays himself back with a percentage of my sales.'

'How big a percentage?'

'Forty.'

'That's surely too much.'

'Not really. From his point of view this is a high-risk speculation. He's got to trust me to work like hell. He's got his eye on a studio. If that works out it'll be almost free.'

'There must be a catch in that.'

'Yes, I'm alert for the catch. But I bloody well need the studio.'

• • •

'There is a complication,' said Graham, 'which quite frankly involves a blatant illegality. Personally I don't mind.'

'Go on,' said James, scenting the promised catch.

'Your landlord's lease specifically forbids subletting for any commercial or professional purpose. I see the point. It's a classy residential area which has become very expensive in the last few years owing to enforcement of this policy. The estate doesn't want a rash of dentists or betting-shops or wholesalers. You'd think your harmless activity would be immune, but it isn't. You'll be a house-guest with a hobby involving the smell of turpentine.'

'I hope he doesn't mind the smell.'

'She.'

'Ah.'

'No, I don't think she'll mind. What we have to preserve is secrecy. This is not to protect you but to protect her. You could plead absolute ignorance of the terms of her lease, but she can't. So when a van arrives unloading canvases, they must be camouflaged as something else. You must be camouflaged as something else. You may not wear a beret or a flowing, artistic cravat. You may not set up your easel in Battersea Park. You may not use that address or telephone number for anything remotely touching your professional activities. This is an absolute condition of your even being allowed to see the place—of your even meeting the landlord. Name, address, everything must be totally secret. I think the lady is being over-careful, but these are the conditions she is making. When you set off, from wherever you set off from, for your day's work or your week's work, since I suppose you will principally live there, you will drop off the face of the earth, like the enraged artisan whom we are to imagine destroying that porcelain . . . Before *any further proceedings*, I must extract from you a solemn oath that even to your nearest and dearest you will not say where your studio is or to whom it belongs.'

'My friends can be trusted, Graham.'
'Not by your landlord they can't.'

'Why?' said Rudi. 'Why do you want to get him *there*?'
'Those rooms are perfect and that space is wasted.'
'Giles doesn't think so.'
'Who cares what Giles thinks? James is more important than Giles. James has got to have a studio which I can afford. I am now an expert on the availability and cost of studios in London which have the facilities James needs. He is an expert on what he needs, and I accept his word in the matter. Never will he find a better place, and the cost to myself will be almost nothing.'
'There is more in your mind than that,' said Rudi.
'Yes, but you may not believe it.'
'Maybe not.'
'I want to help that girl, that Lottie. I like her. She's had a lousy time and she deserves a change of luck. There's no way I can help her directly, except by spending money that I haven't got and she wouldn't accept, but I can help her like this. This is what she'd most want in the world, the best turn anybody could do her.'
'But *there*? In her mother's house?'
'She won't know it's there. She wouldn't let him go if she knew. Then James would never paint a picture and I would never make a fortune.'
'I think it is sick,' said Rudi, 'that you should send James *there*.'
'I don't mind being sick as long as I get rich.'

'You must be James Drummond. How do you do? My name is Debonnaire Courtenay.'
They shook hands and sat down, in a corner of Jules Bar in Jermyn Street.
She was not in her first youth, but she was not so very old, either. James found it impossible to guess her age, and would have felt impertinent trying. She had long, straight,

raven-black hair, grey eyes, and a very smooth pale skin. She was dressed in a long maroon silk coat, with a brooch in the form of a spray of diamond flowers in the lapel. Her make-up was unassertive. Her scent was disturbing, and to James unknown. (He was more familiar, from his childhood, with the scent of carbolic soap.) She unbuttoned her tent-like coat when she sat down; this revealed her pregnancy, previously to be guessed at only by a certain languor of movement. The baby looked pretty imminent.

'I understand,' she said, 'Mr Whittingham-Barnes is joining us. But since you were obviously you, I decided not to wait.'

'Why was I obviously me?' said James, smiling in response to the warmth of her smile.

'I didn't think you were a public-relations man or a gossip-column journalist. I was told to look for a very tall young artist. Actually I'd steeled myself for a beard and a fisherman's jersey.'

James laughed. He was glad he had dressed as he had. He was not actually wearing a suit, but he came close to it: he had decent grey flannel trousers and a dark brown tweed coat (found by Emmee and fitting adequately), with a collar and tie and rehabilitated dark brown American loafers. His corn-coloured hair (cut two days before by Emmee) was no longer than that of many a financial whizz-kid. He did not feel strange, dressed up as respectably as this. Lottie had been pleased with his appearance, and Emmee had passed it. It was an occasion for unobtrusiveness, for protective coloration. If he had to prove he was an artist, he could do so by way of his paintings.

'What I can't contemplate,' she said, 'is any upheaval just at the moment.' She gestured humorously at her own vanished waistline. 'I'm afraid you'll have to stand in the queue for a few weeks. One arrival at a time is all my household can cope with. After the dust has settled . . .'

Drinks arrived, already ordered by Debonnaire Courtenay. It was a bottle of champagne.

'It sounds very lavish and ridiculous,' she said, 'but it's actually the only thing I can drink. The doctors say I should have whatever I fancy.'

'How lucky for me,' said James.

'The creature's booked in for the beginning of February,' she said. 'A little over six weeks off. Then I shall be lying about for a bit, and then perhaps we can be in business. Ah, here's Mr Whittingham-Barnes, isn't it? I thought I remembered you. We have made ourselves known to one another, as you see. Sit down and have some of my medicine. Mr Drummond, fill all the glasses. I'm going to call you James, and you are to call me Debonnaire. The trouble is that everything with me is in the pending-tray at the moment. My brain is addled. I don't know what I shall decide in the middle of February. I think I know, but I'm not sure, and until the party's complete I can't commit myself. Does that sound very stupid and feminine? It does to me. Shall we have something to eat, now that we're here? What about smoked salmon sandwiches?'

Graham paid for them. He said to James, 'I'm putting these down on your account.'

'What's he like?' said Lottie.

'She.'

'Oh. What's she like?'

'Friendly. Very chic and expensive. Nothing can be decided for about two months.'

'But you can't wait two months!'

'I won't, if anybody can find me another studio. My parents can't find one in Fife and my grandparents can't find one in Wales—'

'Thank God for that.'

'I'd have to have heat and light, as well as hundreds of pounds worth of materials. So I'd have to have a job. If I had a proper job I wouldn't have time to work. In the old days I would have found a patron. Probably a church.

Then they would have told me what to paint. I don't know what to do, Lottie. I'm stuck. Debonnaire's attic sounds by far the best bet I ever heard of, but it's at least two months and it's odds against anyway.'

'She can't be called Debonnaire.'

'You wouldn't have thought so, would you, but that's what she says.'

'Where does she live? Is the studio where she lives?'

'I don't know where she lives. Yes, it's the top floor of her house. I don't know if she's even married. She never mentioned a husband. It must be somewhere in London.'

'Would you live there?'

'It depends where it is. If it's round the corner from here, no. But if it's in Hampstead Garden Suburb, then I'd have to be there some nights.'

'Can you work by artificial light?'

'Some jobs. The days will be getting longer soon. Apparently it's two rooms, one with a north window. Water's laid on. I could heat it with a blower.'

'I should think you'd want to go and see it.'

'Of course I do, but until she's decided she wants a tenant like me there's no point.'

'Debonnaire. Was she wearing a wedding-ring?'

'I don't know. She had a lot of rings. I think she's a witch.'

'How does Graham Whipsnade-Zoo come to know her?'

'I expect she buys things. She looks as though she does.'

'She might be a good contact, then, even if you don't get the studio.'

'That's what Graham says. But if I don't get a studio I might as well not have the contacts.'

'Inner cities. Derelict buildings. Factories that have gone bust. There *must* be places.'

'I know, and the minute I find them I'm booted out of them.'

'Be of good courage. Thurber's bringing some wine.'

'Debonnaire gave me champagne.'
'I don't want to hear about it.'

December was mild, but the calendar excused voluminous clothes.

Victoria had never looked better. Cosette said so (sharp Gallic observation) and Victoria knew it was true. Pregnancy gave a bloom to her skin and a lovely languor to her movements. Her son was quiet. He would be born in the harshest season of the year, but the cold claws of winter would be kept away from him by central heating, double glazing, thermal blankets, and love. The nurse had been interviewed, a comfortable and reassuring body. She would come in the middle of January. The rooms for nurse and baby were all ready, and had been for two years.

Victoria watched her diet, and took care of herself. It was not herself but her son of whom she was careful. She was the custodian of the future. Giles was excited. He was frightened for her. He worshipped at the shrine of her motherhood. He tried his very best to anticipate her every want. Sometimes she laughed at herself, for the whimsical things she wanted at all hours of the day and night.

Victoria entertained, from the sofa in the drawing room. People said it was a levée, but Victoria laughed at herself as a Bourbon monarch. She did not take herself as seriously as other people took her. Christmas presents began to pile up on the table in the hall, where the glass-fronted cabinet had been.

There was apparently to be some kind of Christmas party at the place in Haslemere where Cosette's child was kept. Cosette wanted to go to it; she said they wanted her help at the party. The idea was preposterous. A roomful of idiot children would not notice one adult more or less. Victoria needed her. Victoria had looked for greater loyalty, after all her kindness. Cosette left the room with no expression on her face. Probably she had not really wanted to go to the party; probably she was glad of an excuse not to go all that way in midwinter to organise games for children who were incapable of playing games. She was needed where she was, night and day.

They planned to spend Christmas very quietly. 'Just the two-and-a-half of us,' said Victoria to her friends, laughing. It did people good to hear that merry laughter. Victoria did all her Christmas shopping by telephone. She gave Giles a bit extra to buy something special for herself. Victoria looked forward to sitting up in bed and unwrapping it on Christmas morning, after Giles had brought her breakfast. Of such little things is happiness made.

James fumed. He was stuck. He was in a Catch-22 situation. He could not ask his father to cancel his subscription to the golf club, or his grandfathers to give up their televisions. The sacrifices such as these of which they were theoretically capable would have made no real difference.

Some of his friends were struggling more successfully than he was against equal odds. He could not work if he was shivering; he could not work in mittens. Because he was thin, he felt the cold. He could prepare a canvas, draw, paint an interior by artificial light, but not paint a landscape. He could not satisfy himself working in oils on cardboard or hardboard.

'I'm unreasonable. I expect too much,' he said.

'You're not. You don't,' said Lottie. She would have done murder for him, but she had no money to give him.

James's mother sent him the money for a return fare to St Andrews. This was a way of making sure that he came to them for Christmas. He knew that it was time he saw them; he had spent the previous Christmas night on the sofa of friends in Shepherd's Bush. He took sketchbooks and pencils and ballpoints, although he doubted if East Fife in late December was promising outdoor material.

Thurber's parents did not really expect him in Jersey. If he got there it might be impossible to get back. He was wanted for some gigs in pubs over Christmas. He would not be short of company. He would never be short of company.

Emmee was booked in as usual with her mother. Any other arrangement would have been impossibly cruel. Mrs Black expected Lottie, and Lottie expected to be expected.

James so filled a sketchbook with drawings of his fellow passengers on the crowded train—women asleep, men drinking, fretful children—that he had to buy another one in St Andrews for the return journey. He knew that, if he ever had the chance to work them up into paintings, he would have to fight off the too-obvious influence of the chilly, monumental realism of Edward Hopper. He had become skilful, in the restaurant kitchens, in hiding his sketchbook behind a newspaper—in hiding what he was doing in a pretence of solving a crossword or picking winners at a race-meeting. This was not because he was self-conscious about drawing, but because people became self-conscious about being drawn. They sat primly, straightened their ties, arranged their skirts over their knees. He wanted them relaxed and messy, with drooping eyelids and newspapers slipping off their laps. He wanted children with smeared faces, untidy hair, sucking their thumbs or upside down in their seats.

He wanted to show the drawings immediately to Lottie and to Graham Whittingham-Barnes. He showed them instead to his mother, who was quite kind about them.

The previous Christmas with Emmee's mother, Lottie had not had anybody to miss. She found that she had missed not missing anybody. There was something incomplete about a life when you went away and there was nobody to yearn for. This second Christmas, the gap was well and truly filled up. Lottie missed James dreadfully, all the time. She hoped very hard that nobody let James carve a turkey or chop up kindling. He would be no kind of an artist, and not much of a lover, with his hand lopped off.

She had tried all year not to be too obtrusively maternal. Now that he was out of sight she could *feel* as maternal as she wanted.

It was comforting to know at last, with lovely certainty, what the future was.

Thurber came down, in a borrowed car, for lunch on Boxing Day. Emmee's mother was in a flutter at having a man in the house. She expected Thurber to eat as much as the rest of them put together, which he did.

Victoria's Christmas morning was all beautifully as she had planned it. China tea, then breakfast on a tray in bed, the room warm, Giles in the brocade dressing-gown she had given him in response to one of her whims, the presents shyly brought in and eagerly unwrapped, the kisses of gratitude, the happy companionship, the gurgle of her bathwater, and the waft of Floris from the open bathroom door . . .

Victoria let Giles have a second pink gin before lunch, because it was Christmas Day.

Victoria made a Boxing Day Resolution, which was to stay in bed until her son arrived. She was warmed by efficient central heating and by fleecy shawls. She was warmed by the love that surrounded her.

James found it impossible to work while he was in Fife. It was too cold out of doors, and too distracting indoors. It was not that his parents looked over his shoulder, but that they took such trouble not to do so. It was not that they expressed their lack of faith in his artistic future, but that they were at such pains not to do so. It was not that his mother underfed him, but that she thought she was doing so. It was not that his father failed to find interesting things for James to do, but that he thought James thought he failed. They were too full of anxious goodwill to communicate with. James struggled unsuccessfully against feeling ungrateful. He longed for the train and his sketchbook; he longed for Lottie.

Victoria's levées became more Bourbon than before, although she did not, like the king, actually get out of bed. People came from all over London, many bringing flowers and so forth. Giles said that it was a pilgrimage, that her bedside was a place of pilgrimage. She laughed at herself (as, thank God, she was still able to do)—she laughed at the image of her little self in a niche or on an altar, flower-bedecked, offerings piled at her feet, censers swung, prayers intoned. Yet, for all she laughed, there was something of such a feeling during that January. Voices were hushed; the air was scented. There was something of worship in the faces of her friends. There was something votive in their gifts. No dirty shepherds came, but there were certainly wise men. There were men who were almost kings; baronets, anyway. They brought gold. If not frankincense and myrrh, they brought Floris bath essence. Victoria laughed at herself, for the turn her fancy was taking. Her visitors wondered at her merry laughter, at such a time, and went away with a new courage.

James was obsessed with his work, and Lottie was obsessed with James. There was nothing either of them could do about it.

James paced about the narrow rooms of Peckham like George Gambol in a bad mood; Lottie could have sworn that the black cloud over his head was visible, tangible.

Graham Whittingham-Barnes was excited by the two sketchbooks of James's train journeys. He could have lent James money—he did lend him some money—but without studio space there was no point in the kind of investment that was needed. James said apologetically that he knew from experience that he needed room to spread himself about—that the result would look like a gipsy encampment, but that was how he needed to work. He said that when he started he would be working on never less than two and probably three or four canvases at once. Graham waved away these explanations as though he were using a cigarette holder.

Just at the moment there was no news of Debonnaire's intentions.

Debonnaire became a mythical figure to Lottie. She was not sure that this person existed. James had said he thought she was a witch.

Always alert and diligently searching, James, Graham, Marcus, Emmee and other friends heard of studios or places that might be used as studios. James saw some, Graham others; sometimes they went together, and sometimes took Rudi or Lottie. There were problems of heat, light, gigantic deposits, unacceptable terms in the lease—problems that appeared singly or, more often, in combination.

James fretted. This had an effect like that of a pebble thrown into a pool. Lottie fretted, in anguished sympathy, which caused to fret the people she worked with and waited on. Emmee fretted, and so did Thurber, and other people in the street markets, and the people who bought and sold things. Marcus Hills fretted, as he tried to make James eat a proper breakfast, and so therefore did other deeply serious people in the fringe theatre. James's Catch-22 predicament became well known throughout that extensive subculture, and well-wishers crowded forward with suggestions. None of the ideas, from any such source, were any good to James at all, for all the familiar reasons and for various new reasons.

It was reasonable of Victoria to want Giles with her whenever she wanted him to be with her. At such a time it was her right. At any time it was her right. It was no good if he was reading, because he pulled the blinds down on himself. He might as well have been a mile away for all the attention he paid to what she said. To her mind, that was simple bad manners; she knew she was old-fashioned in the value she put on good manners; but she did, and there it was; she often said so; people respected her for it.

Sometimes she sent him away, because, like a little girl, she wanted a girl-to-girl chat with a friend, or a girl-to-boy chat with a friend. Then he went upstairs to his workshop or downstairs to the drawing room, until she rang the silver bell that she kept by her bedside.

She did not really like him to be either upstairs or downstairs, out of her sight. Upstairs he was probably reading, showing off by reading something in a foreign language. Downstairs he might be reading and he might be drinking too. He came to her with gladness as soon as she rang her bell.

One day she was having a long and cosy talk with Freda Beery, who had arrived at the rather strange hour of three in the afternoon. Giles went upstairs. It was exactly a fortnight before Victoria's son was due. Freda wanted to talk about her own confinements, and her then husband's infidelities at those times. Victoria said that was a terrible and treacherous way to behave, and Freda heartily agreed. Freda left soon after four, because she was meeting somebody for tea at Fortnums.

Giles was slow answering her bell. Victoria thought she heard bumps from upstairs, perhaps a laugh or giggle. Giles was long minutes coming down, and when at last he came he had a rumpled, tousled look, as though he had just pulled on all his clothes in a hurry.

Cosette.

Cosette was only thirty-two, skinny, with narrow hips and thin legs; she was one of those skinny women whose breasts are all nipple. She was handsome enough in a peasant way, with corkscrew black hair, heavy eyebrows, bold black eyes.

Mrs Mollam had left before lunch; she would not be back until the morning. Mrs Calloway had left after lunch;

she would not be back until seven. It was not one of Mr Childers's days. Dagobert was three streets away. Except for herself, marooned in her bed, Giles and Cosette had the house to themselves.

Victoria would never have thought of anything so horrible, unless Freda Beery had told her those stories.

The sense of anger and betrayal filled Victoria's mouth like vomit.

She said nothing and showed nothing.

Giles said he had been asleep, on one of the wooden chairs in his workroom. He had fallen heavily asleep, unusually, probably because of the wine Victoria had encouraged him to drink at lunchtime.

Victoria let him talk, watching and listening, herself giving away nothing.

He said he had woken slowly, no doubt because of the wine. He had been stiff, because of falling asleep in an upright chair. His hair and clothes were probably a mess, because, hearing at last Victoria's bell, he had come at once without even looking at a mirror. He said he hoped she had not been ringing long, that he had not kept her waiting.

Cosette came in, with some ironed and aired night-dresses. She went silently to the chest of drawers, and put the nightdresses away. She glanced at Giles, but she avoided Victoria's eye. Her own eye looked sly and secretive.

She was French, a harlot. She already had one bastard. Victoria saw that as she crossed the room she was walking in a new way which was meant to be seductive and suggestive. Victoria was suddenly certain that she was wearing no underclothes. No line was visible across her narrow buttocks, when she leaned to put the nightdresses in the drawer. She hardly needed to wear a bra, so flat was her chest; Victoria was certain she was not wearing one; no strap showed under the thin black stuff of her dress. She was wearing stockings or tights. She had given herself time to pull those on. Giles had given himself time to pull all his clothes on, though not to make himself tidy. Cosette was wearing no make-up. She never did wear make-up. Her corkscrew curls, cut short, were of the kind that look the same tidy or untidy.

How long had this been going on?

Victoria was not one to jump to hasty conclusions, which might be completely unfair or a little bit unfair. Giving nothing away, she looked and listened; she watched them both for signs of guilt.

A look passed between them, as Cosette straightened from the drawer. She glanced at him and he at her. Victoria intercepted the glance. She was angry to think how stupid they must think her, to exchange 'speaking looks' in front of her.

Cosette shut the drawer, using her thighs to push it shut. She made a highly suggestive gesture out of shutting the drawer. It was insulting to Victoria. It was treacherous and disgusting.

It came to Victoria that she had a duty—she owed a debt—not only to herself but also to her son.

Victoria knew exactly and with heaven-sent certainty what she might possibly, probably, conceivably, under certain circumstances, do. She was not yet able to decide how to do it, or capable of doing it even if she had decided, because she was In Waiting, a Lady in Waiting, a Hand-maiden. She figured herself to herself as an old purse enclosing a new sovereign.

'A scruffy, worn-out old wallet,' she said, once again disarmingly laughing at herself.

She watched them, careful to jump to no premature con-clusions: and their guilt was writ large on their faces.

C·H·A·P·T·E·R

12

Lying like a lovely statue, motionless as marble, Victoria could allow her mind to race. Of course it always raced, but she noticed it more when she was doing nothing else.

She never had time to waste over jigsaw puzzles, but now her busy brain was fitting together a thousand odd-shaped, odd-coloured pieces in a large design. She was not inventing but reproducing, recreating, interpreting, seeing lines and colours assume a horrible coherence under her busy mental fingers.

Looks. Absences. Noise and silence. Words spoken for which there was no need; words expected but unspoken. Why should he not say 'Good morning' in the morning? Why should he say 'Hullo' in the middle of the afternoon? Dishevelment, touslement, delays, bumps, half-heard insolent giggles. Why should there be no bumps when he was supposed to be up in his workshop and supposed to be mending something? Why should there be bumps when she was supposed to be resting in her room? How long? How often? Exactly when and where? In the middle of the morning? In the middle of the afternoon? Absent-mindedness. Preoccupation. Brusqueness. A hint of thumb to the nose, of 'if only you knew!' And then excessive politeness, considerateness—your cushion is just right? The lamp just so? Enough ice in your drink? Out to the kitchen for more ice. She there, ironing. Fumble and fondle. Not now. Oh you are awful. The roar of the tap over the ice-tray hides the sound of whisper, giggle, zip, the snapping of elastic, the suck of a tongue.

Victoria found it difficult to bring herself to believe that it had been going on from the beginning. She did not believe it. She was used to being ruthlessly honest with herself, and she did not allow herself to abandon the habit now.

It was in the spring of the previous year, between their return from Jamaica and the Mayday conception of her son. The delusive and tempting spring, full of the phallic thrust of daffodils and tulips exposing their vertical urgency in the beds. Full of girls leaving off their woollies, windows being opened onto sunsets, dawdlers in the parks, nasty goings-on in bus stations . . .

With a slut like that there would be no need of wooing. The flash of a ten-pound note and her skirt's round her waist and her knickers round her ankles.

Victoria was suddenly disgusted and terrified. What had Cosette caught, from the chauffeurs and waiters who screwed her in the backs of cars? What Giles from her? What Victoria from Giles? What disgusting disease, caught at those removes, would disfigure Debonnaire's boy?

Perhaps the languorous summer, dawdling August, when a drawn curtain turned an afternoon room into a magic cave . . . golden September, when wheat-straws and virgins lay helpless in sun-flooded fields . . . Autumn, when the glow of one bar of an electric fire in an attic room conjured romance out of furtive gropings, and saucy girls tittered to find their buttocks chequered by the weave of the carpet . . .

Victoria remembered and remembered, and pieced together her memories. She looked and listened, and pieced together her observations. She screamed at herself for a gullible fool. She laughed at herself for the trusting ninny she was—laughed wryly at herself, even at this time of sick anger and disgust.

It began with her pregnancy. Yes, it began in July, many warm weeping afternoons when she herself slept deeply between lunch and tea. They took advantage. She began it, then they both took advantage. He was in that damned workshop. She went to her bedroom and took off her clothes. She put on a dressing gown, some cheap thing she had half undone at the front. She came to his room asking for help, like Mimi asking for a match, all helpless, needing a man to fix a drawer that was stuck. He struggles with the drawer. She is close to him, struggling also, giggling; her thigh brushes his, her hand . . .

He is bored, deprived, randy, easily aroused, immediately aroused . . . Hush! It's all right, she's out like a light, quickly, then . . .

And through the months since, as her own body thickened and her movements slowed, August glare, September gold, the electric fire and darkening windows, snuggle up in a warm cocoon naked together under the duvet, frost on the window, Christmas lights . . .

Smiles, solicitude.

They were very skilful, very discreet. It was almost impossible to find chinks in that polished armour of correctness. Cosette went on being a super-efficient, self-effacing lady's-maid. Giles went on being a gentle and considerate husband, there whenever she needed him. Victoria had often admired convincing performances on stage and screen, and had sometimes had the opportunity to give the actors pleasure by saying so: but never had she been privileged to watch performances like these. Privileged! That was a comical thought, typical of the wry turn her humour sometimes took. If God had not given Victoria that moment of revelation, she might never have known the truth. She had to hand it to them. From anybody else but her (her eyes having been opened by God) their corrupt and treacherous intrigue would have been hidden.

It occurred to Victoria to catch them at it. She could slip out of bed, put on her fleecy floor-length robe, creep mouse-quiet up the stairs, and fling open the door of Cosette's bedroom. She could. It was an option. She decided against it. The physical disgust would be too much for her, physically dangerous for her son. The effort would be overtaxing, perilous. There were draughts on the stairs. It was her duty to her son to stay quiet and warm in bed, whatever the temptations offered by that dramatic moment.

And there was this about it: that it was not like her to pry and spy, to lift the corners of rugs to see if dust had been swept there. It was revolting to her, to contemplate becoming a person like that, a snooper, a *voyeur*. It was demeaning and humiliating. She had more pride.

And there was this about it: it was needless. With God's help, she knew. She did not have to be shown, by upreared buttocks, what she had been shown by God.

She wondered if they would try to kill her.

She knew a trick worth two of that.

She made a new will. She called the lawyer to her bedside. She left everything to her daughter, er, Charlotte Bramall.

They had better keep her alive, the two of them. After her son was born, she would make another new will.

She wondered if they drugged her food and drink at lunchtime, so that they could safely indulge their forbidden perversions in the middle of the centrally-heated January afternoon. She used Giles as a taster. It was comic to think that he might thereby spend the afternoon in a stupor, unmanned, flaccid as a dotard, useless to the French bitch.

Nurse Wilkins arrived, and took up residence. She smelled of starch and talcum powder. She showed a proper concern. 'We owe it to ourselves to look after ourselves,' she said. She imposed her personality on the household, Victoria's trusted agent upstairs and downstairs. She treated

Cosette and Mrs Mollam and Mrs Calloway as servants.

Her bedroom was immediately below Cosette's, on the floor above Victoria's. That would put a damper on their frolics.

It was funny to find oneself with so much time to think. Victoria's normal life was full to bursting with friends and interests, with her love of art and beauty; it was one long buzz. It was an unfamiliar luxury, to have this enforced leisure; it was a new challenge, to use the time for long and hard thinking.

She thought about ever so many things. Starlight and roses. What sort of scraggy, gawky appearance Cosette presented in the nude. The tragedy that she had never been painted on horseback by Sir Alfred Munnings, or in a flowered hat by Renoir. Would it, in a year or two, be time to have two tiny tucks taken each side of her eyes, by the best cosmetic surgeon in the world? Would she one day write a masterpiece, a long novel with an enchantress as heroine? The men in her book would be men who did things, men of energy and gallantry and easy charm. The easy charm was good but it was not everything. Pondering, Victoria thought that, measured on an absolute moral scale, men who did things achieved more than men who did not. Men with achievements in the world of the arts—they were not only the custodians of civilisation, they *were* civilisation. By their work, societies were judged by posterity. By their work, and by the imperishable legends woven round certain individuals. Helen of Troy. Cleopatra. Guinevere. Garbo.

Victoria dictated many of her thoughts onto the Dictaphone which she used for her letters. She could either incorporate them into her novel, or make them a series of luminous essays. Both, perhaps.

Victoria laughed at herself. She would never be a busy scribbler, because she would never have the time. It would

not be fair. Her work of art was her life. She shared it with
the world as Botticelli shared his paintings.

The lawyer knew how to get in touch with Charlotte
Bramall, because, some time before, Mary-Emma Black
had given him an address. The lawyer got in touch with the
Bramall girl only in order to be sure of being able to do so
again, if need arose. He was to be given any change of per-
manent address; if there was the possibility of prolonged
absence, he was to be given a forwarding address. His duty
required these precautions. It was his duty to go no further
than to take these precautions, because it was supremely
obvious that the will might be changed, possibly within
three weeks. It would have been unkind and unprofessional
to raise hopes which were almost certain to be dashed.

The lawyer had his own views. If he wanted to keep
Mrs Lambert's business, he was obliged to keep them
to himself. He did not so very much care about Mrs
Lambert's business but he had a duty to his partners.

What he could not prevent was the birth of speculation
along the warrens of Peckham. He was checking up. He
had never done so before. That meant something. Conversations on the subject were widespread, but they were not
held in front of Lottie.

As a matter of policy, of commonsense, Victoria made
very sure that all her household knew all about her new
will, of which the original was safe in the lawyer's office.
It would not have been very wise to have had any of them
enriched by her death—that just created more allies for the
conspirators, accessories before and during and after the
event. They were enriched by the fact of her being alive;
they were honoured; they were over-rewarded and molly-
coddled. Well they knew it. Victoria had played the cards
she had been dealt, and she had scored a grand slam.

Cosette looked a bit sour. She had always looked a
bit sour. It was something to do with a working-class

French background. It was what they were given to eat as children—greasy, indigestible food, not enough greens.

Giles was bland about it, apparently untouched.

'I expect you'll outlive me anyway,' he said.

'I expect I shall,' said Victoria silently, laughing silently that he should be speaking so much more truly than he knew.

'Is she always like this?' said Marge Wilkins, 'or only when she's preggy?'

'Like what?' said Beryl Calloway.

'Lying around like a slug. It's more than my job's worth to tell her, but she'd be better active and out in the fresh. There's been some lovely mild days for the time of year, bulbs coming up in the garden . . . Thank you, dear, I shouldn't but I will.'

She'd settled into the life of the kitchen as though she'd always been there. She said she'd been to all kinds of billets, and she'd learned to take the rough with the smooth. She never struck anything smoother than this. There was always a kettle just boiled, and little cakes from the shop at the corner. Bob Childers would come in, and Cosette and Ivy Mollam would come downstairs, and sometimes Albie Huxtable took time off from his moonlighting job at the betting shop; and then the kitchen table was where the action was.

Of course the bell rang pretty often. It might be for Cosette or Marge or Mister. There ought to have been a system, like one clang for Cosette, two for Nurse, three for Mister, but there wasn't. Whichever one went, it was one of the others she wanted. That was one thing you could be sure of—whichever went through that door, it was the wrong one.

Albie and Bob and Mister had bets about it. The trouble with that was, that when Mister lost he couldn't pay.

He would have come to the kitchen more often than he did, Mister would, only he didn't seem sure of his

welcome. Truth to tell, he wasn't very welcome. He was a
nice enough fellow, very nice mannered, but they couldn't
let their tongues run on as they did when he wasn't there.
Marge Wilkins said that what he had was an inhibiting
effect. She had a way of using big words like that. It
made her sound toffee-nosed, but that she wasn't. She
had some wonderful stories (girls only) and she'd seen
some bloody funny things. She said she'd never struck
anything like Mister and Her.

She said she'd heard about the home where Cosette's
kid was. A friend of hers had worked there temporary. It
was pretty good as those places went. Cosette shouldn't
feel guilty, having her there, it was best for them, they
were best with their own sort. The trouble was later, when
they grew up. Some local authorities were good, but some
didn't want to hear. They cut back all the social services,
and then gave each other bigger salaries and hotter offices.
The difficulty when the poor things were grown up was
to find them things to do, to make them feel busy and
useful. In a lot of those places they sat and stared into
space, with a telly they couldn't understand jabbering in
the corner.

'But I never saw one of them,' said Marge Wilkins,
'with as little to do as our friend Mister.'

The bell rang. Cosette went, so it was Marge she wanted,
so Bob Childers lost ten p to Albie Huxtable.

They all wondered what went on in Mister's head.

Nothing much did. He had developed the habit of mental
lethargy, which, living as he did, was a precondition of
survival.

He had wondered how long his luck would last. He
knew. It was running out. He was eating Dead Sea fruit,
and drinking wine that tasted of boredom.

As a boy in Ireland he had had dogs. He had wondered
what it was like to be a dog.

He was not sure how much longer he could stand it. He remembered Peckham with passionate nostalgia. He wanted to wake up in the morning and see Marcus Hills, in his khaki dressing gown with a cup of tea. He wanted the graffiti on the stairs and the draughts under the door.

He was Huckleberry Finn, set to knot his sheets together one night, and escape at three in the morning.

He was nothing of the kind. He was the prisoner of laziness and cowardice. He shied from introspection, as violently as a pony he had had as a child. The pony had shied at the reflected glare of the sunlight on the metal holder of a salt-lick, bolted to the wall of the loose box. The sun went behind a cloud and the glare disappeared. The pony looked again, with an impudent curiosity not to be found, perhaps, in a full-sized horse, in a delicate neurotic thoroughbred or a great, steaming, cart-bred hunter. The pony looked again. There was no glare; he was mollified, and settled to his feed. Such unbidden memories were upsetting, because they were those of somebody who could then pretend, to the world and to himself, that he was normal, that he would one day be a man. Everywhere Giles looked there was a glare; there was the image of himself, in a little tartan coat and with a bell on his collar.

He was asphyxiated by mink and rose-petals. When he had too much to drink he was sick.

He conjured, without wanting to, memories of Lottie's laugh and of her strong uncultured hands. He found that after eighteen months he had forgotten her face.

He looked across the drawing room at the wig-stand, on which somebody had put a bowl of white hyacinths. He looked across his workroom at a lamp, and at the thirteen-amp plug he was supposed to be attaching to the flex of the lamp. He was filled with apathy at the thought of the labour involved.

As a boy in Ireland he had had dogs. One of his dogs, a setter called Nellie, had gone off by herself into a barn; she had gone there to die, and she died. Giles had looked at her silky body, and had buried her in a private place marked only by private grief. He had wondered what it was like to be dead.

On the gynaecologist's advice, Victoria went off to the hospital. It was the newest and most expensive in London. Dagobert took her in the car, with Nurse Wilkins and Giles. Giles was much more anxious than Victoria, who laughed and joked all the way.

It was like heaven in Battersea, the silence of the silver bell. Mister came back from the hospital and drank half a bottle of whisky. He joined them in the kitchen for a bit, but he cast a damper. Albie Huxtable went off to the betting-shop for the evening dog-racing, which went on whatever the weather. Beryl Calloway left something in the oven for Mister and Cosette.

Victoria was betrayed again, by God and by Giles.

When they said she had a daughter she thought at first that they were lying, teasing her, being cruel because they envied her.

She had to pretend to be pleased about the disgusting purple bundle.

At the edge of her consciousness hovered an irritating awareness of Giles, self-effacing, smiling like a fool, wet and unproductive, a wimp and a sponge, a failure.

It was silly of him to bring her flowers, when they both knew the flowers had been put down to her account at the florist's.

Giles was bleating something about names. Names? What names? Names for what?

Debonnaire Courtenay, perfumed and languorous in her hospital bed, telephoned Graham Whittingham-Barnes.

It was about that nice young artist, the very tall one, the one Graham said was brimming with talent, and needed only a little wherewithal and a place to work.

Debonnaire had come to certain decisions.

Graham assured her that the artist she had met, the very tall one, was genuinely talented, hard-working, strongly motivated, a producer, a man who refused to be a sponge, a man who would pay back with interest anything he was lent, a man they would in years to come be very proud to know.

Debonnaire said that Graham was to telephone the house in Battersea, having given her twenty minutes to do so first. He was to make an appointment with Cosette or Mrs Mollam, to take the tall young genius to the house to look at the attic rooms. Not Cosette's bedroom, as for the moment it was, but the other two rooms. Any lumber already in those rooms could be ignored; anything that was of use to the artist could be kept; the rest would be removed.

Nobody was to know about this arrangement: nobody at all, until Debonnaire was ready to tell them. It was to be a secret between the three of them, and Debonnaire's utterly discreet servants.

Graham hardly knew what to do for the best.

The doubts that Rudi had expressed had stuck in his mind. What *was* he doing installing James in the attic of Lottie's mother's house?

Was he afflicted by sympathy for Giles? He had sympathy for Giles, but Giles would not be losing anything important. He did not need a workshop in the sense that James needed a studio; if he wanted to read in peace, there were a dozen rooms in that house where he could do so.

Still Graham dithered, his dilemma, unusually, being purely moral.

Ironically, Rudi persuaded him. Graham's earlier words had stuck in his subconscious, as had his own in Graham's. Lottie did deserve a break, and this was the break she would most like. It did not matter in whose house James had a studio, as long as he had one. Rudi liked James, and admired what he had seen of his work. Rudi reminded Graham of the investment he had already made in James's future. Actually the investment was about thirty pounds, but it was not a factor to be ignored.

Graham telephoned James in the evening, in Marcus Hills's flat. He wanted to know James's availabilities before he made a date to look at the studio. James had unlimited availabilities.

The arrangement was at last made, after much telephoning, the leaving of messages, and calls to and from Debonnaire.

James was excited.

He knew that Graham was venal and manipulative, but also that his enthusiasm was genuine. Graham had not himself actually seen the studio, but it had been described to him. He knew the house where the studio was.

James was meeting Graham in the West End, and they were going together to the house. They would go in a taxi which Graham would pay for. They were expected. Debonnaire was away at the moment. James was not told where the house was. He would know when he got there. If he then told anybody else, Graham washed his hands of him. There were compelling reasons for this secrecy, not all of which Graham himself fully understood.

'Is this the one you said was a witch?' said Lottie. 'I still don't believe in anybody called Debonnaire.'

Lottie was excited for James and for the future.

'Eet ees zees two room,' said a thin dark woman of about Graham's age, who had opened the front door to them and led them upstairs.

'These are heights I have never scaled,' said Graham.

James had no idea whether to believe him; he could not see that it mattered.

'Complete seclusion, all mod cons,' said Graham in a jokey house-agent's voice. 'Hot and cold running water. Power-points. That big table might be useful to you. This north room, as you see, is simply begging for an easel to be placed in the light of the window. It will be emptied of those trunks and things. The days are lengthening, James. The tools in this other room, I am told, are also to be removed. The occasional handyman who uses them will practise his craft in other places. The shelves will be cleared for the jars and essences of your mysteries. There is a loo next door, presumably to be shared with our friend Cosette, but I imagine neither of you will mind that. A bathroom on the floor below. I see no reason why you should not have a bed in the corner of this room. You can heat both rooms, of course. I would recommend a hot-air blower, if you don't mind the noise. You could be as snug as a bug in a rug.'

James had a faraway look when he came back to Peckham. Like a man in a dream he began to collect together all the things that he had, and to make lists of all the things that he needed. Marcus Hills was nearly crowded out of his own flat, by James's reassembled clobber. The inconvenience was temporary, so he could stand it.

To Lottie, it was as though James was already paint-ing—already realising on canvas his mountains of studies on hardboard, his sheaves of sketches in pencil, ballpoint, felt-tip and crayon. He said he had given himself six months' work. Though he spoke aloud he was talking not to Lottie but to himself. Lottie knew better than to distract him when he was in this mood.

She felt left out, by his preoccupation.

'You can't have it both ways,' said Emmee. 'That's exactly what you admire about him.'

'He won't even tell me where this studio is. I don't believe he really knows. He'll never find it on his own. I don't think it exists. Debonnaire. I don't think she exists.

It's all a plot of Graham Whizzy-Bum's.'

'Yes, James knows that. But it's a plot for James's benefit. James makes pots of money, and Whizzy-Bum takes his cut. Whizzy-Bum has faith in James, otherwise he wouldn't be taking the trouble or spending the money.'

'Yes, but I don't have faith in Whizzy-Bum or in Debonnaire. Something dreadful's going to happen.'

'Not to James.'

'Yes. He'll be opening cans of baked beans, and trying to cut slices of bread.'

'The whole point about James is that he doesn't need his hand held.'

'Yes he does,' said Lottie.

James emerged briefly from his busy trance, as though he were a creature of the sea whose head had popped up from the surface.

'One of the points,' he said to Emmee, 'is that Graham thinks I ought to be completely undisturbed.'

'For six whole months?'

'No, of course not, but for several days at a time. He's right. I feel a pig, but I know I've got to do it.'

'Why couldn't you be a motor-mechanic or a computer programmer or something,' said Emmee crossly. 'Why did you have to be a bloody painter?'

For Giles, fatherhood transformed life. What had been empty was full; what had been shameful, proud; what had been purposeless had a clear and shining destination, a pale mountain peak shining in the morning sun. What had been loveless was forgotten, since he was filled with wondering love as he looked at the miracle of his infant daughter. Everything that had been meaningless was given meaning, everything that had been dark was bright, and everything that had been tasteless suddenly acquired a sweet and tangy and heady savour.

He remembered a sermon he had heard as a boy in the chapel at Winchester: the preacher, a visiting bishop, had talked of the Copernican Revolution, which replaced in astronomy—and by implication in philosophy—the earth for the sun as the centre of the Solar System. Giles underwent a Copernican Revolution: his daughter was the centre of his universe.

Staring dumb-struck at the buttoned-up face which was smaller than a man's hand, he tried names to fit the face and his feelings. Imogen, Artemis, Chloë, Amaryllis, Phyllida; Jane, June, Jean, Joan, Jeanne, Joanne, Joanna. Soon they would be home. On bright March mornings he would wheel the pram in Battersea Park, and during firelit evenings in the nursery he would tell her stories of giants and lovely princesses remembered from the nursery of his own Irish childhood.

They told him at the hospital that his daughter was a very nice baby, a perfect baby, certain to be beautiful, absolutely healthy, normal in all respects, all systems functioning.

Giles returned in a haze of happiness to Battersea. He did not go up to his workroom. He did not see that, in the meantime, Albie Huxtable had packed up all his tools in a tea-chest and put them in a skip in the next street.

Things were hanging fire. James was all ready to go. He was in contact with the self-drive van hire firm. There were people on call to help him load; Graham would send people to help him unload. The green light remained unlit. The hours ticked by like days and the days like weeks. James was frightened that his high sense of energy and dedication would taper off in delay, frustration, distraction.

It was a difficult time for Lottie.

Victoria started to do her exercises, under medical supervision. She seemed to be in a tearing hurry to recover her

fitness and her figure. She had to be restrained, to be made
to rest.

Sometimes, first thing in the morning, she looked her
age.

Albie Huxtable knew which side his bread was buttered.
He was earning two livings, one in the black economy. It
wasn't for him to fret about the rights and wrongs. All he
had to do was what he was asked (short of murder) and
keep his nose clean.

He knew nothing about Mr Lambert's tools. A burglary?
Surely not—nothing else was gone. None of them knew
anything about the tools. Ivy Mollam had not been in the
room, having enough to do with the rest of the house; Beryl
Calloway had not even been upstairs; Bob Childers had not
so much as been in the house, except for a cup of tea in
the kitchen. Cosette? Cosette shrugged. She could be very
Gallic. There was nothing to be got out of her.

The loss of a couple of screwdrivers would not destroy
Giles's new and miraculous happiness.

Cosette was able to get down to Haslemere three times
to see her little Jeanne. She was happy and heartbroken.
They said at the home that her visits were wonderful for
the child, that she perked up and took an interest as at no
other time. It was right that Jeanne was in the home, but it
was right that the mother should come more often, much
more often, to see her.

They allowed Victoria home after twelve days. Dagobert
came for her, with Nurse Wilkins. Dagobert carried the
bags and Nurse Wilkins the baby thing.

Victoria went straight to bed when they got home.

She realised within minutes that the intrigue between
Giles and Cosette was still going on, was going hot and
strong. They could have been open and shameless about

it while she was away, much of every day and all of every night: they had taken blatant and cynical advantage of her helplessness.

Giles crooned over the baby thing. It was ridiculous that a grown man could simper and say 'Goo-goo'.

The following Thursday was Nurse Wilkins's day off. She would be out from the middle of the morning until the early evening, spending the day with her married sister in Esher. It was not afterwards obvious who made the suggestion: that Nurse Wilkins should take the baby, in the car with Albert Huxtable, to show the lovely baby to her sister and her sister's family.

'Small will enjoy herself,' said Nurse Wilkins. 'It's ever so kind of Mother to lend us the car and the chauffeur.'

'It won't really be a day off for you,' said Ivy Mollam later in the kitchen.

'It will do the scrap good to see a bit of normal life,' said Nurse Wilkins.

Albie Huxtable did not at all want to spend a day twiddling his fingers in Esher, but he had to look cheerful about it.

That Thursday was one of the days when Mr Childers did not come to do the garden. Mrs Mollam would leave shortly after midday, Mrs Calloway shortly after two. Cosette would have charge of the house and her Mistress. Giles would be wherever he was told to be.

Debonnaire rang up Graham Whittingham-Barnes and confirmed that James Drummond would come in a hired self-drive van whenever summoned. Debonnaire said that he was to come on Thursday afternoon, not earlier than three-thirty nor later than four-thirty. Since James was bringing some things in his van, he could take away some other things, rubbish too bulky for the dustmen to take, heavy, valueless, to be dumped somewhere. It should be dumped with full regard to the rules, to the amenities, to ecology. Debonnaire thought James could reasonably be asked to do that for her. Graham thought so too.

James thought so, when Graham told him of Debonnaire's request. Lottie thought so, when James told her of it.

During the eighteen months since his arrival in Battersea, it had occasionally occurred to Giles to wonder what the servants thought of him, living a life so grossly unlike anybody else of his age.

He did not suppose that they thought of him as the Master. He did not suppose they referred to him as the Master, in conversation among themselves. He supposed they discussed him, sitting over all those cups of tea in the kitchen. He knew that the Irish servants of his childhood had discussed the Family interminably, adhering to their roles in a hundred novels, in Trollope and Dorothea Conyers and Somerville and Ross. He imagined English servants were the same—Anglo-French in the case of Cosette, who reportedly came from Jersey. Cosette was the one he saw most of, in Victoria's bedroom; and he was aware of her sometimes moving about in her attic bedroom down the passage from his workshop. She was a dark, silent, efficient presence, completely enigmatic to Giles when, about every six weeks, he idly wondered about her. He gathered that she had suffered a personal tragedy, but Victoria did not want to talk about it and Giles would not have dreamed of asking Cosette about it.

The other three women (to include Nurse Wilkins, as she presumably did not include herself) and the two men were, in comparison, transparent. You knew what was in their minds, on all indifferent subjects, because they said it. They were as open as the day in their stated views about the weather, the football results, the arrest of a pop-star on drugs charges, the merits of a new TV series. Cosette did not talk about those things or about anything else, in Giles's hearing. Yes, she was enigmatic, which was something Giles had never succeeded in being and never tried to be.

He hoped that, at her age, she had a sex life, but she did not look as though she had.

Victoria got up in the middle of the morning. She felt well rested and fit for anything. She knew she should still take things easy. She intended to. The things she proposed were easy.

Debonnaire found, as she knew she would, the keys of the two old school trunks in the attic. She was very tidy-minded; she liked her life to be minutely ordered. She had troubled to keep the keys, labelled with small brown tags. She put the keys in the pocket of her soft tweed skirt.

Nurse Wilkins put her head in to say that they were off. Baby was all wrapped up and they had everything they needed. Mr Huxtable was at the door with the car. Nurse renewed her thanks for Mother's kindness.

Mrs Mollam left not long afterwards. Unfortunately she, like Nurse, had to go out of the front door. There was no way out to the street from the garden.

Debonnaire ground up three of her sleeping-pills between two teaspoons. The result would not knock anybody out but it would make anybody drowsy. She put the powder in a brown envelope, and put that in the pocket of her skirt with the keys of the trunks.

Victoria asked Giles to be very sweet and do something for her. He bobbed his head and grinned in a silly way. He was not a proper man, doing anything creative or useful. He followed her to the attic, and pulled the two old school trunks out from under other things in the north room.

Victoria came down to lunch for the first time since her return. Mrs Calloway was thrilled and thankful to see her.

Victoria encouraged Giles to have a second pink gin before lunch. Humorously, she calculated that the little bottle of Angostura bitters would now last her for years.

• • •

Victoria heard Cosette come downstairs to have her lunch with Mrs Calloway in the kitchen.

Mrs Calloway cleared away lunch and offered them coffee. Often Victoria refused coffee after lunch because it made her wakeful when she needed her nap. But she would not have time for a nap that day.

Victoria heard Mrs Calloway washing up the lunch things. The servants' things could go into the dishwasher, but not the good china or silver or glass.

Victoria went out to chat with Mrs Calloway for a moment, because it was that sort of household, full of goodwill and laughter. Mrs Calloway was by then in a bustle of leaving. She had finished the washing-up and put it to drain; she would give it all a polish when she came back in the early evening. Cosette was a silent presence. She had been sitting at the kitchen table with a cup of coffee, but of course she stood up when Victoria came in.

Mrs Calloway left, taking a casserole in which she would bring back the main course for dinner. Victoria called out to Giles to get out some red wine to go with the casserole. At Victoria's suggestion, Cosette went with Mrs Calloway to open the door, the silly old thing's arms being full.

Debonnaire emptied the powdered sleeping-pills into Cosette's coffee, which was an extravagant half pint, black and sugared.

Victoria herself left the kitchen as Cosette returned to it and to her coffee.

'I'll leave you to drink it undisturbed,' said Victoria.

Cosette nodded. Out of the tail of her eye, Victoria saw her sit down and pick up the big cup in both hands.

Victoria told Giles not to go out yet, to give his lunch time to go down. He was a little drowsy, as he always was after a second glass of gin before lunch. She did not want him too drowsy, as she had work for him to do. He had *The Times* on his lap, folded back for the crossword. He had a snobbery about solving the crossword without filling it in; Victoria never knew, therefore, whether he actually solved it or not; luckily she did not care.

Victoria glanced into the kitchen on her way upstairs. Cosette was sitting there, heavy-eyed.

'For goodness' sake go and have a nap,' Victoria said to her with affectionate impatience. 'You're out on your feet.'

Cosette nodded and mumbled her thanks. She went upstairs to the attic as though she were sleep-walking.

Victoria waited ten minutes. She looked out at the winter-prisoned garden, and even from those stark branches and bare stalks she derived spiritual comfort.

She looked into the drawing room. Giles was asleep, or nearly so, although the crossword was still on his lap.

Debonnaire went upstairs. In her own room she took off her shoes. She put on thin cotton gloves she had worn the previous summer at Ascot. She went on up to the top of the house in stockinged feet. She softly opened the door of Cosette's room, and found the girl on her back on the bed, her mouth open, breathing noisily.

Debonnaire took a cushion from the armchair and smothered Cosette. She probably held the cushion over Cosette's face much longer than necessary, but she thought it best to play safe. She had no difficulty pulling the stringy, small-boned body off the bed and into the next room, the unused north room. She opened one of the old school trunks and put the body in, folding it into a foetal position. She covered it with various oddments that had been cluttering the room for too long—a pair of long-broken binoculars, a non-functioning kitchen clock, a tray missing a handle, some old clothes. She got Cosette's night things from the other room and put them in the trunk, with a purse, toothbrush and sponge, a few underclothes and tights, and Cosette's passport.

Soon the trunk was full. Debonnaire closed it and locked it with one of the keys in her pocket.

She straightened Cosette's room. In doing so, she found £42 in cash. Obviously it was Debonnaire's money, stolen from her bag or her dressing-table. Possibly stolen by Giles and given to his whore. Debonnaire put it in the pocket of her skirt.

She went down the two flights of stairs to her room. She put on her shoes, and she put the money in her bag. She went down to the kitchen. She was still wearing gloves.

She took the long butcher's knife out of the drawer by the sink. With the steel of the carving set, she put an extra edge on the blade and a needle sharpness to the point. She put the knife on the kitchen table.

Beside the knife on the table she put a cardboard shoebox in which there were some dozens of old, anonymous unlabelled keys. They had been in a drawer of a desk that had come from Court Farm. Debonnaire had always thought that there might one day be a use for them.

Debonnaire woke up Giles and asked for his help again.

He took off his coat, at her suggestion.

He brought the full trunk all the way downstairs from the north attic room to the hall. He brought the empty trunk down, and put it in the kitchen.

'The men are coming later to take the rubbish away,' she explained. 'There's a lot of old kitchen stuff to go in this one. I'll go through it with Mrs Calloway.'

He nodded. He looked exhausted already. The full trunk had been pretty heavy. He might have suggested waiting until Huxtable or Mr Childers was there to help, but he had not done so. He thought he was proving something, to her and to himself, by managing the trunks on his own.

'Do you think you can find the key that fits this trunk?' said Victoria. 'It will burst open if it's not locked, and spill old saucepans all over London. The key might be one of these.'

Giles took the box of keys, and knelt by the empty trunk. He tried the keys in the lock of the trunk, one after the other. The position stretched his shirt tight across his back, so that his spine and shoulder-blades were delineated. Debonnaire picked up the butcher's knife, and stabbed him a little to the left of the spine and well below the shoulder-blade. He died almost at once. There was surprisingly little blood. Debonnaire did the one thing which was heavy work, which was putting this body in the empty trunk. She got some of his older clothes from his dressing room and packed them round and over the body. She put in some other useless rubbish. She put in Giles's razor, the pyjamas he had been wearing, and his cotton dressing gown. She put in the butcher's knife, in case after the most thorough washing it would carry microscopic traces of Giles's blood. She put in Giles's passport and his cheque-book. She had let him have a cheque-book so that he would feel a man, but he was not allowed an overdraft.

Like the other trunk, if this one was forced open it would appear to contain valueless rubbish.

Debonnaire closed the trunk and locked it.

She cleaned up the floor of the kitchen with disposable paper tissues, which she flushed down the downstairs lavatory. No doubt a scientist would be able to find traces of the blood. That was to be explained by the accident with the chisel, which Mrs Calloway and Mrs Mollam and the doctor would all perfectly remember.

In her bedroom, she took off and put away her gloves, and put the keys of the trunks back with the others.

At half-past three a van arrived, and in it Graham Whittingham-Barnes and the tall, nice-looking young

artist that Graham said was a genius. He was a strong
genius. He and Graham, who was in stylish old clothes,
unloaded a mass of things from the back of the van,
and stacked them by Debonnaire's front door. As soon
as the van was empty, they lifted in the two trunks.
Then they began transferring all James's things to the
top of the house, to the empty north and north-east
rooms.

At four-thirty everything was upstairs, though there was
still much sorting to do. There were still a good many
things to buy. Graham and James had been through the
list together. It was a lot of money, to James an impossible
sum. Graham's serious investment was beginning.

James was overwhelmed by gratitude to Debonnaire,
which he struggled haltingly to express.

It was necessary to dispose of the trunks of rubbish.

'No problem,' said Graham. 'The City of Westminster
runs a central tip. They squash it all and put it on barges
and squeeze it onto the Isle of Dogs. They're going to build
tomorrow's soaring cities on today's rubbish. I want a lot
of clients in high-rise developments there, with a lot of
blank walls. I shall be proud to have contributed to the
foundations.'

'So shall I,' said Debonnaire, laughing.

The boys went off in the van, with the useless, valueless,
battered old school trunks full of rubbish. They promised
to return.

At five o'clock Victoria telephoned the police, sounding
tentative and embarrassed, sounding as though frightened
of making a fool of herself. Her husband and her maid
were not at home, and they seemed to have taken a lot of
things with them. Not her things, as far as she knew, but
their own—clothes, toothbrushes, that sort of thing. She
was worried. She did not know when they had gone out,
or if they had gone out together.

It was already dark, a bleak February evening.

The police came, with an air of not knowing why they had come: a detective in a coat that looked inadequate for the weather, and a policewoman in uniform. She was a nice girl.

Very tactfully, really quite nicely, they asked Victoria if there had been a relationship, any kind of relationship, between her husband and the woman called Cosette.

'No,' said Victoria, suddenly and loudly, seeming to startle herself as much as her hearers. She said, 'I don't know why I said that, so certain, so quick. I don't know. I don't think so. I never had reason to think so. It's a horrible thought. I'm sure it couldn't be possible . . . Why am I sure? I suppose I'm not *sure*. I couldn't swear on a Bible that there was nothing . . . I mean, how could I know, for certain . . . ?'

She had gone to sleep, as she nearly always did in the afternoon. She had awoken to find herself alone in the house; she had been puzzled, then frightened. She was still puzzled and frightened.

The boys came back in the middle of this.

Their presence was explained, fully and frankly— James's predicament, Graham's professional and financial interest, Victoria's desire to have her unused rooms made use of. Everything in the attic rooms confirmed that James was exactly what he said he was.

Everything in Cosette's room was consistent with her having slept there the previous night, and with her intention to sleep elsewhere that night.

Everything in Mr Lambert's room had the same message.

Wherever the two of them were going, alone or together, they were not coming home to Battersea.

As far as Victoria could tell—just quickly, there and then—nothing of value had been taken: no spoons, glass, rugs or pictures.

Nurse Wilkins came back, earlier than expected, with the baby. She knew of no relationship between the Master and Cosette, but of course she had not been in the household for more than a few days.

Albert Huxtable the chauffeur had known the two of them longer, but he was not, so to say, inside the household. If there had been a carry-on, it was unlikely he would have seen anything.

There was a tweed coat hanging over the back of an upright chair by the writing-table in the drawing room. This was so normal an object in a lived-in family house that it caught nobody's attention, until it caught the policewoman's.

Was it a coat Mr Lambert had been wearing earlier in the day? At lunchtime?

Nurse Wilkins was sure he had had it on in the morning. Victoria thought he had been wearing it for lunch. Mrs Calloway would probably remember.

Mrs Calloway arrived, with the casserole ready to put in the oven.

Yes, Mr Lambert had been wearing the coat at lunchtime.

Why would a man take off his coat and hang it over a chair before going out in mid-afternoon in mid-February? He chose, for some reason, to wear a different coat. There was a notecase in the breast pocket of the coat, but nothing much in it—no letters, no credit cards, one five-pound note.

Would a man go away with empty pockets, leaving a fiver behind? Was there a coat missing? An overcoat? Any kind of hat? Perhaps Cosette would have known.

The missing persons had passports? Their passports were not to be found.

There might still be some perfectly simple, reasonable, acceptable explanation. The probability, never great, grew smaller as each minute passed.

The boys kept out of the way, busy upstairs. Whatever had happened, they had arrived after it had happened. They might be curious, or anxious to help, but none of it was anything to do with them.

Victoria remained dry-eyed, but it was evident that she was consumed by worry. Of course she was. Anybody would be.

The trunks by now would be on their way to the Isle of Dogs. By dawn they would be completely buried, incorporated in reclaimed land on which there would soon be acres of concrete.

Mrs Lambert, Mr Whittingham-Barnes, Mr Drummond, Nurse Wilkins, Mrs Calloway and Mr Huxtable would be available for further questioning if necessary, if it seemed that any crime had been committed. Mrs Mollam and Mr Childers would be available, if required, in the morning.

'I must warn you,' said the policewoman privately to Victoria, 'that if they want to run off together the law can't make them come back. It may be horrid, but it's not a crime. This isn't really a police matter at all.'

Victoria apologised for wasting the time of the police. They said they wished they could have been of more help.

The police left.

Graham Whittingham-Barnes came downstairs saying that he had to leave; after only one drink he left.

Mrs Calloway got on with dinner, for herself and Nurse Wilkins and maybe Cosette in the kitchen, and for Her, it seemed, alone in the dining room. Mrs Calloway had never been less surprised by anything in her life.

After seeing Graham off, James went upstairs to finish off sorting out his stuff. Debonnaire followed him after a little, because she could not at such a moment sit by herself doing nothing, and because she wanted to see James's paintings.

To her the paintings looked extraordinary, but she knew they were wonderful because she had Graham's word for it.

She said, 'You're going to be filthy and exhausted and famished after all this. Why not have a bath here?

You'd better use my bathroom. And stay for dinner. Mrs Calloway has cooked that huge casserole. It seems a pity to waste it.'

Later she said, through the steam, 'Do you mind if I come and talk to you? Is it very unseemly? I can't bear being alone just now. I'm sure you understand. I don't see how I'm going to bear it. I don't want your pity, just your company. Oh, that does look inviting. Is there room for me? I think I shall have your bath too.'

Graham said to Rudi, in the underground garage of their 'chambers', 'She's so ignorant about what she's got that there's quite likely to be a treasure or two in what she calls rubbish.'

'If you find a treasure, what will you do with it?'

'Something ought to go to that stepdaughter. Felicity. In Wales.'

'Yes, I think that is right.'

They jemmied open the locks of the trunks and began picking through the contents.

Domini Taylor is the author of three previous novels, *Teacher's Pet, Gemini,* and *Mother Love.* She lives in Hampshire, England.